LOVE
from
A to Z

Also by S. K. Ali

Saints and Misfits

LOVE
from
A to Z

S. K. ALI

SALAAM
READS

NEW YORK LONDON TORONTO SYDNEY NEW DELHI

An imprint of Simon & Schuster Children's Publishing Division
1230 Avenue of the Americas, New York, New York 10020
For information about special discounts for bulk purchases, please contact Simon & Schuster Special Sales at 1-866-506-1949 or business@simonandschuster.com.
The Simon & Schuster Speakers Bureau can bring authors to your live event. For more information or to book an event, contact the Simon & Schuster Speakers Bureau at 1-866-248-3049 or visit our website at www.simonspeakers.com.
Jacket design by Lucy Ruth Cummins
Interior design by Hilary Zarycky
The text for this book was set in Adobe Garamond Pro.
Manufactured in the United States of America
First Edition
2 4 6 8 10 9 7 5 3 1
Library of Congress Cataloging-in-Publication Data
Names: Ali, S. K., author.
Title: Love from A to Z / S.K. Ali.
Description: First edition. | New York : Salaam Reads, [2019] | Summary: Eighteen-year-old Muslims Adam and Zayneb meet in Doha, Qatar, during spring break and fall in love as both struggle to find a way to live their own truths.
Identifiers: LCCN 2018056836 (print) | LCCN 2018060096 (eBook) | ISBN 9781534442726 (hardback) | ISBN 9781534442740 (eBook)
Subjects: | CYAC: Muslims—Fiction. | Arabs—Fiction. | Prejudices—Fiction. | High schools—Fiction. | Schools—Fiction. | Multiple sclerosis—Fiction. | Dawḥah (Qatar)—Fiction. | Qatar—Fiction.
Classification: LCC PZ7.1.A436 (eBook) | LCC PZ7.1.A436 Lov 2019 (print) | DDC [Fic]—dc23
LC record available at https://lccn.loc.gov/2018056836

To the best of good peoples, my parents.
And to other good peoples, Anu and Haju,
without whom this book could not be.

This is a love story.
You've been warned.

MARVEL: TWO SATURDAYS IN MARCH

ON THE MORNING OF SATURDAY, MARCH 14, FOURTEEN-YEAR-OLD Adam Chen went to the Museum of Islamic Art in Doha.

A thirteenth-century drawing of a tree caught his gaze. It wasn't particularly striking or artistic. He didn't know why this tree caused him to stride forward as if magnetized. (When he thinks about it now, his guess is thus: Trees were kind of missing in the landscape he found himself in at the time, and so he was hungry for them.)

Once he got close, he was rewarded with the name of the manuscript that housed this simple tree sketch: *The Marvels of Creation and the Oddities of Existence.*

He stood there thinking about this grand title for a long moment.

Then something clicked in his mind: *Maybe that's what living is—recognizing the marvels and oddities around you.*

From that day, he vowed to record the marvels he knew to be true and the oddities he wished weren't.

Adam, being Adam, found himself marveling more than ruminating on the weird bits of existing.

We pick up his Marvels and Oddities journal on March 7, four years after that Saturday at the Museum of Islamic Art.

Eighteen now, Adam is a freshman in college, but it's important to know that he has stopped going to classes two months ago.

He has decided to *live*.

On the very late evening of Saturday, March 11, sixteen-year-old Zayneb Malik clicked on a link in her desperation to finish a project. She'd promised a Muslim Clothing Through the Ages poster for the Islamic History Fair at the mosque, and it was due in nine hours, give or take a few hours of sleep.

Perhaps it was because of the late hour, but the link was oddly intriguing to a girl looking for thirteenth-century hijab styles: *Al-Qazwini's Catalogue of Life as It Existed in the Islamic World, 1275 AD.*

The link opened to an ancient book.

The Marvels of Creation and the Oddities of Existence.

A description of the book followed, but Zayneb could not read on.

"Marvels" and "oddities" perfectly described the reality of her life right then.

The next day, after returning from the history fair (and taking a nap), she began a journal and kept it going for the next two years, recording the wonders and *thorns* in the garden of her life.

Zayneb, being Zayneb, focused on the latter. She dedicated her journal entries to pruning the prickly overgrowth that stifled her young life.

By the time we meet her at eighteen, she's become an expert gardener, ready to shear the world.

She's also just been suspended from school.

A NOTE TO UNDERSTANDING THE STORY
ABOUT TO UNFOLD

OTHER PEOPLE'S PRIVATE JOURNALS ARE TRICKY THINGS. IT FEELS strange to read them.

And if you do get to read one—say, if a diary were to fling open and stick to the window of the stalled subway car opposite your stalled subway car, and you had highly trained vision that allowed you to read tiny, tilted, cursive writing—even then, while devouring the details of a stranger's life, you would be overwhelmed with guilt.

You may even look around to see if there are witnesses to your peering-and-gulping reading behavior.

In this case, rest assured that you are free to enjoy the thoughts of Adam and Zayneb shamelessly. They have donated their diaries in the cause of . . . yes, love . . . on three conditions. One, that I cut out two incidents (the first involving a stranger's coffee cup, misplaced, that they both drank from by accident, and the second something I cannot write about here without quaking).

The other conditions are that I change their names and that I rewrite their entries in narrative form.

Done. Done. Done.

ZAYNEB
WEDNESDAY, MARCH 6
ODDITY: *HATERS*

I HATE HATEFUL PEOPLE. *

Exhibit A: The woman seated beside me on the plane.

She swore under her breath when she saw me. Hijabi me.

Muslim me, on an airplane.

She lifted her carry-on suitcase and slammed it into the overhead bin so hard, I was sure she damaged the wheels on it.

Then she rolled her eyes and whisper-swore again when I took a long moment to get up from my aisle seat to let her in.

My lap had been full. I'd had my Marvels and Oddities journal, a pen, my phone, headphones, and the food I'd bought right before boarding—a saran-wrapped breakfast sandwich and coffee. I had to gather these and, while clutching them to me, slide out.

After Hateful Woman got into her seat, her actions were executed in staccato, each orchestrated to let me know she was mad at my presence. Setting her purse down on the floor, *slam*, snapping the seat pocket in front of her to punch her newspaper in, *pow*, pulling her seat belt strap from under her, *yank*.

"I'm going to need to get up to go to the bathroom quite a bit, you know," she growled at me.

Nice to meet you, too.

"Okay," I said, smiling my smile of deadly politeness. I'd recently learned that smiling calm-evilly in the face of haters, well, *stranger haters*, gets them more inflamed.

"You've got to be ready to move out of the way faster than that," she said.

I tilted my head and blinked at her sweater-set self. "Okay."

"Shit. Bitch." She pretended it was because she couldn't find her seat-belt slot.

"Okay," I said again, popping headphones on and scrolling on my phone to find the right selection. I turned up the volume and drew the left earphone away from my ear a bit as if adjusting it.

A bit of Arabic, a traveling dua, filled the space between Hateful Woman and me.

She stared. I smiled.

*I know, I know. *I hate hateful people* was so ironic.

But I was born this way. Angry.

When my siblings and I were young, my parents had this thing where they liked to sum each of us three kids up by the way we had entered the world.

"Sadia had an actual smile on her face. Such a happy baby! Mansoor was calm, serene. And our youngest, Zayneb? She screamed nonstop for hours. A ball of anger!" Dad/Mom would say, laughing when they got to the punch line: me. When I was way younger, I'd get angry at *this*, their one-dimensional descriptions of us, their reducing us to these simple caricatures, their using me as a punch line. My face would redden, and I'd leave the room, puffing. They'd follow, trying to douse me with excuses for their thoughtlessness.

After a while they learned to follow up the punch line with

descriptions of my positive qualities. "But Zayneb is the most generous of our kids! Did you know she's been sponsoring an orphan abroad with her allowance since she was six? He's two years older than her, and she's been taking care of him!" They'd beam at preteen me, at my newly developed guarded expression.

Then, two years ago, when Mom and Dad had stopped this rudeness, I began not to care that they'd called me an angry baby.

Because by then I'd discovered this about myself: I get angry for the right reasons.

So I embraced my anger. I *was* the angry one.

Though, Marvels and Oddities, the right reasons got me suspended from school yesterday.

Exhibit B: The prime villain of the hater squad, Mr. Fencer.

I've written a lot about Mr. Fencer in here. But I've never given him a whole section in my oddities entries. I guess it's because oddities are like the nagging parts of life, things that you can sort of escape.

Fencer is inescapable. Every senior has to take at least one of his classes at our small school.

And he is evil personified.

Yesterday, in social science, he rubbed his hands together before passing out his carefully chosen handout:

GIRL BURIED ALIVE IN HONOR KILLING

Police in Gazra have discovered the body of a sixteen-year-old girl apparently buried alive for talking to boys. Her father and grandfather have been charged with the crime, having admitted that they had been upset at the girl for being friendly with several boys in the village. Her lungs and stomach were filled with soil, indicating that, at the time of burial, she was still alive.

I stopped reading. I knew what Fencer was doing. He was adding fuel to the fire he'd kindled since the semester started in February.

"You're going to use this article to do an analysis with the graphic organizer I modeled last class. Assignment due Wednesday, before break, no extensions. Questions?"

He stared right at me, the only Muslim in class.

He had parked himself in a corner of the room, on top of an empty desk, in order to get the best view of the class, a look of perverse satisfaction on his face. Like he was *tun-tun-da*-ing us.

From glancing around at the other students, I saw that it was working pretty well. Mouths hanging open, sighs, frowns, shifting in seats.

I turned the handout over to begin a note to Kavi.

Mike's hand shot up, already homing in to ace this one. "Sir, do we compare American culture and this particular culture?"

His laptop was open, an iPad beside it. My bet was that Mike was going to start the analysis as soon as Fencer answered him.

"Well, technically you can do any culture you're familiar with. But you must do this culture, Turkish—or actually Islamic—as the comparing culture."

I raised my hand. "Islam isn't a culture. It's a religion."

"A religion that permeates every aspect of one's living, right?" His legs began swinging. Excited. "Like art and architecture, for example."

"Well . . . yeah, some people call it a way of life."

"I define that as culture. A mode of living."

"But in this case, this buried girl is not an example of Islamic culture. You're stretching again." I made sure not to add "sir." Ever. Never.

"Anyone else want to answer that? People keeping up with notes can look back a couple of classes. When we did that extensive chart comparing women's rights around the world."

Mike's hand shot up. He had his iPad up in the other hand for everyone to see. Its brain held *his* brain, so no one else bothered to flip through their own notes. "Sir, we came to the conclusion, with the chart, that certain countries were weaker at upholding women's rights."

"And was there something that these countries had in common? Come on, people. Someone other than Mike?"

"They were all Muslim?" said Noemi, a girl with long blond bangs covering her eyes. She was staring at Fencer with an expression at the intersection of Practiced Boredom and Mild Curiosity, Freshly Piqued. "Is that what you're saying?"

Fencer jumped off the desk and awarded us with his you-got-it stance: hands on his corduroy hips, legs apart, face beaming. "Yes, or, to put it more precisely, you can say that it looks like the majority of those countries follow Islam. Anything else? Zee-naab?"

He deliberately mispronounced it that way. I'd told him it was Zay-nub many times. Even writing it phonetically on worksheets for him: *ZAY-NUB*.

I now bent down over the sheet of paper on my desk and pressed hard with my pen. *Fencer is not going to be here. I'm going to make sure of it.*

The dream: get Fencer fired.

The reality: raise my hand, challenge his BS, get my words twisted, sulk, and, to finish off, pen my anger on a piece of paper.

When Fencer went to the projector, I tossed the note to Kavi behind me. She added something and passed it back to me.

#EatThemAlive.

I smiled. She was talking about the online movement our friend Ayaan had recently joined, #EatThemAlive. Its primary function is to take down your regular neighborhood-variety racists and supremacists through Internet sleuthing. But Ayaan is in student council, so she does everything underground. Her way is to collect receipts quietly until she has enough to dismantle someone in a foolproof, methodical manner.

She'd told me she had some stuff on Fencer. Though she hadn't shown me anything.

But at this moment, I let the glee light me up inside—*Ayaan has stuff*—which meant we'd be taking Fencer down soon. I'd already told her I wanted a part in it.

Fencer is not going to be here. I'm going to make sure of it.

I stared at Kavi's words underneath mine. *#EatThemAlive.*

A doodle of a pair of hands holding a fork and a knife would go well on either side of Kavi's contribution. She'd appreciate my attempt at art, *her* forte.

I began drawing a sharp-looking butter knife with exaggerated jagged edges and a slender, spiky tip.

A hand clasped the paper from my desk and yanked so hard, my pen trailed ink off it onto my desk.

I looked up at Fencer, my eyes wide, brain registering what I'd just drawn.

A knife. A fierce-looking one.

"Zee-naab, office. Now." He had the calm face of someone who already knew they'd won before the game had started. "I'll be there in five with this threat of yours."

. . .

It was easy for Principal Kerr to suspend me. It was a two-step process.

1. After repeatedly asking *Why would you do something like this?* and getting nothing out of me, Kerr called Mom. She promptly left the travel agency where she works.

2. Holding up my "threatening" note, Kerr outlined, for Mom's benefit, what I'd done, while I stayed mute, staring so hard at Fencer's shoes, willing two holes to be burned in them, that he shifted uncomfortably a few times.

Kerr repeated "Eat them alive?" two times, the second time in a higher-pitched voice, and I pictured Kavi's face, dark hair parted at the side, thin brown arms crisscrossed over textbooks affixed to her chest, her lips doing that barely there smile she does.

I saw her by my locker, waiting for me at lunch, as she'd done almost every day for the past few years.

I'd never give her away.

"Miss Malik, do you realize this could be considered expulsion worthy? A threat, with a weapon, directed at a teacher?" Kerr stared at me.

The anger inside me got switched, without my permission, and traded places with worry.

I want to go to UChicago in the fall. That's where my sister, Sadia, goes, and she promised to move out of her dorm so we could get a place together.

I wilted in the chair beside Mom. She glanced at me, worry flitting her own eyes, so I shot her a pained look: *Say something.*

But she was a people pleaser, so she nodded at Kerr, almost groveling-like.

My stomach clenched. Mom wasn't going to help me out.

I dropped my gaze and saw Fencer's dark brown loafers again.

The sight stilled the tears that had begun pooling. I blinked them away and concentrated on boring more holes in Fencer's shoes.

But maybe Kerr saw my wet eyes. Because suddenly she cleared her throat, and when she next spoke, her voice was calmer.

"The only reason we've decided to give Miss Malik a week's suspension instead—which will go into her records, by the way—is due to her exemplary academic record over the years. I'll see this as a terrible, terrible decision she's made. Mr. Fencer agrees with me on this." Her voice hardened again. "But give me one more thing to make me reconsider, Miss Malik, and we may be seeing your college future at stake. I will not hesitate to make that so."

Beside Mom, Fencer sighed as if he were pondering college-less me.

Anger welled and churned inside.

Eat them alive.

I'm going to get him. I'm going to get Fencer.

As soon as we got in the car and she turned the ignition, Mom began. "I never thought we'd have this sort of trouble with you, Zayneb. A threat against your teacher? A knife?"

"It wasn't a threat! It was about getting him fired. And the knife was a butter knife. I was just about to draw the fork." I frowned at the front of Alexander Porter High with its ugly green double doors.

"We didn't bring you up like this. I'm ashamed." Mom's voice was small, which meant it was going to be the crying kind of lecture.

"You didn't say anything!" I turned to her. "Nothing about what he's doing! You acted like it was my fault!"

"I can't prove anything about your teacher. Every time Dad

and I offered to talk to him before, you said no." With the car stopped where the entrance of the school parking lot met the road, she glanced at me, mouth trembling slightly. "Can't you just graduate in peace?"

"You mean, *Shut up, Zayneb! Don't make a scene, Zayneb!*" I put my hand on the door handle. "Can I get out? I'll just walk home like I always do."

She let me.

Ayaan had alerted me to Fencer before I entered his class this semester. There are only a few Muslims at Alexander Porter High, so we've gotten into this looking-out-for-each-other thing.

She told me Fencer was an Islamophobe. That she'd had two classes with him—one in junior year and one first semester of this year—and, somehow, he brought an uncanny number of topics and discussions around to how Islam and Muslims were ruining the world.

The thing is, Ayaan has wanted to become a lawyer since forever, so she's about building up a case. She doesn't say anything, *didn't* say anything to Fencer, and just kept collecting information when she'd been in his class. Collecting *evidence*. Including, recently, data from his online personas. She was supposed to show me some screenshots soon. She said I had to come over to see them, as she wouldn't risk sending them via messaging or e-mail. She didn't say it outright, but I'm pretty sure she was worried I'd pass it on somehow and ruin everything.

The other thing is that Ayaan doesn't wear hijab. She's Muslim, and Fencer knows it from her full name—Ayaan Ahmed—but he's not sure what kind.

Like, he doesn't know if she cares about her identity or if she practices her faith. Or if she simply has a Muslim name.

He doesn't know what I know: that Ayaan is a devout Muslim who goes to the mosque more than hijabi me. That she prays and believes and is on a million Muslim committees.

She's been able to keep track of Fencer quietly, stealthily. Undercoverily.

But from the moment I arrived, I wouldn't stop challenging his bullshit to his face.

Which made him more excited. And caused him to dial up his antics. It's like, when I walk into his class, I can practically see his glasses train their crosshairs on my hijab.

What riles me is that people think Islamophobia is these little or big acts of violence. Someone getting their hijab ripped off, someone's business getting vandalized, someone getting hurt or, yes, even *killed*.

No, there's the other kind too, and it's a more prevalent kind: the slow, steady barrage of tiny acts of prejudice, these your-people-are-trash lightsaber cuts that tear and peel strips off your soul until you can't feel your numbed heart any longer.

Angrier than angry, because then you've got almost nothing positive left inside.

Then the truth reveals itself: The world doesn't make sense, doesn't work for you.

For me.

And I know it won't ever work for me, no matter how much I fight or how angry I get.

That's how I felt unlocking the door to let my suspended self into the house.

After dinner, Dad knocked on my bedroom door before opening it gingerly. He'd already given me a lengthy speech while we were eating (*The best way to challenge these Islamophobes is by succeeding in society. Getting suspended is not succeeding! Don't you want to join your sister and brother at university?*), so I wondered what he wanted now. On the bed, cocooned in my ancient, raggedy but cozy blanket, Binky, I paused the reply text I'd been composing to Kavi, slid my headphones off, and stopped a comforting episode of *The Office* on my laptop, my questioning eyes on Dad.

He stroked his beard and cleared his throat. "Okay, I don't want you to see this as a reward, but Auntie Natasha is on the phone with Mom. Trying to convince her to let you come earlier."

"To Doha?" I couldn't stop the stunned joy from escaping me. The blanket cradling my head dropped back as I uncrossed my legs. "Like, what do you mean, 'earlier'?"

"Mom looked at flight options, and you could leave tomorrow afternoon if we drive you to Chicago. Auntie Natasha said instead of moping here, you should spend the next week with her, before Mom joins you guys."

"Oh please, could I?" I shrugged out of the blanket, got up from bed, and went to the suitcase Mom had wheeled into my room last night with orders to fill it over the course of next week for our planned spring break trip to visit her sister in Qatar.

But with this news, I'd potentially be getting to Doha on Thursday, when everyone else at school had a week to go before break!

If Dad and Mom agreed to Auntie Nandy's idea, that is.

I dropped the orange hard-case luggage on its side on the carpet and knelt to unzip it. "Please? I'll pack right now?"

"But this is not a reward, you understand?" Dad crossed his arms. "You'll have to do whatever Auntie Natasha says. She's still working, you know. She's not going to appreciate you giving her problems."

"I promise, Dad." I let the two halves of the suitcase fall open and looked up just as Mom came up behind him. Her face was sad, so I smiled to prove I'd gotten over being angry at her. "I won't bother Auntie Nandy. I'll be quiet and compliant."

Mom and Dad looked at each other and exchanged weird expressions, in between amusement and disbelief. Then Mom spoke. "The only flight you can take has a layover in London. I'm a bit worried about that."

"Mom, all I have to do is get out of the plane and wait in the airport for another one. Please?"

She turned to Dad. "Well, it *is* just two hours. Not a long wait, really."

He nodded.

I couldn't stop myself from jumping up. I went to stand in front of them, my arms open slightly, a hug cue.

They took it, enveloping me in forgiveness. Mom spoke into my hair. "When we come back from Doha, you'll only have a couple of months of school left. Can you promise us you'll do your best until the end?"

I nodded. Everyone has a different definition of what "doing your best" means. For Mom and Dad, it means not rocking any boats.

For me it means fixing things that are wrong.

Dad let the hug go first, but it was to address me. "Going away on your own often changes you. Maybe this bit of time in Doha is just what you need."

"I'm going to try to leave the angry part of me here for the next two weeks," I said, turning back to the suitcase.

When I glanced up, Mom and Dad were exchanging looks again, so I felt the need to emphasize my commitment to calm.

"I promise you I won't cause any more ruckuses. Anyway, it'll be easier, with less rude people around me."

The less-rude-people thing hasn't worked out.

Exhibit A: The hateful woman I'm stuck next to on the plane.

We've been in the air just under two hours, and this woman has made me get up from my seat four times already. I've been writing in you, Marvels and Oddities journal, on and off since the plane took off, and she won't stop peering at my words.

I promised Mom and Dad I wouldn't make a scene, so I've kept my responses limited to unrelenting smiles, but now . . . I think it's time to get to her.

So to really freak her out, here, journal, have some Arabic words, written nice and big.

إن شاء الله

MARVEL: AIR

Air, as in what I'm flying through. Well, the plane I'm sitting on is flying through. Air.

(Also, air holds the cellular signals that will allow further communication between Kavi, Ayaan, and me. So that we can plot Mr. Fencer's takedown.)

إن شاء الله

Oops, that went into oddities territory there.

ADAM
THURSDAY, MARCH 7
MARVEL: TOUCH

SINCE I STOPPED GOING TO CLASSES TWO MONTHS AGO, MY DORM has gotten crowded.

It's a good thing my roommate, Jarred, is practically never here. I mean it's a good thing his girlfriend has her own place.

The tools are on my side, spread across my desk mostly, but somehow the things I make end up on his desk while they wait to be finished.

Jarred's desk currently holds a working clock made out of an old marble chessboard, with chess pieces for numbers, awaiting another coat of sealant. A plastic-robot phone-charger station awaiting wiring. A tiny Canada goose, midflight, glued together from bits of discarded wood chips, awaiting painting. Several parts of a foam Boba Fett helmet awaiting assembly.

Also awaiting assembly: a gift for my sister, Hanna.

Yesterday I took the thin pieces of grooved balsa wood and fit them together in a grid pattern inside the box I'd already made. As the square compartments revealed themselves, smooth and flush without any screws or nails, I thought about touch.

I thought about how, without the ability to feel the wood, the plastic, the foam, the metal, without the sensation I get when I clasp the ryoba saw and the jolt from snipping a thick wire or the hum that goes through my fingers when I'm sanding, without all this I wouldn't have anything, wouldn't be happy.

I like that I still have the ability to touch. And that I can use it to make stuff.

So, since January, since second term started, I've just been making things.

I've dropped out of school.

I don't want to run out of time.

Speaking of touch, I haven't had a voluntary *human* touch in a long time. A real one, I mean.

In September, I hugged Dad and my little sister, Hanna, at the airport before leaving for London.

The last I-love-you touch.

Technically, you could say, *what about on Fridays, Adam? At the mosque, after prayers, when everyone says salaam and hugs one another, you included?*

Those hugs are cursory. They don't go much beyond the shoulder-slam, hey-I-see-you-bro.

There's another kind of touch: the *kind* kind. It means a lot— well, to someone who craves it.

I crave it. I haven't stopped thinking about how much since I realized how long it's been.

It was the tick marks above my bed, underneath the bunk on top of mine, that got me thinking about when I'd last extended my hand to anyone. Or anyone extended their hand to me.

Someone who lived in the dorm before me had recorded their days at university like a prison sentence, carving into the wooden slats under Jarred's bed, and, one night a week ago, reaching up to run a finger over the tallies, I touched the gnawing in me.

I realized it had worked its way around inside, gouging, for a while.

It must be a hole I've carried since the start of freshman year. (Though sometimes I wonder if it carried over from years before that.)

Simple tally marks etched with a pocketknife woke me to my hollowness.

Now it's Thursday morning, and I'm supposed to be getting up and getting going, but instead, I reach up and touch those tally marks again, wondering if people can get used to this feeling.

Like they get used to other sad stuff.

Anyway, this journal entry is a marvel, so it's supposed to be positive.

Positive: It's spring break, and this afternoon I'll be on my way to Doha.

In about eight hours I'll hug my family again. Show love to Dad and Hanna again.

And be loved back. For a bit.

Ryan was waiting for me in the common room, sitting in one of the worn-out armchairs, a laptop open on his legs. "Where's your luggage?"

I lifted a shoulder. "Here."

"A small duffel? For two weeks?" He closed his laptop and slid it into his backpack before getting up.

"I already got clothes there. This is just stuff I can't live without," I said, holding up my guitar case. "You know about the detour we have to take, right?"

"The Rock Shop, aye, aye, sir. I didn't know you were into metal music." He led the way down the stairs to the door opening onto the side street, the only place you could find parking, if you were lucky. "That's not the kind of stuff you play."

I smiled but kept my mouth shut.

We opened the door labeled THE ROCK SHOP, written out in pebbles. The storefront had no window, so your first taste of the Rock Shop's wares was literally on the door.

The door yielded the rest of the shop's treasures. Rocks, pebbles, gemstones, fossils assembled in little baskets placed around the tiny store.

Ryan looked at me. "What's this? Why are we here?"

I laughed. "Present for my little sister."

"We could have got some for free near the maths building," Ryan said, picking up a nondescript-looking gray rock from a tray. "You know, all those shiny white rocks they have around the planters out front?" He turned over the rock in his hand. "Three quid for this? Really?"

I headed straight to the minerals section.

Hanna had asked me for azurite, a blue mineral, to add to her collection. When we were talking on FaceTime, she showed me the space she'd made for it, and I couldn't help noticing the old Ferrero Rocher tray she kept her favorite rocks in. I knew she liked the candy box for its rounded compartments, perfect for holding each stone, but I could imagine how excited she would be to have her own *real* display case.

Like the one I'd made for her, now packed between my clothes in the duffel.

• • •

After we stopped to eat, Ryan dropped me at the airport. I checked in the case containing the guitar that I'd carefully bubble wrapped, silently praying it would safely reach Doha.

Finding a seat near my boarding gate, I set my duffel between my feet and leaned back into the vinyl.

A couple was right in front of me, their arms draped around each other, laughing at something they were watching on a tablet propped between their laps.

I looked to the left and was met with the sight of another two kissing each other by a mobile-device charging pole.

I glanced over the whole place. Yup, couples dotted here and there, everywhere.

Spring break.

I don't dare bring up my predicament with Jarred, my dorm mate, or Ryan, my closest friend here in London. They're both in kind of steady relationships and will tell me to start my own.

They'll tell me to get a girlfriend. Get it on.

But it's not physical. (Though that's mixed in there somewhere too.)

It's this thing beyond that. I know that may sound weird.

But that's me.

Besides, Jarred and Ryan don't get how, for the type of Muslim I am, it's a one-relationship deal. With one person. Without trying it out or half investments.

And so I gotta be right about a relationship. Before I get too into it.

When you think about it, that seems scary. Impossible.

How do you meet that one *exact* person who's right for you?

• • •

I've met only one person who I thought could maybe be *exact* for me.

She was a freshman orientation tour guide, and then I saw her again, working as support at the computer lab. The next time I'd noticed her was at the Muslim Student Union welcome dinner.

We started talking every week, mostly at the lab or the MSU.

I liked her because she smiled easily and her voice had this *sure* quality to it. Like she was confident of whatever she was talking about.

By the end of October I'd made up my mind to ask her if she'd want to get to know each other seriously, and not just at MSU stuff. But then in November, I'd gotten news I didn't want.

And when I looked up from being so preoccupied with it, she was gone. Literally. She went to Lebanon over the winter holidays and came back engaged.

It was a good thing, too. She couldn't have been the right one for me.

My November news told me I had other things to deal with.

So I've been training myself to make my peace with aloneness.

I rubbed my eyes to clear the happy coupledom scenes from my brain, and, just as I was about to take my laptop out of my duffel to go online, a girl came and sat two seats to the left of the couple in front of me.

She had on a hijab that was almost exactly the same shade as the azurite I'd bought for Hanna. Brilliant blue.

I'm pretty sure that's why I noticed her. That and how she didn't take her eyes off the phone in her hands, the one she was speed-clicking on, not even to check if the seat she took was clear, not even when her carry-on suitcase fell over, with her coat on the handles, and lay on the floor in a pile.

She left everything there, and then even let the flowery purse on the crook of her arm slip down and join its mates on the floor.

The handles on the purse sprung apart to reveal its jammed contents.

An orange book sticking out caught my eye. In big, bold, black handwritten letters it said *MARVELS AND ODDITIES JOURNAL*.

I think I must have made a sound, because she looked up, her eyes inquisitive.

I looked down at her feet. At the jumble around them.

She looked down herself and gave a start, setting her phone on the seat beside her to gather everything up and set them properly.

I took my laptop out and opened it on my knees—but I'd be lying if I said I was browsing online.

Instead, shielded by eyes staring at the log-in screen, my mind was in scrambles, wondering how, sitting across from me, was someone with a journal exactly like mine.

ODDITY: SECRETS

The kind of secret that punches people in the gut.

The kind written on the folded paper in my duffel, ready to be carried onto the plane to Doha.

The reason I avoided flying back home for Christmas holidays. The reason I stopped going to classes.

After I received it, in November, I spent too much time incessantly unfolding it to pore over it. Then, one day in December, I folded it up for the last time and kept it that way.

I haven't looked at that bit of news since then.

ZAYNEB
THURSDAY, MARCH 7
ODDITY: *RUMORS*

I'D WANTED TO GET AWAY—MAYBE EVEN FIND THAT ELUSIVE THING called *peace*—but everything followed me.

Exhibit A: The messages I got on every social media platform when I landed in London.

Somehow someone had gotten a picture of my note—*Fencer is not going to be here. I'm going to make sure of it.* (Bad knife drawing flanking #*EatThemAlive*)—and shared it with others who were then sharing it on and on.

Some people thought it was funny, but those people were few. Fencer wasn't exactly popular, but he wasn't considered mean, either, so most students were giving my suspension a thumbs-up.

And then *i* and *t* words started showing up underneath my profiles.

She's ISIS.

ISIS girl should have been expelled.

I can't believe Kerr let the terrorist off.

You terrorist cunt.

Then it became crazy stuff.

Heard your father is in ISIS.

Someone should tell the cops to check her house.

I already did. Told my dad who's a cop.

They already found stuff on her.

Then I got a slew of private messages from Ayaan: *What did you do?*

I mean Kavi told me.

But what did you do?

SUSPENDED?

AND you blew everything.

And you take off for Doha?

WTH Zayneb

These messages came flooding in as the plane taxied on the tarmac at Heathrow and my phone got service again. After disembarking and walking to the gate for my connecting flight to Doha, I was able to start answering Ayaan once I found a place to sit.

I clicked apology after apology to her, imagining her sad, sad face looking at all the evidence she'd been collecting on Fencer for so long going up in flames.

Kavi had already told me this morning, after apologizing in tears to me last night for *her* contribution to getting me suspended, that she'd apologized profusely to Ayaan for writing *#EatThemAlive*, possibly alerting Fencer to what was going on.

If he googled those words, I'm pretty sure he'd come upon the hashtag and then see the many people who'd been removed from their jobs for their racism. He'd get a whiff that he himself was being tracked, and, *poof*, he'd delete his online presence.

The one Ayaan's been researching.

The one she needs to turn over to the school board, because they'd probably not believe her screenshots, so easily photoshop-pable.

Yes, I did blow everything.

I kept sending a string of apologies, but deep down I knew Ayaan would never trust me again.

And to think, I'd considered what had happened on the rest of the flight to London with Hateful Woman had been bad.

When she saw the Arabic I wrote in you, Marvels and Oddities, she pressed the flight-attendant call button incessantly.

"Either I move or she does," she hissed at the attendant who came by. "She's threatening me. Writing something about me the whole time."

The flight attendant, a guy with dark hair and white glasses, looked at me.

"I'm just writing in my journal. I don't get how that's threatening," I offered.

"Move me *now*." She began gathering her things.

I swept my stuff together, put my tray up, and stood to let her pass. She stepped out in front of me, into the aisle, her eyes on other passengers, her head shaking hard in an attempt to solicit sympathy for her plight.

"Ma'am, please stay seated. I haven't found a spot for you yet." The attendant put his hands on his hips and looked down the aisle.

I turned away, to the back of the plane, willing myself to be calm. Willing myself *not* to tell the woman off.

Or even explain myself to the flight attendant.

You promised Mom and Dad.

Stay quiet.

Shut up, Zayneb.

Some of the other passengers peered at me, and I beamed back at them. Maybe if I looked like a happy Muslim teen, someone would offer to trade places with Hateful Woman or even with me.

No one moved.

I turned around so I wouldn't make it even further awkward for everyone.

"Sit down, please, ma'am. I'll come back after I check," the flight attendant said to Hateful Woman again, his gaze then falling on my face.

Maybe I looked weird in my attempts to appear nice, because he shook his head slightly before turning to walk to the front of the plane.

Hateful Woman and I were still standing, me in the aisle, her in front of my seat so I couldn't even sit down, her back to me as she watched the flight attendant go in search of "comfort" for her.

I clutched my things tighter to me and looked around again, at the passengers' faces—some blank, some frowning, some whispering—my stomach squeezing over and over.

Most of them probably believed everything bad that they'd heard about Muslims, the headlines, the "news" stories, the online comments, the rumors.

Was there anybody on this plane who wouldn't look at me and think *troublemaker*?

Or worse, *terrorist*?

Hateful Woman was moved to first class, and, even though I had both seats to myself, I stayed tight and unmoving, fuming.

Then I noticed a girl my age across from me, up one seat. She was working in a sketchbook, a container of colored pencils in her lap along with headphones, snacks, and a stuffed animal.

Coloring girl was white and blond.

The sight of her tore a hole in me.

The way she was bobbing her head while her pencil moved rhythmically across the paper, like she was immersed in some happy music only she could hear, though her headphones were not even on her ears.

Part of the coat she was sitting on stuck out into the aisle— cutesy for her, but if *I'd* let that happen? *Belligerent.*

Seeing her totally okay, completely comfortable in life, made me tear up.

I mean I'm sure that girl might have all sorts of other problems going on. Most probably she did.

It's just that when people first saw her, a bunch of crap thoughts didn't instantly load into their brains.

Her coat sticking out didn't sum *her* up.

My coat sticking out could. Because of all the years of rumors about *people like me*.

I didn't have to open my mouth or do anything for people to judge me. I just had to be born into a Muslim family and grow up to want to become a visible member of my community by wrapping a cloth on my head.

I just had to be me.

Angry people are not known to be public criers. They usually don't succumb to displays of grief.

But I let the tears fall and fall without a care of who saw them. I didn't sob or heave or make any movements. I just sat there staring at the white girl coloring happily and cried.

Maybe it was Fencer's sigh in the principal's office yesterday, the suspension note in my student file, and the fact that Ayaan hadn't replied to any of my messages before I'd left home this afternoon.

Maybe it was imagining Hateful Woman enjoying first class, getting rewarded for her rudeness to me.

Maybe it was *everything* for a long time.

I succumbed to the sadness I'd held at bay.

And the questions flooded in:

If I had been that white, blond girl with a lap full of a journal, a pen, headphones, phone, and a sandwich, a coffee in my hand, would Hateful Woman have slammed her carry-on so hard above me? Would she have excused the time I'd taken to get up, thinking of her own daughter or granddaughter and how it took them a while to get their stuff together? Would she have made small talk and gotten to know me a teeny bit? Then would she have smiled fondly at me like the flight attendant walking by the coloring girl had smiled at her *right now?*

I just held myself, alone on a full plane, and mourned silently until I fell asleep for the rest of the flight.

And then, Marvels and Oddities, I landed in London.

She's ISIS.

ISIS girl should have been expelled.

I can't believe Kerr let the terrorist off.

You terrorist cunt.

MARVEL . . .

I can't even think of one at the moment. But I know I promised a marvel for every oddity, so . . .

Okay, here, I'll give you one: cute guys.

Well, the cute guy across from me as I write. He's preoccupied with his laptop, so I'll describe him.

Exhibit A: Cute guy at the airport.

He's tall, his legs so long that if he didn't keep them propped up kind of high, he'd be tripping people walking in front of his seat.

He looks like he's of Asian background, like me.

Well, one half of me, because Dad is from Pakistan, which is in South Asia, but then Mom's family being Guyanese (grandpa) and Trinidadian (grandma) makes her of West Indian background, which is considered to be Caribbean.

This guy looked like he was of East Asian ancestry—either Chinese or Korean or from another country—plus something else.

Plus something else, like me.

I think what pinged CUTE GUY ALERT immediately was the way his face was angular, including a perfect jawline, and inaccessible-seeming, but then his expression was so open.

Like the first time we locked gazes, his eyes had looked lively somehow.

Like he wasn't closed up.

Like there's this easy smile on his face, even while reading his laptop screen.

His hair was—okay, that's all. He saw me looking at him a few times, so I'm going to stop.

Besides, if my big sister, Sadia, were here with me, she would text, *Lower your gaze like a good Muslim, Zu-zu.*

I LOOKED AT MY FIRST MARVEL ENTRY, AT THE VERY BEGINNING OF my Marvels and Oddities journal, which I'd uploaded onto my laptop, and it was *trees*. That's when I was sketching in my journal, so there were tiny drawings of a few tree specimens found in Doha.

Every subsequent marvel entry was an observable item like *sand*, *birds*, *water*, *potatoes*, and a whole long entry on *rocks* when Hanna got crazy over them. Typical thoughts recorded by some-one who loved cataloging things. Almost entirely nature-oriented observations.

I guess at some point it was natural I would move on to less-tangible things. That point occurred just this past year, when I noticed the things I needed to hold on to, marvels you couldn't necessarily grasp in your hands.

Like *smiles*. And how instantaneously a genuine one can set you at ease.

The brilliant-blue-hijabed girl stopped tapping away on her phone and pulled out her Marvels and Oddities journal, propped it on her carry-on suitcase, and began writing in it without pause, without glancing around, a frown on her face.

I was still floored that we had the same journal, so I kept stealing glances at her. And then she stopped with her pen to her lips and looked straight at me.

Luckily, I saw it coming and moved my eyes in time. I hope.

At one point I had this sudden urge to strike up conversation: *Isn't it weird we're doing the exact same thing? Recording marvels and oddities?*

Isn't it absolutely wild?

But I let it pass, and then the flight happened.

And the smile happened.

Around midpoint in the flight, I got up to use the bathroom, and there she was—sitting in the very last row in a single seat, almost right across from the bathroom. She had the reading light turned on above her, so she was bathed in its glow, her face—big eyes now behind round glasses—lit.

When she looked up and saw my tall self advancing toward the back of the plane, I nodded at her for some reason.

Great.

Creepy guy on plane.

I had to explain the nod.

It was basically the Muslim-to-Muslim nod, but, looking at me, she probably didn't think I was Muslim.

Without a marker like a skullcap or something, it's sometimes hard to distinguish us Muslim guys.

So as I got right across from her seat, I said, "Assalamu alaikum," and disappeared into the bathroom.

"Walaikum musalam," she said when I emerged. "I hadn't realized you were Muslim. Sorry."

Bam.

"Yes. Since I was eleven." There was a nice space in front of the bathroom as it was also connected to a kitchenette, so I was able to face her from where I stood.

"Like my mom," she said, tilting her head to look up.

"Your mom's been Muslim since she was eleven too?"

"No." She laughed. "She converted when she married my dad. Well, right before she married him. In her twenties."

"Aha," I said real sagely. I crossed my arms and looked down the aisle. Someone was coming to use the bathroom.

"But wow, you, at eleven years old? I've never heard of that." She tilted her head again, her eyes even wider. "A little kid converting."

And then she smiled. Big, open, and honest.

I indicated the guy heading our way. "Maybe I'll tell you about it . . . on my next bathroom break?"

She laughed again.

Back in my seat I decided my next bathroom break would be in forty minutes. I watched an episode of some reality show where contestants had to drive cars that they'd tinkered with to make more powerful, and then bent to retrieve my journal from the duffel bag.

I had to show her the cover. *Marvels and Oddities.*

There were a few people waiting for the bathroom now, so I joined the line until I noticed that the girl was sleeping, her arms crossed in front of her chest, her face lying on a pillow she'd propped next to the window.

I glanced away—it felt weird to look at someone sleeping. And then I went back to my seat.

・ ・ ・

The next time I ventured back there, she wasn't in her seat. Maybe she was in the bathroom herself.

I put the journal back in my duffel.

I thought I'd try one more time. I didn't care that everyone around me must have thought I had diarrhea or something, the amount of times I was making my way back there.

I don't know why I just had to show her the journal—maybe to let her know there were two of us?

No, I think maybe it was to see that smile again.

The flight attendants were blocking the aisle with the food cart. I ended up taking a few steps toward them before returning to my seat.

From behind the cart, I had glimpsed the blue-hijabed girl. She'd been watching something on the screen in front of her, so she hadn't seen me.

Even though I had made up my mind to try one last time, I fell asleep until the flight landed in Doha and the guy beside me nudged me to get a move on. I picked up my duffel and got in the exodus line, thinking of Dad and Hanna.

The Doha airport was so quiet that the whir of luggage wheels formed a hum that accompanied those of us who disembarked. It followed us to the visa counter and then to the luggage carousel.

I glanced around a few times but didn't see the girl from the plane.

Real strange. First, that I saw the journal, and, second, that it was preoccupying me so much.

At the luggage carousel, as the belt went around empty, awaiting the luggage, I put my hand in the pocket of my jeans and pulled out the azurite. It was kind of small, but it was the deepest blue one at the shop, and I knew Hanna would appreciate that the most.

"Found something?" Girl in blue hijab. Smiling.

"No, just a gift for someone." I held up the rock, hoping my face hadn't lit up too much at the sight of her. "She's a rock connoisseur."

"Nice." She nodded. "There's my luggage."

She left to grab an orange suitcase off the carousel. She pulled up the handle and slid her carry-on onto it so that she only had one item to pull behind her.

And then she didn't come back but just waved at me before heading to the wide, automated exit doors.

I felt a need to raise my voice to ask her name or her Instagram, but it was so quiet in the place.

I also realized I'd let my guitar go by on the carousel.

I decided I'd let it go around again.

I walked fast enough to catch up with her just as she reached the doors.

I just need her name.

The arrivals doors flung open to reveal those waiting.

And there stood Ms. Raymond.

I turned back to the carousel, back to my guitar.

Ms. Raymond was my teacher in the fourth grade at Doha International School.

I had no idea why she was here at the airport now, but it was unnerving.

The folded paper in my duffel, the one with my diagnosis, flew out and punched me in the gut.

It literally didn't, but that's what it felt like.

ODDITY: FIRST IMPRESSIONS

How do you decide you like or don't like someone? Like, when you meet someone, there's a point when you form one of two thoughts: *I like this person enough to want to know them a bit more* or *STOP! Go no further in your attempts to know this person.*

For me, it takes at least four times being around someone. I like to let things unfold, so I rarely rely on first impressions. I'm generally a four-impressions kind of guy.

First impressions don't reveal anything. They're just about you—well, the person looking at someone, listening to them, observing them—projecting your own self to assess another.

I guess I'm trying to say it's okay I didn't get her name.

BY THE TIME I WOKE UP, I WAS IN A BETTER MOOD. THE UNEVENTFUL flight from London to Doha—uneventful except for the fact that the cute guy from the airport said salaam to me!—and the three episodes I'd watched of *Sweet Tooth*, a dessert-making show where there's no talking, just music and people making complicated desserts step-by-step, had calmed me down a lot.

Then, to see Auntie Nandy! The hug she wrapped me in as soon as I got out of arrivals had almost swept me off my feet.

Auntie Nandy was Mom's younger sister, but she was taller and had a more squarish face, with a prominent jawline and a big smile. Ever since I could remember, she'd worn her hair in a pixie cut.

She was no-nonsense but in a super-kind way.

The entire ride to her place from the airport had been me listening to testimony of how much she'd missed me, how she'd watched every Instagram story I posted (mental note: remember this), sometimes several times, and how she'd felt like she'd won the lottery when my parents agreed to let me come visit her earlier.

Basically, I was engulfed in love.

Cute guy saying salaam, eating desserts with my eyes on the flight over, Auntie Nandy professing her love—this almost erased the dumpster fire Tuesday had been.

But while Auntie Nandy is warm and cheerful, her apartment isn't.

Exhibit A: Cold spaces.

Her place is hard and crystal clear and unforgiving. Each room has windows from the ceiling to the marble-tiled floor, with glass tabletops and steely reflective surfaces everywhere to further emphasize the clean, cold clarity of the space.

It's like a crisp-suit-and-cufflinks-wearing stern man lives here instead of a smiley, talkative aunt who calls me Zoodles.

Last night I'd rolled my luggage into the minimalist guest bedroom—white-duvet-covered bed framed by a huge, mirrored wardrobe, sleek with no knobs or handles—and promptly unzipped my carry-on suitcase to pull out some essentials.

I knew it had been a good idea to pack Binky and Squish.

The cuddly factor was a must in this place. Especially after my soul had been drained over the past few days.

As I set Squish on the night table, I realized on first sight of it, someone might gag and pick it up with two fingers to hurl it into the nearest garbage can. But if they looked carefully, past the matted brownish-gray fur and squished ears (hence the name), five letters would come together to form in their heads: L-O-V-E-D.

Squish is not a stuffed *animal* per se but some sort of cross between a puffer fish (round and spotty with bulging eyes and knowing lips), an elephant (longish snout), and a cat (perky ears—well, previously perky, now loved to nubbins).

Squish was my first stuffed *being*.

I have no idea whether someone weird gave it to me as a baby or whether Mom and Dad found Squish at some stuffed animals–factory mishaps sale (they don't remember its origins either), but the most important thing about Squish is it's the first thing I learned to love—after Mom and Dad, I mean.

Before my sister, Sadia, or my brother, Mansoor, took shape in my eyes as beings, Squish was there, squat and dependable for tears-and-fears duty, for soaking up rages and confusions.

I lay in bed now, not ready to completely wake up to a new day just yet, and saluted Squish on the night table, and pulled up Binky the blanket, my second cozy must, to my chin.

Sigh. Old, soft, and comfortable. Like Daadi, my grandmother, Dad's mom, who'd knit it for me when I was five.

Who passed away in October in Pakistan.

My whole life, she'd lived six months of the year with us in Springdale and six months in Pakistan. Every year she'd leave us in November to spend the winter months there, but last year she'd wanted to go earlier in order to attend a grandniece's wedding. Even though Dad had not wanted her to.

He always worried whenever Daadi did something different. Like leaving the city of Islamabad, where she lived in Pakistan, for any reason—out-of-town wedding or not.

I don't know the exact details of how she passed, but I know it had something to do with a car accident. Dad and Mom claim they don't know everything.

I wonder if they're just protecting us kids.

Our entire family was wrecked for months.

I closed my eyes and brought the bunny-white, bunny-soft blanket up over my nose, even over my eyes, trying to hold Daadi's face still in my head. Graying black hair loosely parted and spun daily into a slack knot at the back; quiet, studying eyes; and a small, ever-present smile—these features wove in and out of my mind's canvas.

But the image of her hands stayed static and accessible. Because those hands were always moving. Toward my face to cradle it in gentle greeting when I came home from school. Holding out food for me to try. Knitting me winter things in a mix of Gryffindor and Slytherin colors, like I'd request whenever she asked me what I wanted.

And, before that, knitting me Binky.

I wondered, if I'd seen her before I left home—if I'd felt her arms around me—would I have cried so easily on the plane here? Would her hug have transferred some of her calm—because she was the essence of peace itself, being the purest, softest, gentlest soul?

I miss her so much.

Exhibit B: Cold food.

Just as I was getting ready to fall back to sleep, Auntie Nandy, not only taller than Mom but louder, too, startled me by singing something about someone who left her, who hurt her, who was now back, but *She Will Survive!*

I got out of bed, grabbed my glasses—it being crazy early for my contact lenses—and opened the guest room door.

"'Oh no, not I! I will survive!'" she sang, advancing from the kitchen with a plate of scrambled eggs. She spotted disheveled, just-woke me. "Hi, Zoodles! You still love eggs, right? Because I made them three ways."

I nodded and emerged into the combination living-dining room. The center of the dining table was covered with small plates of food. "Thanks. Do you always sing in the morning, Auntie Nandy?"

"Only after nine a.m. on weekends. And only the best seventies hits. Grandpa's fault, sorry." She pulled a chair out for me and patted it. "Eggs: French toasted, scrambled, or omeleted? Also, mall or souk?"

"I haven't gotten up yet. I'm jet-lagged." I sat in front of the French toast, which promptly called on me to take a bite. It was strangely cold. "I thought you didn't cook. Mom even warned me not to ask you for anything. She told me to just fix my own stuff. What happened?"

"I'm glad you're bringing this topic up early on. Okay, time for operational details of your stay in Doha. I only cook breakfast, and it's usually a lot of choices, like so," she said, indicating the plates of charred tomatoes; boiled potatoes; yogurt with muesli flecks on top; cheese cubes and slices; several types of shelled nuts; chopped cucumber, celery, and green peppers; oranges, figs, and grapes; and the aforementioned eggs. "And then it's nothing until I order dinner in or we go out. This is like a nibble-whenever-you're-hungry table, like a buffet."

"So no lunch?" My stomach rumbled in anticipatory upset. "I'm into lunch."

"Worry not! I stuck a sheet on the fridge with the names of local restaurants that deliver here, plus my ordering info. Just go online and choose your lunch when I'm at work." She punched my arm. "I am not going to starve you. I've heard teens are ravenous creatures."

"Good, because I like to sleep in, eat a lot, and go out at night during vacations." I ripped French toast with my teeth to emphasize my wild nature.

"Then you'll love Doha. It comes alive at night, especially the souk."

"I remember from last time. Remember I shopped so much, Mom had to buy more luggage?" Last time I visited was when I was ten, but it was one of my favorite trips, so I've held on to the memories. Auntie Nandy had worked in Dubai and other places in the Arabian Gulf, but she'd stayed in Doha the longest. She said she found it a "less hectic but happening" city.

"Which brings me to operational details, part two. When I'm at work, you can move around on your own using my Uber account."

"What about the bus?"

"The bus system here is not the best, kiddo, but, woo-hoo, a subway is on its way!" Auntie Nandy grinned wide suddenly, and *now* she looked more like Mom—their lips thin out the same way, almost turning inward, so you see two rows of neat teeth. "I'm so happy you're here, Zoodles! Earlier than your mom, I mean! We can LIVE IT UP, GIRL."

She leaned over, punched my arm again, and then drew her hand away for a high five.

I paused nibbling the corner of a cheese cube and fived her. "Can we go out tonight? To the souk? Shopping?"

"Ah, no. Sorry darling. Tonight is a no. We're going to a party." She fixed herself a plate with a bit of everything, but she did it in a circular way, so that in the end it looked like a strange flower with part of an omelet as the center. "I'm on a clean-eating regime. I want to be toxin free by the end of summer."

I reached for the serving plate and tore a piece off the omelet to try. Also cold.

Auntie Nandy took her plate to the black leather sofa in the living room adjacent to the dining area. Tucking her legs under her on the couch, she picked up a remote and looked at me while turning on the TV. "If you want, we can go to the souk now and then come home in time to get ready for the party?"

"That's okay—I'm going back to bed. It's the middle of the

night back home. Thanks for the breakfast. I'll heat it up and eat some more when I'm really awake." I stood up. "About the party . . . do I *have* to go? Isn't the party invite just for you?"

"I thought you said you like to go out at night? It's absolutely not just for me. The other teachers are bringing their families," Auntie Nandy said.

"Oh, it's a school thing?" I frowned. Now I really didn't want to go. I was done with school.

But I guess that's what I got for spending my suspension week with an international schoolteacher. And Auntie Nandy *had* taken me in, instead of letting me stew at home, which meant I had to act grateful to her. She was watching car racing and hadn't seen my frown, so I undid it quickly.

"Don't worry; it'll be a nice party." She turned to me. "Lots of kids your age."

This Is What You Missed, Bulletin I by Kavi Srinivasan, filed as FYI for Zayneb Malik:

Fencer talked to the class about rage and how much of a destructive emotion it is.

And how rage is the root of a lot of world problems, namely terrorism and genocide, and how he wanted to apologize to everyone for how rage had disrupted the class yesterday.

I tapped my laptop keyboard furiously: So I'm terrorism and genocide?

I'm not done.

Noemi, blond-bangs girl on the lacrosse team, put her hand up and asked if, in Fencer's estimation, rage is ever justified.

He said in an ideal world no, but he recognizes we are not ideal, and so we get enraged over so many things.

What about rage at being victimized? Noemi asked.

He said sometimes victimization is in our heads, a perception problem.

(I'm pretty sure I heard a small group of people gasp at this.)

Noemi then said that she's studying sexual assault for her art project and how that's NOT a perception problem.

He said OF COURSE NOT. I'M TALKING ABOUT WHAT HAPPENED IN CLASS YESTERDAY WITH A STUDENT WHO FELT IT WAS WITHIN HER RIGHT TO THREATEN A TEACHER BECAUSE SHE WAS ENRAGED AT HEARING FACTS.

He actually raised his voice to say that. Then the bell rang, and Noemi said "asshole" under her breath as she was leaving.

So, again, I'm terrorism and genocide?

And also enraged at facts. Don't forget that part.

You know what? I'm going to a party tonight. It's a boring party, but it's a party nonetheless. I'm going to forget demon Fencer.

And, in a nod to my previous botched cutlery-drawing attempt, I added a long train of knife and fork emojis to finish off our communication.

For the boring party, I wore one of the nicer things I'd brought: a beige shirt with flared sleeves. I wore it with jeans and a dark blue chiffon hijab, and Auntie Nandy, in jeans herself and a tunic top, said I looked great.

She slipped a shawl around her shoulders before we left the apartment. She wasn't Muslim, but maybe having lived in Arabian Gulf countries for so long, she was used to scarves.

"Each year, the week before spring break starts, the head of the school, David, hosts a get-together at his house. It's like a *thank you, you've made it this far* party." As Auntie Nandy drove, she went on describing the people who'd be there and how much she liked this school compared to the other international schools she'd taught at, but I was drifting in and out of her words.

I was looking at Doha at night.

It was a strange mix of unbelievably glamorous, futuristic architecture and industrial concrete boxes, aka apartments. And, being a city in a predominantly Muslim country, the whole landscape was also dotted with the spires and domes of traditional-looking mosques.

It was like the old and the new and the future joined together in a small explosion, because there was also construction debris here and there that contrasted with the glitzy look of some of the neighborhoods.

I peered more and noticed there *was* a lot of construction happening. Within a kilometer of Auntie Nandy's apartment, I counted ten cranes.

Maybe I was kind of a weird person, because I liked the old-looking stuff more than the new. There was something inviting and even comforting about the round domes we passed by.

Maybe I was done with dealing with coldness.

Cold people in particular.

I wanted to be surrounded by warmth.

I lowered the window and let the warm air touch my face. Then I leaned back, closed my eyes, and listened to Auntie Nandy singing along to a song asking if I've ever seen the rain.

MARVEL: SEVENTIES MUSIC

Exhibit A: "Have You Ever Seen the Rain."

When the song ended, she started it again, turning the music up this time.

After the third time, I found myself singing along to the refrain, asking about the rain out the window as we paused at a stoplight. Three men in an SUV beside us, with shemaghs rimmed by black cords on their heads, the traditional Gulf Arab headdress, thought I was asking them a question. The driver lowered his window to check.

Auntie Nandy started laughing, which made me sing "Have you ever seen the rain?" out the window again. The men looked perplexed and then, laughing themselves, rolled up their window.

Realizing I'd asked them about the rain in a dry, desert country, I began giggling, pausing only to catch my breath and yell the word "RAIN!" whenever the band said it.

I was so giddy and happy and felt free to be away from scrutiny, to be around people who didn't look at me weird for the way I dressed, for how Muslim I looked, but only for how weird I acted.

And that's how I arrived at the party, with a big smile capping the happiness beginning to percolate within.

And that's how the cute guy from the plane opened the door to me.

The cute guy from the plane *was* the cute guy from the airport *was* the cute guy at the door at this party I hadn't wanted to go to.

I floated into the house on the giddy bubbling inside.

Maybe this party is going to be all right after all?

Maybe I can finally not be on guard and just be happy and FREE?

ADAM

FRIDAY, MARCH 8

MARVEL: COINCIDENCES

OR, IN THIS CASE, MAYBE I'D CALL IT *SERENDIPITY*?

Though if I did, I'd be saying it was a happy thing that the girl from the plane yesterday was standing on the front steps of my home.

Let's call it serendipity, then.

Of the infinite number of occurrences possible, this was the one happening: The person who I'd thought about last night when I'd unpacked and threw my journal in a dresser drawer, wondering how and when she'd begun *her* journal, that person was standing here looking at me, the hugest of grins on her face, surprise in her eyes.

Standing beside her was Ms. Raymond. I'm pretty sure this made my welcome smile falter a bit.

I knew *she'd* be coming over today, so it wasn't as bad as seeing her yesterday at the airport. But still, it felt like my heart skipped a beat.

Just even a glimpse of her reminded me of Mom's passing.

"Adam! How wonderful to see you!" Ms. Raymond took a step into the foyer and threw out both arms to me. "How's university?"

"It's good. Thanks for asking, Ms. Raymond. It's great to see you." I held a hand out for her shawl.

"No, I'll keep this with me. We're sitting outside, right? It's a bit nippy." She looked at the girl who had stepped in behind her, that dazzlingly big smile still on her face, cheeks flushed. "That's the thing about Doha—it can get cool at night at this time of the year, especially near the water. Adam, this is my niece, Zayneb, my sister's daughter. She's visiting from Indiana on her spring break. Zayneb, this is Adam, son of the head of my school. I used to be his teacher when he was a wee little one."

For a second I wondered if I should say we've met before. Zayneb and me.

Or was that between us?

"You wouldn't believe it, Auntie Nandy. We kinda met each other on the plane here," Zayneb said, beaming.

"No, really?" Ms. Raymond tilted her head back. "That's awesome. How serendipitous!"

Ms. Raymond *would* say that.

"Yeah," I said, nodding at them, wondering why things got weird for me. A minute ago it was like a bright light went on inside when I opened the door.

Now I was standing in my foyer in Doha in front of a girl I'd first noticed a continent away in London, wondering what to say next.

I couldn't believe it: I'd tried so many times to talk to her yesterday—even at the airport, before she got away—and now she was right here in my house.

But nothing came out of my mouth.

Butler. Doorman.

That was my job tonight.

Yes. *Stick to the script, Adam.*

And then . . . later . . . you can talk to her . . . Zayneb.

"Everyone's either in the kitchen or on the patio." I led the way down the hall. "There are some people in here, as well," I added, pointing to the sunken living room on the right.

"Not me. I go to where the food's at," Ms. Raymond said, continuing ahead. "Zayneb, have fun."

"What do you mean?" Zayneb stopped at the entrance to our large kitchen, buzzing with guests. "Are you saying I can't follow you?"

"Of course you can, Zoodles, or Adam can show you where the young people are, right, Adam?"

"Sure. But I think you should get food first. It may be the best thing at the party." I nodded at Zayneb. "Sad to say, but it's true."

"Okay. Then tell me what I should try." She stepped into the kitchen and turned to me, standing in the hall. "My aunt told me your dad caters interesting cuisines."

I followed her. "He went South Indian today. You've got to try the masala dosa. It's this type of crepe with spicy potatoes. Those are my favorite."

"This is too funny. My best friend is Tamil, and I've eaten this food tons of times." She took a plate and put two round, spongy rice cakes on it. "My favorite. Idli. You just pour the sambar on top, and the idli soaks it in, and it tastes amazing."

She ladled vegetable curry on top of the cakes. The curry had been kept hot on burners, so when she returned the ladle to the pot, wisps of spiced steam scented the air between us.

I took a plate and added dosa and potatoes to it. "I guess I can eat too. Energy for my door-duty shift."

"It looks so good." Zayneb scooped some of the sauce with a spoon and tasted it. "And it *is* good."

We stood there for a minute not saying anything, just eating. Then she paused and looked at me. "So where are all these people my aunt wants me to meet?"

"Mostly outside. I'll point the way, but I gotta stay back.

Committed to the doorbell." We walked to the living room with our plates, Zayneb looking at the pictures on the stucco walls along the way, mostly single-subject photographs taken by Dad.

She paused in front of a close-up of a bee and then glanced up at the dark wood beams running across the ceiling. "I like your house. It's like how I imagined a Spanish villa would look. Like when you read stories where people live in pretty villas, you know? This is what I would picture."

I don't know why, but when she said that, the light went back on inside me, like it had at the door.

She was pretty open. Okay sharing what she liked.

I felt a need to show her the best part of our house.

"Then I think you're going to like this." Now that we had taken the two steps into the living room, I pointed to the left, where the three sets of arched French doors were flung open onto our large, cobblestoned patio, beyond which lay a neat lawn. Beyond *that* were steps leading down to a boardwalk edging the Arabian Gulf, with the white sails of small yachts and traditional dhows dotting the water along the horizon. It was my favorite scene to look out at, especially on a night like this, with stars flecking the vast dark sky.

"That is beautiful. Oh my God." She set her plate down on a side table and went toward the middle set of doors.

The doorbell rang, so I put my plate beside hers and went to answer it.

When I got back from walking the latest guests in, she and her plate were gone.

Dad beckoned me over to where he was standing with some guests when I stepped out on the patio, doorbell duty done. "Adam, come say hello to some new DIS teachers. This is my son, Adam."

I shook hands and, in between learning names, glanced around. And saw *her*.

She was sitting cross-legged on one of the enormous fake white rocks that the landscapers at our residential community thought would be perfect scattered around everyone's lawns. She held up a bubble wand while talking to my sister, Hanna. Or, most likely while *Hanna* was talking to her.

"You must be so thrilled to be studying in London," said one of the teachers I'd just met.

I nodded.

Zayneb blew bubbles as Hanna whacked them with a badminton racket.

Dad looked at me. "Adam, why don't you go talk to your friends? They've been asking for you since they got back last week."

I guess he knew my mind was somewhere else.

I nodded and made my way to Connor, Tsetso, and a few other guys from my graduating class at Doha International School. They'd gone on to universities in different parts of the world, and most had gotten back for spring break earlier than me.

Beyond the initial hellos and quick catch-ups, I hadn't sat down with them yet.

They were on lawn chairs near the steps to the boardwalk, their backs to the water, watching the guests who were playing badminton on the lawn. I joined their semicircle, sitting on the grass.

"Adam. Right on time. Right person to tell us, who invited *that* guy?" Connor pointed at a kid swinging a badminton racket round and round until it hit him in the face, at which point he screamed and ran to a woman dressed in the uniform many nannies in Doha wear. After she consoled him, he went back and attacked himself with the badminton racket again.

"I have no idea." I laughed. "But practically everyone here is a teacher at DIS, so he must be a teacher's kid?"

Tsetso put his plate down on a rock next to him. "Okay, who invited *that* guy?" he said, nodding at a man who, while talking to a woman, was also getting a good scratch in, moving his back up and down on the trunk of one of the date palms separating our yard from a neighbor's.

I shook my head. "Drawing a blank. Not a teacher."

Connor pointed in Hanna's direction. "And who invited her? With your sister."

Zayneb was still blowing bubbles for Hanna, who was now popping them with a magic wand.

"She's Ms. Raymond's niece. Visiting for spring break. Zayneb. From Indiana. Sorta met her on the plane over here," I said.

"That lady with the dog is Ms. Raymond's niece on spring break? That's one *old* niece." Connor laughed.

There was an elderly woman behind Hanna, standing by herself, rubbing her nose on the head of a Chihuahua in her hands.

Oops. I'd been looking at Zayneb. Why couldn't I stop looking at her?

"Remind me why you guys think this who-invited thing is fun again?" I stretched out my legs on the grass and leaned back on my elbows. The kid out to get himself with the badminton racket was at it again, so I decided to entertain myself watching the next episode.

"ADAM!" It was coming from behind me. "CONNOR, ALL OF YOU GUYS, COME DOWN!"

I sat up and turned to look down the steps. More students from our graduating class, on the boardwalk. I'd noticed them taking pictures of the water when I first came outside.

"WHY?" Connor shouted, standing up. His long, plaid shorts

paired with a differently plaided, scruffy shirt paired with a white boater hat over his bushy brown hair told me he hadn't changed his crazy style after leaving for university in California. "WE'RE BUSY PLAYING ADAM'S FAVORITE GAME."

"Madison has the video of you guys doing If Harry Potter Went to DIS from our grad party last year." It was Emma Phillips. I could recognize her voice anywhere.

"YOU GUYS FOUND THAT?" Tsetso stood up. "I'm outta here."

The rest of the guys got up too and began bounding down the steps behind Tsetso, simultaneously trying to pull one another back to be the one to get there the fastest.

Before he went down, Connor turned to me. "Your Zayneb? Playing with your sister? She's coming over."

I watched the badminton kid go running to his nanny for the hundredth time. This time she tried to take the racket away from him. In response, he threw himself on the ground.

"I think I met your sister. Hanna, right?" Zayneb sat on the chair Connor had just exited from. The only part of her I could see directly was her hands—left hand holding the bubble-solution container, right hand on the cap, a thin silver bracelet with a pendant dangling on her wrist.

"Yeah. She's super friendly."

"Also, a big fan of yours. I think I know everything about you." She laughed and began opening the bubble container. "But don't worry—I pretended to act surprised when she told me about the blue stone you got her for her rock collection."

Maybe it was looking up at her and seeing the remnants of her secret smile before she blew more bubbles that made me blurt out, "Do you want to come see the water?"

Or it could have been how her scarf blended into the darkness of the sky behind her so only her profile was lit up, surrounded by bubbles and stars.

Or maybe I just needed to stop.

Stop projecting more meaning into her than she deserves.

"Sure. Your friends are down there, right?" She stood up, screwing the bubble cap back on. "I'm pretty sure on the way home Auntie Nandy's going to ask who I met here. I can't tell her that I met a ten-year-old girl named Hanna. So I better meet some other people."

I nodded and let her go ahead of me on the steps.

"Adam." As soon as we stepped off, Emma—Emma Domingo, as there were three Emmas in our class—waved me over. "Come see yourself pretending to be Lupin."

Zayneb hung back to let me go ahead. I hesitated, not sure if I should lead her to everyone periodically breaking into howls of laughter in unison, clustered around Madison's phone.

Or if I should lead her to the best place to see the moon above the water.

Then I remembered she wanted to meet people, so I led her to them.

I was pretty certain they'd love her.

ODDITY: HOGWARTS HOUSES OR HOW EVERYONE SEEMS TO WANT TO BE GRYFFINDOR

They did love Zayneb, enough to give her their social media stuff. And tell her their Hogwarts houses.

She said she was mostly Gryffindor but also a bit Slytherin.

"You're Harry Potter!" Emma—Emma Zhang—said. "He was part Gryffindor and part Slytherin."

And that just made everyone talk about who among us was *really* Gryffindor. Brave. Inspiring. Remarkable.

That got me quiet.

I may be the most un-Gryffindor person there is in existence.

Like, I'm lying here in bed after the party, proud that I passed a full day at home without once thinking about how I have to tell my father about my multiple sclerosis.

There should be an un-Hogwarts Hogwarts house, one that doesn't have any traits attached. Like bravery or wit or loyalty or cunning.

A house for people who just want to appreciate the good things in life—the marvels, simple and extraordinary.

Which reminds me: I didn't tell Zayneb that we have the same journals. I never got the chance to.

Maybe I'll wait for her to bring it up somehow. When we next meet.

I'm going to see her again. Zayneb.

Tomorrow.

I made sure of it.

Because, yeah, I'm counting, and today was impression number two.

I have to get to a fourth.

ZAYNEB

SATURDAY, MARCH 9

ODDITY: UNPREDICTABLE CREATURES

EXHIBIT A: THE THREE EMMAS I MET YESTERDAY.

Emma Zhang, Emma Domingo, and Emma Phillips. Black straight hair with short bangs, dark brown curly hair with no bangs, and reddish-brown wavy hair with long bangs.

The three Emmas were different from one another but strangely similar, too. They had clear skin and lengthy limbs. Even the shortest one, Emma Domingo, had long limbs on her petite frame. How?

They were also similar in mannerisms. Getting excited at the same things and then, just like that, without a glance at the others, becoming suddenly subdued in unison.

It was hard to know when the switch would occur, so I'd decided to observe carefully, without once getting excited. (I, myself, have a tendency to get easily excited about *everything*, so with this type of crowd, I stand out.) I figured if I played it cool the whole time, I could learn what got them abuzz. (And then I could disappear into them, peacefully.)

I learned it was mostly their favorite movies and games, online and in real life.

The Emmas weren't the only ones like this. Most of the "young people" Auntie Nandy thought I should meet at the party were the same. Like they had an unwritten code organizing them.

Maybe it was an international-school thing.

I was getting into their rhythm, laughing along, sharing along, and shutting-up along, until the girl finding and sharing videos on her phone, Madison, paused a clip and said, "Amazing. I'm so glad I saw *this* again. I need to bring the whole outfit back to college with me. Connor and I got Coachella tickets, guys, and I'm rocking *this*, even though it's fake-shit DIY."

She passed her phone to Emma Phillips, who hooted on sighting whatever it was and passed it to Emma Domingo, who did a cringe-smile and passed it to Emma Zhang, who said, "WHAT? Oh God, that's so Coachella but also . . . DON'T, Madison," before passing it to me.

My anticipatory smile fell.

In the frozen video clip, Madison had on a headdress—a handmade one by the looks of it—with big feathers arranged in layers and a long train of feathers falling over one shoulder onto a see-through black shirt, under which she wore a colorful, beaded tank top. Her cheeks were vividly marked with makeup in an attempt to replicate face paint. I frowned. "Um, are you indigenous?"

I'd heard a slight Australian accent whenever she spoke, but I couldn't assume she didn't have an indigenous background. A North American one, I mean.

Emma Domingo shook her head at me and whispered, "She's not Native American."

"I made that myself. With expensive feathers my dad brought me back from a business trip. And it took me two entire-ass weeks. Remember, guys, for our fake Coachella party?" Madison took the phone back and smiled. "Connor, how cool would this look when we're at the real thing, huh?"

She passed the phone to a guy with clothes that screamed *I want to be noticed in the worst possible way*. They actually looked like brother and sister, this guy and Madison, with similar coloring— skin and hair. Except his hair was a bushy brown, and hers was a thin, stringy brown.

Something about the way he laughed when he saw the outfit enraged me.

I swallowed my anger, remembering this was my first day with these people.

But then . . . maybe I'll never see them again.

"I mean, are you of native background. Like, is that part of your culture, or . . ." I paused, cautioning myself, *Remember—you came here in peace*. But the three Emmas were waiting for me to finish speaking, even though Madison ignored me, leaning back into another guy, who immediately draped both his arms across her shoulders. "Were you using someone else's culture to have fun? Because you know it's sacred, right?"

If I had been back home, I would have added more to this and been spicier, been louder, but here, surrounded by people I didn't know, in an attempt not to rock boats, I said it like I was talking to a fragile, elderly person I'd been ordered to show respect to.

Kavi wouldn't have recognized me. Ayaan would have given me a long, hard look.

All it did *here*, my lukewarm tackling of Madison, was get me further ignored.

Madison took her phone back from Connor, closed the video, and flicked at her screen. Snuggling into the guy behind her, she held it up and snapped a picture of them both.

I looked at the Emmas. Emma Zhang widened her eyes at me and then called me over to her, and Emma Domingo looped her arm through mine. Then, like nothing had happened, the Emmas and I took pictures together with our backs to the water.

I'd melted into them.

It was the weirdest thing, and a part of my brain had a thought, as I smiled and shifted poses serenely for Emma Phillips's phone: *If this is what peace feels like, I need to take a crash course in learning to like it more.*

Because I just wanted to yank Madison's phone from her, superglue her to a chair, and force her to watch the longest video on cultural appropriation. And a marathon of videos on the more than five hundred tribes living on the land Coachella takes place on. And a video on . . .

Only Adam, the guy from the plane, wasn't completely in sync with the crowd around him. He was quiet mostly.

I didn't even know where he was when I feebly tried to take Madison on.

The only time he spoke up a bit was when we were talking about where we'd been in the world, and Connor, who seemed to like the limelight, started a chart on his phone to see which continent had the most visits from all of us.

To record our answers, he barked names out one by one like he was a teacher. And funnily enough, he said Zayneb properly when his eyes landed on me.

Geesh, I don't even know how I let this simple thing—him saying *Zay-nub*, my *name*—immediately earn him a sliver of respect from me. I duly listed the four continents I'd visited, like a good li'l student.

Emma Domingo has been to every single continent except for Antarctica. She's also visited her father's "ancestral homeland," as

Connor put it, the most, having been to the Philippines *twenty-four* times.

Adam is the one who's been to the least amount of places.

Other than Doha, he's only been to Canada, where he's originally from, two school trips to Belgium and France, and then England for college.

"So you're the only one who hasn't visited your parents' country of origin?" Connor asked.

"Well, I have. Because my parents are Canadian," Adam said.

"I know your mom was. But your dad is originally from China." Connor lowered his phone.

"My dad's grandparents are originally from China. Like how my mom's grandparents are originally from Finland." Adam shrugged. "And, yeah, I do plan on visiting China and Finland one day. And the rest of the world."

After that, he hung back, observing, smiling sometimes, and looking at the water and the night sky at other times. Not talking much.

Except when we were leaving and he walked Auntie Nandy and me to the door and suddenly asked me if I wanted to volunteer with him on Sunday at Hanna's class at DIS. They were going on a field trip to an animal sanctuary outside Doha.

So he, too, was unpredictable. Maybe. Kind of?

I said yes. Even though I'm not into animals, except for whatever animal Squish ended up being.

I said yes, because I wanted to be around him more.

It was almost five in the morning here in Doha, after Fajr prayer on Saturday, but I looked through the pictures on my phone from last night to find him.

I knew there was at least one shot from yesterday that Adam had ended up in inadvertently.

There it was. There *he* was. In the background behind us, the Emmas and me. He was standing with his back to the fence skirting the water.

An angular face with the trace of a sad smile. Eyes that could faze with their gaze, so carefully did they look at things.

And yes, like I thought, he had those eyes turned to the sky again.

This Is What You Missed, Bulletin II by Kavi Srinivasan, filed as FYI for Zayneb Malik:

Ayaan got an e-mail asking her to come see Kerr Monday morning. Sent on a Friday evening, the e-mail was.

From the principal's own e-mail address and NOT info@alexander-porter.

Fri. Day.

Oh. No. Do you think it has something to do with you-know-who?

Probably. We can't figure out what else it could be. Ayaan is quaking.

Quaking happening here, too. You have to let me know what it's about as soon as you find out.

I don't know if Ayaan will fill me in. She's become quiet around me at school. And then does one-word replies to texts.

Gulp. My fault. Crying.

I wrote the words that got you in trouble. Crying more.

Okay, I believe in prayers, so I'm praying that she doesn't get in trouble for her part in #EatThemAlive. I'm okay with trouble. But Ayaan is our purest star. She must be protected by all, at all costs. Let me falter, let me fall, but let Ayaan rise above us all.

Wow, poetry.

No, it's a prayer. Just made up now. Hey, did you hear back from SAIC admissions?

No. I'm getting worried. I keep thinking maybe I shouldn't have included the picture of a skateboarding seahorse in my portfolio. It wasn't good quality.

If they say no, I say we do a sit-in at the admissions office. Holding your drawings up as protest signs.

Wish you were back here. I went to check out the Purdue campus with Nhu yesterday, and the whole time we filled in what *you'd* be saying if you were with us. ONE BATHROOM FOR THREE LECTURE HALLS? NO WHEELCHAIR RAMP TO THE CLOSEST DOORS?

DO NOT MAKE A COLLEGE DECISION WITHOUT ME, GIRL.

WE won't. Though we are going to see the rest of the campuses during break.

Without me.

Hey, you have Doha.

I do. And so far, it's been okay.

I sent her the picture of the three Emmas and me. And Adam.

Looks like fun?

All of them are named Emma.

Even the guy looking up?

No, that's Adam.

She shared a picture of her and Nhu making faces at each other through the openings of a holey sculpture on the Purdue campus, and it looked like *real* fun.

The weekend in Doha is Friday and Saturday, so Auntie Nandy said we should go to Souq Waqif today, before she went back to work on Sunday.

Thankfully, she first let me sleep in in complete silence and only turned on her music—very obviously seventies-sounding music—when I emerged from my room at two p.m.

In the dining room, everything was loud and tinny and plucky and distinct and strangely groovy, too.

"Wow, is this what they call disco?" I began gathering a plate of food—food *shivering* while it awaited me to transport it to the warmth of the microwave. When the words of the song began, I paused on my way to the kitchen. "Wait. Is that Urdu? Or, I mean Hindi? Seventies *Bollywood* music?"

"I'm going to pretend it is." Auntie Nandy, sitting at the table with her laptop, smiled. Then she whispered, as though the Rock and Roll Hall of Fame had her place bugged, "It's actually from 1980. But isn't it great? Nazia Hassan singing 'Aap Jaisa Koi'? 'Aap jaisa koi meri zindagi'!"

She got up and began dancing. Raising one hand in the air, she shook it a few times then swung it down across her body dramatically before lifting it up again in a sudden whoosh, all the while shaking her shoulders and hips. Her eyes were closed, but her expression was serious.

Auntie Nandy's hips and shoulders looked like they belonged to two different people, while her arms didn't seem to know whether they were taking turns flailing for help from a helicopter hovering over a deserted island or pointing earnestly at something someone lost on the ground.

I couldn't look away, so I stood in the doorway of the kitchen, holding my plate up to my chest, trying hard to keep my lips at an appreciative-smile level and not let them venture where they wanted to: side-splitting, bust-out-laughing, this-is-perfectly-too-funny-to-be-cringey level.

But then came a point when she twisted-shimmied her way down while one hand did jazz hands and the other tried to pull her pants up, and I had to run to the table and put my plate down to use both *my* hands to cover the laughter exploding from my mouth.

She saw me and tried to straighten gracefully, giggling at the way she had to yank her pants before she made it even halfway up. "Oh, so you think I don't know how to dance? Or is it you think *you* know how to dance?"

"I actually do, Auntie Nandy." I laughed. "And you actually don't."

"This is disco, Zoodles." She pulled my arms to get me to join her on the carpet. "Listen to the rhythm. It's different from your music."

I laughed again and reached for my phone. "My friend Nhu's mom runs a dance studio. And she even teaches disco. I'm going to FaceTime her to show us some real moves."

"Perfect. Let's hit it from the top!" Auntie Nandy pressed a remote, and her sound system started again.

Kavi, I like disco music.

    Also, here's the best song: "Aap Jaisa Koi."

    Aap jaisa koi meri zindagi mein aaye.

    Which means: If someone like you entered my life . . .

Souq Waqif was beautiful at night. We ate at Damasca, a Syrian restaurant, and then wandered the bustling market.

The cobblestone streets, polished smooth, were lit by lights attached to the buildings, in alcoves and atop the structures as well. The buildings themselves were traditional Qatari style, low and with wraparound balustrades and second-story balconies overlooking the market below.

There were all sorts of shops selling everything from trinkets like camel key chains to rugs to perfumes and pure-gold jewelry. And clothing shops with tons of scarves stacked in piles near their entrances.

I couldn't stop myself from buying a few hijabs.

I bought one for tomorrow's field trip with Hanna's class.

It was the color of the sky before a storm, a sort of grayish baby blue, but the best part was the print on it. Darker gray silhouettes of tiny birds flying.

When we reached the car in the parking lot across from the souk, I draped the hijab around my head to model it for Auntie Nandy. "Good for a trip to an animal sanctuary?"

"Perfect." She put our purchases in the trunk. "We leave at seven thirty, so get to bed as soon as we get home, Zoodles."

"Yes, Mom-sub."

On the road, she turned off the radio. "I should tell you something about Adam. You'll be spending time with him tomorrow."

I looked at her. It was like her voice had become muffled. Or dropped an octave.

The glistening in her eyes told me it was sadness. She blinked a few times, and a tear dropped.

Whoa, that was sudden.

I didn't say anything and instead focused on the palm trees lining the avenue we were driving down. The night sky was visible between the buildings behind the trees, and I thought about the photo of Adam looking at the same sky yesterday.

Yes. There was something sad in his eyes.

And now maybe I was going to know why.

I glanced at Auntie Nandy again. She was still blinking.

Then she turned the car into a plaza parking lot and reached into the glove compartment for a tissue box.

I pulled my arms in tight and clutched myself while she blew her nose, wondering if I should hug her or something.

Auntie Nandy drew a breath. "Adam's mother passed away when he was in my class in the fourth grade."

"Oh God." I gripped myself tighter. "That's so sad."

"It was obviously devastating for him, for the whole family. She was diagnosed with her illness, MS, many years before, in her late twenties, and she coped, even did well, but then, after she had her second child, it progressed rapidly." She began crying again.

I reached my hand out and rubbed her arm. She wiped her face with a folded tissue and swallowed before turning to me. "I'm telling you because Tuesday is the anniversary of her death, and I see it in him, the remembrance of it."

"Thanks for letting me know."

"She was one of my closest friends. She taught at DIS too. High school art."

"I'm so sorry."

"I'm usually not like this. I think it was just seeing Adam again last night after not seeing him for months." She started the car again. "Anyway, just a heads-up. In case you see him quiet."

"Hanna must have been really young?"

"One and a half years old. Of course she doesn't recall Sylvia." We were waiting to turn onto the road from the parking lot, so she looked at me for a moment. "Adam was nine, and he'd been very close to his mother."

The rest of the way to the apartment we were quiet, me looking at the sky the whole time, unable to imagine his pain.

Daadi's death in the fall had been traumatic beyond belief.

But then, *Mom*?

She and I fought sometimes, but she was also the number one reliable factor in my life, Dad being inaccessible at times due to his busyness as one of the few ophthalmologists in town.

I couldn't imagine my rock being removed from me.

As I got out of the car, I blinked away my own tears.

After Maghrib and Isha prayers, combined, I lay in bed but couldn't go to sleep.

Maybe it was jet lag. And how I'd slept in today.

I sat up.

Not jet lag.

It was Adam.

I think I felt something I hadn't felt since I swore off feeling this way.

It was just a twinge and felt very buried, but it was there.

Like a pull inside whenever I thought of him.

After Yasin, this guy who hung out with Ayaan's brothers, who I'd met at her house, I hadn't felt it again. That was a year ago.

I'd liked Yasin, and he had liked me back, and then just like that, after three months, he had stopped liking me. Because he said he didn't know why everything was an issue with me.

What he meant was he hadn't liked me asking why he'd written a whole screed on how hijabi girls who wore makeup canceled their hijabs.

After Yasin, I'd decided nobody was going to get me interested in them unless they had something real to stand for. And brains.

That was my number one criterion.

That and a sense of quiet mystery?

I looked at the photo of Adam again.

He *was* sad.

MARVEL: RESOLUTIONS

Exhibit A: The Better Me manifesto I wrote in the middle of a Doha night.

Tomorrow I was going to be poised and peaceful.

Maybe quieter, too. Well, quieter in the sense that I was going to listen more than talk. Not jump to conclusions.

Just let things unfold. (More than I'd done yesterday; and yesterday, with Madison, I'd *really* pulled punches.)

I will have to pretend to love animals, however unpredictable they are. (Even though I am deathly afraid of dogs, because I was chased and bitten on my ankle by a Doberman when I was eight. And scratched by numerous cats belonging to friends. Not to mention the three instances of bird poo finding its way onto my head.)

Animals are unpredictable creatures for sure, not dependable like my Squish, but I will let them be so.

I am going to be a better version of myself, because this isn't the time for my shenanigans anymore.

Somebody grieving is going to be in my vicinity tomorrow.

I need to rein me in.

HANNA KNOWS MOM THROUGH THE STORIES I TELL HER. A THIRD of the way into whatever I'm sharing about Mom, she'll say, "Stop," and then go and get one of the many framed photos of Mom around the house. She'll hold it and gaze at Mom's picture while I finish the rest of the story.

Last night, when I gave Hanna the case I'd made for her rock collection, I filled her in on the time Mom and I made a house and garden in a jar. This was after we'd been living in Doha for a year, when I was seven, before Hanna was born, before Mom's disease took hold of her.

At the time, I'd kept telling Mom I wanted to go back home, to our backyard in Ottawa. So in our Doha apartment kitchen she propped up a picture of our old house and built a model of it out of toothpicks. Then we worked together to make a yard for it that matched the one I missed so much. We placed the entire thing into a widemouthed jar to preserve it.

Hanna stared at Mom's picture, the one where Mom is sitting on a swing, while I told her this story.

"Where is it? The jar with the backyard?" she said.

"That I don't know. We moved into this house soon after we made it, and then things got busy when Mom had you. Then it got even busier when she got sick." I finished fitting the wooden grid together inside the rock display case and flipped it up to show Hanna the interior. "You can put twenty-four rocks in here."

"Thanks." She took it from me and put it on the kitchen table we were at. "I wish I could see the jar."

I leaned back in my chair. "What about a bird? Do you want to see a bird?"

"I see a lot of birds."

"A bird Mom made?"

Her eyebrows rose high under her bangs. "Where? Is it in a jar?"

"It's behind you."

She turned around to another of Dad's photographs on the wall. A sculpture of a goose, a Canada goose, midflight, hanging on invisible wire.

"Mom made that?"

"Out of clay."

She stared at it, holding Mom's photo up high against her shoulder, so high it was like Mom was looking back at me.

I'm proud of you doing your best to keep everyone happy was what Mom's eyes said to me.

We got to DIS early on Sunday due to riding down with Dad. As head of the school, he was hands-on. Which meant he made sure to get to school an hour early to check on everything in the office and do a school walk-through before greeting parents dropping their kids.

Hanna took off for the schoolyard. I hung around the foyer talking to the reception secretaries, but then they decided to ask a million questions about London and university.

I got away and headed to Hanna's class to wait for her teacher, Mr. Mellon.

Zayneb stood just outside the door to the classroom, reading something on the wall beside it. When she saw me, she beamed and waved the hand that wasn't holding a travel mug.

Then she opened her mouth as if she was going to say something. But nothing came out, and she turned back to look at the display, taking a slow drink from the mug.

I came to stand beside her in front of a bulletin board of student projects on historic discoveries.

I laughed.

Zayneb turned to me, eyebrows raised.

"Hanna did the same project I did in fifth grade. Our dad has mine framed in his study at home. She's pretty efficient, using my research like that!" I chuckled again.

"The Pinhole Camera Based on Ibn al-Haytham's Camera Obscura by Hanna Chen?"

"Her drawings are much better than mine, though." I nodded at the sketches under her write-up.

"Yeah, she's really good. That's one cool panda being projected through."

"That's Stillwater, her stuffed panda." I turned to Zayneb. She was almost my height, maybe just a couple of inches shorter. "He's like a third sibling. Sits at the table, gets blamed for stuff, pretends to do chores, everything."

She laughed loudly. And then closed her mouth quick, with a big smile, but looked away.

I'd been staring. Ugh.

I looked back at Hanna's project.

"So how does a camera obscura work?" Her voice was upbeat,

eager—like she absolutely wanted to know. "Which I feel bad not knowing. Ibn al-Haytham is huge at home, because my dad's an ophthalmologist."

"It's the capturing of light entering through a hole. Images of objects in front of the hole get projected inversely onto a surface. In the case of a pinhole camera, the surface would be the film inside the camera or, like in Hanna's project, a box. Pinhole cameras came about because of the camera obscura discovery."

"A-mazing." She peered at Hanna's drawing of an upside-down Stillwater. "My sister and I have this theory that photos are some kind of magic. Or little jinns—or maybe angels?—anyway, some kind of beings, sitting inside devices, making things happen. Shh, don't tell my dad."

Her blue-hijabed head, light grayish blue today, turned to me. I don't know what she saw on my face, but she quickly added, "I'm talking about digital photos being magic. Not pinhole ones."

I tried not to laugh, didn't want her to think I was laughing at her, but I couldn't stop a chuckle. "Sorry, not laughing at you. Just the idea. Of little beings in my phone."

"It's okay. I know it's crazy. We just like to attribute everything we can't figure out to the unseen realm. Controlled by the greatest unseen being of all, of course." She took a quick drink from her mug and smiled. "Which, I just realized, I'm comfortable saying to you, knowing that you're Muslim."

"Makes complete sense to me. For life in general." *Like meeting you again,* I thought, looking at her bent head as she turned the lid of the travel mug to close it.

I liked that she wore a hijab with birds for a trip to be with animals.

Serendipity?

This would be a good time to bring up the weirdness of meeting her. And our journals.

But when I looked at her again, she was texting on her phone, so I stepped away a bit.

"No, it's okay. It's nothing. Just my mom." She looked up, mug in the crook of her elbow, thumbs paused midair over her phone, face stricken.

Oh.

Oh yeah.

Of course Ms. Raymond must have told her about Mom.

"Go ahead. I'm going to go into the classroom. The teacher, Mr. Mellon, will be cool with it." I tried the door.

Damn. Locked.

I turned to her. "Look, it's okay. I'm okay if you mention your mom, moms in general, or even my mom in particular. Actually, I'm more than okay if you mention my mom."

She clicked her phone and slid it into the pocket of her jeans.

"I'm sure your aunt told you about it, but yeah, my mother passed away when I was nine." I leaned on the classroom door. "And it's interesting, because the next year, in the fifth grade, I did this exact project on the camera obscura that Hanna copied. Because of my father. Because that's his specialty, history of the Middle Ages. He's always been fascinated by everything about that time, but especially the Middle East. The Silk Route, the Crusades and Saladin, scientists like Ibn al-Haytham. And we just engulfed ourselves in that era and then went even more back in time, to Medina and Meccan times. Right after my mom passed."

Zayneb nodded, and, just before she turned back to the bulletin board, I caught a glimpse of her eyes.

The look of fear and worry, that stricken look, had gone from them now. Mostly.

Relief flooded my body.

And I had no idea why.

I examined the sketch of Stillwater. Dad had bought the stuffed toy for Hanna when she turned two. After mom. "My dad converted to Islam a year after my mom passed."

She peered at Hanna's project again and nodded. "And then you did?"

"Yeah. He taught me what he knew, and I converted a year later."

"At eleven."

"Yeah."

"Okay. I was just worried that you'd be affected if I said something insensitive." She swiveled the lid of her mug, took a drink again, and then lowered it. "So moms are okay topics."

"Pretty much everything is an okay topic." *Except my diagnosis,* a little voice said. I pushed it away. "Tea or coffee?"

"Air." She unscrewed the lid and tipped the mug forward to show me the inside. "There's nothing in this mug, and I've been pretending to drink it. I finished my tea before you even got here, but yeah, I saw you and panicked, because I was worried I'd somehow talk about something weird. So I just drank a lot of air."

We looked at each other and burst out laughing.

Mr. Mellon turned the corner, waved at us, and fitted his key in to open the door. Following Zayneb into the classroom, I felt like the birds on her hijab.

Light and intent on soaring.

She was the real deal. That rare type: a WYSIWYG. What you see is what you get.

Third impression notwithstanding, I was pretty sure meeting her went beyond serendipity.

It turned out that for the entire field trip, I wouldn't be seeing Zayneb.

Because Mr. Mellon had extra volunteers, she ended up being assigned to another class. A class that went on another school bus and took another tour.

I glimpsed her once across the macaw enclosure. She was standing back, letting students huddle in between her and the fencing as they watched the colorful birds. I waited to wave, but she never once glanced my way. Her gaze didn't even reach the birds that the kids and their teachers were getting excited about.

When I came closer to the fence, I realized why. She was busy shooing a butterfly, one of the hundreds flying around us in the pavilion.

"Adam, I need it again." Hanna clutched my arm. "Look at the macaw that keeps peeking out of its little home-hole."

I took my phone out of my pocket and handed it to her. She clicked several photos quickly, without even paying much attention to what she was focusing on, and then gave the phone back before Mr. Mellon could see her.

He had declared no devices for students on the field trip. "We're going to be *in* the moment. Here in this real world. Not in another dimension on devices or online."

I scrolled through the photos Hanna had taken.

My sister was such a rebel. She'd taken the pictures just for the sake of breaking Mr. Mellon's rules. Most of the photos weren't even that clear.

Except two. One was a macaw, yes, peeking out of a hole in a tree. And the other was a shot of an empty part of the cage, with Zayneb in the background, frowning at a butterfly fluttering in front of her face.

Was she scared of them? Butterflies? Or, maybe, allergic?

"This is *so* amazing—two of the birds are talking to each other! I need to take another one! Please?" Hanna looked up at me, eyes pleading, tendrils and even chunks of hair escaping from the two ponytails in the back. "Just a teeny video. I want to show Dad!"

I gave in. It was the hair. She'd been doing it herself since she was five. After she declared that Dad made her look like an octopus whenever *he* did her hair.

She looked kind of like an octopus at the moment. An octopus bounding away with my phone.

"Adam, ready for your next stop?" Mr. Mellon and his group had arrived at the macaw area. Which meant I was supposed to have already moved my group of five students to our next exhibit, that of the Beira antelope.

As I began the hard task of herding the kids, I heard my name.

"Adam!" Zayneb waved energetically from across the enclosure.

Her face was the exact opposite of the image captured on my phone—now it was lit by enthusiasm.

I waved back.

She was leading her group of kids in the other direction from where I was scheduled to take mine, so I decided to make an executive decision.

"Okay, guys, I know we're supposed to see the Beira antelope. But." I paused and flipped the pages of the package Mr. Mellon had provided us volunteers.

Aha, found it: the exhibits schedules for different groups from DIS, along with a handy map.

Ms. Nielson's fifth graders, Team C, were the other group that had been at the macaw display at the exact same time my group was.

That meant Zayneb was with Ms. Nielson's Team C.

That meant they were going to see something exciting next.

I addressed my team using my most energetic voice. "How would you guys like to see an elephant?"

"YAY!" The two girls and two boys with me cheered and did dances. Where was Hanna?

Coming my way.

With Mr. Mellon.

"Adam, Hanna has something to say to you." He peered down at Hanna with eyebrows knotted together, his eyes boring into hers with significance.

"Adam, I'm so sorry for taking your phone out of your pocket," Hanna said, holding out the device. "So really sorry."

I accepted and pocketed it.

Mr. Mellon shook his head. "We'll go over field trip rules once more when we get back to school, Hanna. I'm severely disappointed." He turned to me and saw the stapled trip package in disarray in my hands. "Your group is at the Beira antelopes next, Adam."

"No, Mr. Mellon! Adam said we could go see the elephants!" announced one of the girls.

"Oh no, no, no. You must be looking at the wrong schedule." Mr. Mellon undid his own package from the clipboard he carried around and flipped through it. "See, right here. The Beira antelope in pavilion five."

"Right," I said. "Beira antelope."

The kids deflated in front of me.

Hanna crossed her arms.

I led the way to pavilion five.

There was only room for exactly one rule breaker in our house.

On the bus ride back to school, I found Zayneb's number on the volunteers' info sheet Mr. Mellon had stapled onto our package before we left in the morning.

Hope you had fun.

This is Adam.

I took in the landscape whizzing by. We were on the outskirts of Doha, and it was mostly rocks mingled with sand mingled with short, dry shrubs.

Ha-ha I was just going to text you. I did have fun.

I looked out the window again.

Favorite animal?

At first glance, the scene appeared the same throughout, but subtle color shifts in the rocks and sand made it interesting.

Whales.

Wide open spaces and then the sudden introduction of a tumbleweed.

You saw a whale on the field trip?

Or the jarring appearance of a house surrounded by a concrete wall, same color as the land.

No.

Sorry I thought you meant favorite animal ever. On the trip: macaws.

Even though I kinda didn't pay attention to them. Those butterflies distracted me.

And sometimes, if you were lucky, when your bus was stopped for a turn, you could see a lizard of significant size moving across the rocks.

I snapped a picture of the lizard and sent it to Zayneb.

Oh wow. My group didn't get to see THAT on the trip. Let me guess, related to dinosaurs?

I laughed.

It's a spiny-tailed lizard. Or as we locals call them a dub dub. I literally just took this pic. Out the window.

She didn't reply for a while, even though her text bubble kept popping up.

Must be something long she was composing.

The way it should be. Animals in the wild. Not caged. I don't like zoos.

She sent me a picture of the outside through her bus window. I examined it but couldn't see any animals in it, just flatland. And tons of rocks.

But she was obviously into the environment, maybe even the conservation of it.

Maybe even animal rights.

Hey, tomorrow I'm taking Hanna to a rescue shelter for salukis. Want to come?

Oops. This was the second time I was asking her to go somewhere.

She was going to think I was too much.

I glanced at the sky.

Why did I just feel an instant urge to push send on that text? I'm not impulsive. I'm Adam.

I consider, ponder, reflect, and only *then* do I make a move— in any aspect of my life.

I leaned my shoulder on the sill, rested my head on the window above it, and closed my eyes.

My movement caused Hanna to jolt beside me, head lolling, eyes flickering open.

I hadn't realized she'd fallen asleep leaning on me. I sat back up and set her head, hair completely in disarray now, on my arm once more.

My phone buzzed.

Sure, I'd love to.

Rescue shelters are so important.

She added a lizard emoji.

I smiled and looked back at the sky. It was clear, without even a tiny wisp of a cloud.

What was so interesting about the desert was this: It was invitingly ponderable.

I took another photo.

Dad led us for Maghrib, Hanna and me on either side of him, our three prayer rugs facing the direction of Mecca, Dad's sajjada just a bit ahead of ours.

Afterward, he turned to face us. Sitting cross-legged, he said the duas that Hanna was learning out loud, and we, with our heads bent and palms raised, said ameen to them.

"Your turn," Dad said to Hanna.

She gazed up from the gold hijab she'd carefully wrapped around her head for prayers. It was turban style, with the ends brought down and flung around her neck like a fancy scarf. She had dark sunglasses on—something she insisted helped her focus while praying—and the whole effect was of a very fashionable supplicant to God.

"Thank you for everything You have given us, Allah. Like Adam being back." She leaned forward and peered at my face to make sure I saw her being grateful. I returned her smile, and she settled back to continue her prayer. "Please, Allah, forgive me for the things I did wrong today, like if I wasn't aware of it."

She was repeating the words of the prophetic prayer that Dad had taught her: *Forgive us for the wrongs we did, willingly or if we were unaware.*

I leaned forward to look at *her* face so she could see me touch a finger lightly to my pocket, the one holding the phone, tapping it when I had her attention.

"And the things I did willingly, too. Please, Allah, make Mr. Mellon nicer. As nice as the way his name sounds. Melons are one of my all-time favorite foods, so I thought he was going to be my favorite teacher, too."

"Hanna," Dad said.

Hanna sighed and took off her sunglasses. She placed them in front of her on the rug and continued. "Please, God, forgive me for that conflict of interest I just did. I was *unaware* for a moment that I shouldn't talk about any teachers, because Dad's their boss."

"Hanna, your personal prayer of want?" Dad prompted. "You can say it out loud or in your heart."

Hanna looked ahead, way beyond Dad, onto the walls of his study, and paused for a long moment.

Then she announced, "I want to say it out loud."

"We've been working on developing our reliance on God for wants and needs," Dad said to me. "She's getting it. I'm proud of her."

"Please, Allah, I want to see the jar with the house and back-yard that Adam and Mom made together. One year before I was born. The one I never saw. Adam said it was lost. But You can find it because you can just say 'BE!' and it is. You are the most merciful of all. Ameen." She lifted her palms, wiped her hands over her face like Dad always did, then quickly stood up, picking up her sunglasses and her prayer rug to fold it and put it away in one continuous action. She unraveled her turban on the way to the spiral staircase, just outside the family room.

I stayed sitting, saying my own duas, reluctant to look up at Dad.

When I finally did, his head remained bent over his upturned palms, but I could tell he was crying.

ODDITY: PHOTOS TOO

As I folded my own prayer rug, I saw what Hanna had seen when she'd looked up after prayer.

On the wall behind Dad's head was the photo of Mom sitting on a swing. In our backyard in Ottawa.

The same photo Hanna had clutched so tight yesterday while I shared the story of Mom and the jar with her.

Reminders of loved ones, of love, in words, in picture form, were supposed to be good. . . .

Anyway. At least now I know I can't even bring up anything with Dad, my diagnosis, *anything*, until after Tuesday, the anniversary of Mom's passing.

Spring break goes like this. Solemn at first, and then, after the anniversary, as Dad remembered us, Hanna and me, he would get chipper, eager to do things together as a family.

I'll just wait for him to be ready for my news.

Lying in bed, I looked at the photo of Mom, the same one of her on the swing. I brought it into my room so Hanna wouldn't see it and remember the jar again.

Mom looked like she agreed that both of these decisions of mine were the right course: stop Hanna from thinking about the jar and put Dad off learning I have the same disease Mom had.

EXHIBIT A: MY ANKLE, THE RIGHT ONE, THROBBING WITH TRAUMA
as I sat outside Auntie Nandy's building waiting for an Uber.

An Uber to take me to the *dogs* that Google showed me when
I searched "saluki."

Dogs.

I had initially thought they were *lizards*.

When I said yes to going with Adam to the saluki shelter, I'd
pictured sad lizards. Sad lizards being bottle-fed, actually.

Like the desert lizard he'd sent me a picture of on the bus ride
yesterday. The dinosaurish dub dub who looked like he minded his
own business, unlike dogs, who wanted to know *everyone's* business.

I felt the phantom stitches ache on my right ankle. So it was
true what they said about old war wounds. How they flare up now
and then.

But I was bitten ten years ago.

Trauma.

I lowered my phone. What was I going to do?

I mean, the dogs that turned up in a saluki image search were
sort of nice and kind-looking, with their long, pointy, slightly

pretty faces sticking out of the middle of long parted hair.

But then there were some pictures where their mouths were open, sharp teeth ready.

I shuddered and tapped a photo of a kind-looking saluki to enlarge it.

Maybe if I imagined *this* dog's face everywhere at the shelter, I could get through the experience intact.

Without revealing to anyone—well, to Adam—that I was terrified.

I was supposed to let things unfold, not let myself get in the way today.

I was supposed to be poised. Zen.

Meanwhile, there was screaming happening in my brain: *I DON'T WANT TO GO SEE SALUKIS.*

THEY AREN'T EVEN LIZARDS.

I lowered my phone again and tried to take my mind off dogs.

Across from Auntie Nandy's place construction was happening on a new plaza.

Men in blue jumpsuits moved to and fro, carrying tools and materials.

Something was different about them, though. Different from construction workers back home.

One guy turned this way to pick up bags of cement, and some other men came over to help, and I noticed the difference.

All of them were brown like me.

Not one of them was the other brown, Arab, like the people of this country.

I had never seen so many brown construction workers in my life.

With what I hoped was discretion, I lifted my phone and took a picture and messaged it to Kavi.

Yup.

What do you mean, yup?

Yup I've seen this before. My uncle lives in Dubai. It's also full of migrant workers like this. From India, Nepal, Pakistan, the Philippines, etc.

Oh, right.

They're often not treated well. Just like our migrant workers here.

I looked across the street again. One worker took off his hat to wipe his brow.

Then he looked over at me.

I busied myself with pretending to dust off my sandals, but what I was *really* doing was wondering what he saw when he looked over at me, sitting in front of pricey condominium buildings full of Europeans and us North Americans.

As soon as the Uber driver pulled up to the shelter and I saw Adam waiting outside a stucco building with "saluki rescue" in Arabic and English on it, I felt that twinge again.

The same thing I'd felt every time I'd glimpsed him on the field trip yesterday.

And when he'd texted me.

Oh God.

I was really getting into him.

I slid out of the back seat to be immediately greeted by Hanna, who popped up to the side of the car from I don't know where.

"Hi, Zayneb." She had her backpack on. Adam had told me that she'd be getting picked up after school for this. That she was crazy about animals.

"Hi." I grinned at her.

"Did you know we're going to see Ariel first? She's my favorite saluki here."

"Let me guess—does she look like this beauty?" I turned my phone to her and showed her the gentle-looking dog I wasn't completely scared of.

"Oh, that's a pretty one!" Hanna said. She wiggled out of her backpack and unzipped it to take out an iPad. After scrolling through photos for a while, she showed me a white-and-gray dog with its mouth wide open.

Sharp teeth greeted me.

"Wow." I managed to say this with a smile, because Hanna was looking up at my face.

"She's been at the shelter for two years because nobody wants her. Do you want to know why?" Hanna put her iPad away. "Exactly why nobody wants her?"

"Why?"

"Because she bites people when she gets stressed. Like hard. Do you want to know why she does that?"

"Sure." I twisted the handle of my bag. "Why does she bite people?"

"Because she was treated horribly by the people who'd kept her before. She had trauma. It means a really bad experience."

From near the door to the shelter, Adam turned around to look at me, eyes full of mirth. "I think Zayneb knows what the word 'trauma' means."

I nodded, feeling the trauma in my right ankle.

"You're going to love the shelter. They want prospective adopters to see the personalities of the dogs, so they let them run around the warehouse and the pen outside, in the sand, and we can just mingle with them," Adam assured me, holding the door open to my personal nightmare. "Salukis love running long and hard, so it's amazing to see."

"But not Ariel," Hanna said to me. "Ariel stays in a separate area. She can't handle everyone. Even the other dogs."

"Is she in a cage?" I asked hopefully, pausing in the space between the double doors.

"No, don't worry. She's not caged. It's just like a low divider, so we can still be with her but with a barrier," Hanna said. "But it's not in the warehouse. That's the sad part but also a good part for Ariel. She needs it calm."

"I think I'll spend time with Ariel then," I said. "With you, Hanna, of course. Because she knows you, she'll be okay with me there."

Adam turned to me again and smiled.

Twinge.

I decided to *do* this thing.

Be chill with fear—which, if accomplished, meant I could be chill *all* the time.

Ariel began barking and howling when she saw us and then ran around her pen like a crazed . . . dog.

I stopped walking. Hanna and Adam kept going, following the shelter worker down the wide room toward Ariel.

Adam noticed I'd held back and waited for me.

"You guys go ahead. She knows you two. I'll wait a bit," I whispered, trying to summon the right word to make it sound like I cared about Ariel's feelings. "Let her *acclimatize*, you know?"

Adam nodded and caught up to Hanna, who was already sitting cross-legged in front of the barrier, talking to Ariel.

I leaned on the wall and waited.

I was waiting for something to arrive within me: a sense of sympathy for Ariel.

I'd read the mission statement of the shelter: *We are a nonprofit that works to find loving homes for the dogs native to this area (salukis) that we rescue from abuse and neglect.*

Adam and Hanna had filled me in on the stories. Of dogs being mistreated by different sorts of people—some locals, some Westerners, expatriates working in the Arabian Gulf who took them in and then didn't care for them as their canine type needed to be taken care of, some who then even just released the dogs into the streets when they moved back home.

And then there were the cultural taboos about dogs being bad.

That made me sad. But not sad enough to bravely go forth.

I called to mind the Islamic story that I'd been taught in Sunday school, that Hanna had recounted to me as we waited for Adam to fill out papers at the shelter reception desk, because her dad had just taught her the tale.

Prophet Muhammad once told his companions of someone who was forgiven completely by God for every ill deed she'd ever done—because she'd been thirsty and so had climbed down an abandoned well to drink water, and, when she emerged from the depths of the well, she found a dog at the surface, panting from the same thirst she'd felt. She climbed back down and filled her shoe with water and brought it up for the thirsty dog, and thus, for this act of kindness, she was utterly forgiven.

I told myself that the Saluki Mission Shelter was the woman in the well: noble and selfless.

And that I should have a tiny iota of this compassion too. Enough to proceed to see this sad, neglected dog.

Nothing. It did nothing to erase my fear.

I hung back.

Until I saw the change in Ariel. She was sitting down in front of the barrier across from Hanna and Adam, who was also cross-legged. Whatever they were saying to her was making her calm.

I inched forward slowly, stealthily.

Then Ariel whipped her head up, noticing me and, maybe, my intense stare. She began yelping and running around in a frenzy again.

It took my all not to scream and run the other way.

I mouthed, *I'll wait out there,* to Adam and walked quickly to the front office area that we'd entered through.

Afterward, after I'd played twenty rounds of Angry Birds Rio on my phone while I waited for their visit to end, Adam's father picked us up.

Adam kept apologizing on our way back home for me "not being able to enjoy the dogs."

"Totally okay," I said, finally happy and at peace. I loved the feeling of fearlessness again. "I can tell Ariel has had a difficult life."

"She was tortured," Hanna said. "They tied her."

I swallowed.

"Some people think dogs are bad. Like they actually think they're evil. So they hurt them." Hanna crossed her arms.

"Unfortunately, there are so many misconceptions about certain things in Islam," Adam's dad said. "And too often it's us Muslims who have them. Like the thinking that dogs are unwanted. Yet in the Qur'an itself, the surah of the cave describes how loyal that dog was to the young people it was with. How important their dog was."

I nodded and told myself, *You hear that, Zayneb?*

The image of Ariel kneeling calmly in front of Hanna and

Adam came to me. Maybe she'd been okay with them because she knew they cared about her.

But when Ariel had seen me, she'd become agitated. Somebody had hurt her, and it wasn't me, but, still, she didn't know what I was about. And I'd become agitated when I saw her—even though *she* wasn't the one who'd hurt me so long ago.

I teared up. "Does the shelter take donations?"

Adam nodded. "You can do it online or at the shelter itself."

"Okay." I made a note to myself on my phone.

A picture showed up in my messages. It was an AirDrop from Hanna's iPad.

Ariel. Sitting on the floor of the shelter, head settled on her front paws, mouth firmly closed, no teeth in sight.

I smiled at Hanna. She leaned over and whispered, "You're scared, right? Of dogs?"

"No, just when they get hyper," I whispered back. "And do things like biting people, you know?"

She nodded.

For the remainder of the ride I taught her how to play Angry Birds Rio on my phone.

When I got out in front of Auntie Nandy's building, Adam got out too. He looked like he was going to say something, and I waited, spending a bit of time opening my bag to get keys out, so that he could say what he wanted to say.

Like maybe he'll ask me to do something else with him tomorrow?

But he just stood there.

When I glanced up to say salaam, he had a weird expression on his face.

Like it was closed. Even his mouth wasn't turned up in that slight smile he wears.

Instead it was just a straight line that moved a tiny bit to say salaam.

And then he got back in the car.

Maybe he'll text me later.

Yes.

This Is What You Missed, Bulletin III by Kavi Srinivasan, filed as FYI for Zayneb Malik:

Sitting?

Now I am. Was lying down before.

Lie down.

What's up?

Wait, is this about Ayaan? ISTHISABOUTAYAAN

I got off the bed. *I'm standing now.*

Ayaan got removed as vice president from student council. From student council, completely. Fencer provided information that "resulted in Ayaan's removal from student leadership, as her actions contravene school guidelines on responsible social media use."

No.

She's supposed to provide a written explanation of her "online activities running a campaign against a teacher and encouraging hatred toward him."

No.

Kavi.

Fencer "provided ample evidence about her incessant monitoring of him."

I hate him so much.

I got this information from Trevor. He screenshot it for me, the e-mail that student council members got. Ayaan is super mad at us.

I'm done.

We're all done.

I did this. If Fencer hadn't caught me, Ayaan wouldn't be in trouble.

It's not that simple.

My big temper. I have to talk to Ayaan.

I don't think she's ready. This is traumatic for her. You know how long she's been gunning for student council. She's not going to want to talk now.

Okay. We'll have to respect that. But we have to help her. Well, I have to.

We will. Just wait a bit. What's happening in Doha?

I sent her a photo of Ariel.

Pretty. But a dog? You?

Right?

You've changed.

Right. Or am on the way to it. Zayneb, more mellow.

I don't know if I like this.

My parents will. Ayaan will.

Fencer will too.

Topic changed.

Ayaan's Instagram, usually active, had come to a standstill. It looked like she'd stopped posting last Thursday, the day I got suspended.

I sent her a DM, *I'm so sorry*, and then immediately regretted it.

So I followed it up with a sad crying emoji.

And then, disgusted at my behavior, I tossed my phone under the bed.

But what about when Adam texted?

I dove under the bed, retrieved the phone, and turned my volume on to make sure it would ping audibly when a message came in.

When *his* message came in.

I returned the phone to its temporary home under the bed again and lay on the floor, on the cold marble floor, staring at the ceiling.

It was a pretty fancy ceiling, moldings crisscrossing in twirls and flourishes.

It reminded me of Ayaan's dress, the one she wore last Eid.

My hand, with a will of its own, reached for my phone and opened Instagram and sent Ayaan a heart. Four hearts. Ending with a broken heart.

Agghh.

I threw the phone so far under the bed, it came out and hit the baseboard on the other side.

Ayaan was super important to me. She was older, but, because she'd spent a year abroad in Somalia with her grandparents at the end of middle school, she ended up in the same year in high school as me.

When we'd met as freshmen, she'd acted like a big sister immediately. Even though she'd been trying to figure school out too.

I showed up in the foyer on the first day of ninth grade, clutching my schedule, eyes scanning for Kavi instinctively, even though I knew she was in India on a family trip, her flight delayed.

"Are you Mansoor's sister? Mansoor Malik?"

I turned to a girl shorter than me with curly hair clipped back, an inquisitive look in her wide eyes. She wore a roomy sweatshirt over light blue, super-faded jeans.

"Yeah?"

"Mansoor's a friend of Abdirahim, my brother. That makes us friends." She smiled. "I'm Ayaan. Let's check if we have any classes together?"

And, just like that, she'd stuck by my side. Even though, as the years went on, she got involved in tons of stuff at school, running-the-school stuff, and I got involved mostly in the yearbook committee and newspaper club, because I liked making CAPITAL LETTER captions and titles for things and Kavi was also there making graphics and designing pages. Ayaan went on to become a rightful school star.

My phone pinged.

Adam?

I crawled under the bed, only to realize how stupid that was when Auntie Nandy opened the door to see my legs, wearing pajama shorts, sticking out in view, the other half of me hidden, but still too far from my phone.

"I promise I knocked," she said. "What is happening?"

"My phone."

She went over to the other side of the bed and passed it to me underneath it.

It wasn't a message from Adam.

It was one of the Emmas—Emma Domingo—asking if I wanted to meet the three Emmas at the mall, *the BEST MALL IN DOHA*, she wrote, tomorrow. Apparently, there was a Fenty makeup shop pop-up happening, and only Fenty had stuff suitable for Emma Domingo's brown skin, her being part Filipino and part black.

It might be good for your skin too? she offered kindly. I imagined her texting this with some sort of peel on her face, cucumber slices on her eyes.

Which I've always wanted to try, actually.

"Is it okay if I go to Villaggio Mall tomorrow with some of the girls I met at the party at Adam's house?" I asked, emerging from underneath the bed.

"Actually, that would be perfect. I've got some appointments I want to get done before your mom comes on Sunday. I'll try to fit them in tomorrow."

I sent a yes to Emma Domingo. And then checked if there was anything from Adam.

Just leave me alone. I'm not mad at you. I just want to be left alone, k?

Ayaan. She'd finally answered me.

I went back under the bed.

"Dinner is on its way." Auntie Nandy sat on the bed. "Then what do you want to do tonight? We can drive down to the water if you want?"

"I'm kind of tired from visiting the shelter," I lied.

"Oh yeah, how *was* that?" She peered at me. "Is there a reason you've got your head down there?"

"It's cool down here," I lied again, staring at Just leave me alone. "The shelter was sad. But good."

"Aren't you scared of dogs?"

"I'm working on getting over it." Boy, I was on a lying spree.

I clicked out of my DMs and saw one of the Emmas' posts. Emma Phillips, in a white T-shirt and shorts, doing yoga on a white rock, exactly like the rocks scattered in Adam's backyard. She must live in his neighborhood.

She looked like a cool pretzel, one arm twisted over a leg twisted on another leg.

I pressed like.

Yoga was peaceful.

I rolled out from under the bed. "There's a gym here, right?"

"An entire fitness center, including your favorite, a swimming pool. A pretty big one too," Auntie Nandy said.

"Are there yoga classes?"

"Each morning at six a.m. I go sometimes. Wanna come?" Her face lit up. "That could be a great idea. Call it an early night tonight, then hang out at yoga before I go to work tomorrow?"

I nodded, scrolling through posts and stories, liking everything without examining anything.

I was depressed.

MARVEL: ADAM

I can't believe I wrote that.

Why was he even? A marvel?

I mean, I realize that before I even knew him as Adam, I'd called him a marvel, at the airport in London, just because he was cute.

But at this point in time, I think I mean it in a different way.

Because he's calm. Peaceful.

Mellow. Like everything I'm trying to be here.

That's why he's a marvel. Not just because he's good-looking.

Anyway, why wasn't he texting me again?

It felt as if a few words from him arrived on my phone, like *Hey, do you want to go to blah blah tomorrow?*, this down-in-the-depths feeling I had at the moment would just disappear.

But then I remembered his mouth after his dad dropped me off today. The way it was that straight line, like he was done.

Right.

Adam had probably realized I was faking it at the saluki shelter. He'd found out about my phoniness and was over wanting to get to know me.

Well, if he even wanted to get to know me in the first place.

I stared at the ceiling. And sat up suddenly.

I couldn't believe it. I was letting myself be what I'd never ever wanted to be: at the mercy of a guy's whims.

No way.

Dinner was Turkish food. We ate quietly on the couch, watching some house-hunting reality show on TV, Auntie Nandy engrossed, me scrolling through my phone.

Adam posted an Instagram story.

His waterfront with boats, sea, and sky.

I didn't have to be at *his* whims, but I could decide whether *I* wanted to say something to him.

Thanks for today.

I added a puppy emoji.

As of 1:42 a.m. he hadn't replied.

And, huddled in Binky, I noticed my message continued to be unread.

At Fajr, five a.m., still unread, but he posted another story. Another seascape, a dark one this time.

The twinge was disappearing, being replaced by further dread.

ADAM
TUESDAY, MARCH 12
MARVEL: PLANS

I PRAYED FAJR OUTSIDE THIS MORNING, PRAYER MAT UNROLLED BY the water, my back to it.

It was dark, with that inkiness in the sky that hints at more colors to come. I contemplated waiting for sunrise—which would be right over the gulf behind me, promising better pictures than the ones I'd just taken—but then I glimpsed Dad through the blinds he opened in his second-story bedroom.

And I remembered my plans for today.

Today was about avoiding Dad, who, at dinner last night, had already shown signs that this year's anniversary of Mom's passing was going to be the same, as hard as usual.

He'd chewed his food for so long while eating that I passed him the salad unasked to break his reverie, to get him to swallow. He nodded and set the bowl beside his plate.

Then he kept his eyes lowered, strictly on his food.

He'd also let Hanna get away with screen time at dinner, which is usually a huge no for him. The entire meal, she laughed her way through episodes of some YouTube show, earphones on, her iPad propped up against the two cans of tomato sauce she'd boldly brought to the table from the cupboard.

It was quiet, like Dad wasn't there, and yet like he *was*, because I didn't dare talk to Hanna, either, in case she said something about Mom.

I let him have it, his withdrawal from us. Besides, I was busy making plans.

First order of the day was to avoid Dad, like I've said. Second was to hide myself away in the nanny's room, aka my workshop downstairs.

The only time the room had been used before was when Mom's personal support worker had lived with us during the last few months of Mom's life.

Then it had lain unused until three years ago when, in an attempt to get rid of stuff, I'd packed up and given away the furniture inside, leaving it bare and ready for a new start.

Soon after, when I began journaling marvels, I started a project in the room.

It became my making-stuff space.

Today I wanted to pick up on it again, maybe finally finish the installation I'd begun.

Hanna's wanting to see the house in the jar that Mom had made had given me an idea: Maybe I could bring together the bits I'd been working on over the years.

I also don't know how much time I have before I can't do things like this anymore.

I've had a faint headache since I woke up this morning, and whenever I've had any type of physical symptom since my diagnosis, I start thinking of what lies ahead.

I want to make sure I use my hands, finish making things, before the numbness that I know waits for me begins.

The third order of the day was currently staring at me on my phone.

Unread message: @ZayA_01.

Avoid Zayneb.

Avoid a fourth impression.

In the workshop there were cobwebs here and there on the piles of lumber pieces and boxes with paint cans and toolboxes.

Interestingly, the bits of wood for the cosmos installation I'd prepped were pretty clean. And, interestingly again, the pieces had been rearranged from largest to smallest.

Hanna.

I got to work, pulling the extra materials and tools out of the room, into the hallway, clearing it completely again. I wanted the room itself to be part of the project.

I imagined walking into it, like walking into a snow globe, and being immersed in the installation. Becoming a part of it.

The jar had given me this idea. When I'd wanted to go back home to Ottawa so badly, Mom had brought a little of Ottawa to me.

Imagine if I transformed this room into the place where someone would want to escape to?

As I painted the ceiling cobalt blue, standing on a ladder, the phone in my pocket vibrated with another message.

Zayneb?

I couldn't look at it. Her message. Her messages.

There was something about her that drew me in so quickly and intensely.

A few things, really.

For example, her bravery at the saluki shelter yesterday.

I can't believe that I hadn't figured out she was scared of dogs. Hanna told me she'd thought so when we were returning from Ariel's pen. "I saw her face when Ariel was running around. She was standing back there shaking. I think she's just doing this for us. Visiting the shelter with us."

And sure enough, when we got out into the foyer, I noticed the change in Zayneb. She was a completely different person from the one who'd been in the room with Ariel. She was relaxed, smiling.

She'd swallowed her fear to accompany us. Whoa.

And then, on the ride back to drop her off after the shelter, I got that tingling sensation I'd been getting on and off since September. Up my arms and legs, like tiny shocks were running through, the tingling that had forced me go to the doctor in early November. *Paresthesia.*

I'd concentrated on looking out the window, on giving no sign to Dad that something was happening inside me.

The feeling left me before we neared Ms. Raymond's building. Zayneb's drop-off.

Then I got to thinking: Was there any use? Of just hanging around with her? When it wouldn't come to anything?

I couldn't even say a word to her when she got out of the car.

I was trying hard not to so obviously shake off the sensations that had just invaded my body minutes before.

She'd stood there for a bit, then looked up at me and waited a few seconds before saying salaam.

And I'd thought, *No.*

It isn't the time to begin something with someone so interesting.

Someone so cute who I am completely attracted to.

Her eyes when she speaks excitedly are captivating, hard to

tear away from. And the way she keeps rearranging her lips when she's listening. Like she wants to open them to speak but is still making up her mind on what she wants to say.

I could look at her all day.

Add to this how frank and open and sure she is, and there, just like that, she had a hold on me.

That's exactly why I need to avoid her. I was getting drawn so fast and so hard that I was forgetting the things I had going on, the things I had to deal with.

I'd just stood there yesterday, grim, muttering a salaam. Steeling myself within, closing the door.

Bye, this girl I met on a plane who showed up at my house, who showed up in my heart.

There's nothing ahead for us and nothing comes out of wishing it weren't so.

I'm pragmatic that way, have always been so, through everything. Including Mom's passing.

I guess you could call it my survival mechanism.

The dull ache spreading behind my forehead reminds me I need some of that pragmatism to transfer to dealing with my illness, too.

After spurts of the phone buzzing on and off, things completely stopped, and it became silent while I painted the entire ceiling blue and the walls a white base.

Then the door opened.

Connor stood there. "The cleaning lady let me in. Where were you, bro?"

I put the paint roller in its tray and wiped my hands on the old T-shirt I had on. "That was *you* messaging?"

"Incessantly." He looked around at the room. "What's this? Guest bedroom?"

"No." I kept my answer simple. None of the other guys understood that I liked to make stuff. They got it when I showed them something cool I'd made, but this sort of stuff? That was actually art? They wouldn't be on board. Except maybe Tsetso, who did digital drawings.

"We're meeting for lunch, then catching a movie. At Villaggio, like old times."

"Gotta finish in here."

"Come on, Adam." He carefully tested the door trim for wet paint before leaning on it. "You gotta come out with us. Tsetso's leaving on Friday, and he's got a bunch of family stuff, so today's it for him."

"I'll go over to his place tomorrow or something." I moved the roller in the paint tray, avoiding his eyes.

"Okay, I'm staying here then to help you so you can come too. I'll just tell the other guys we'll meet up later." He crossed his arms.

I looked at him. Connor is the kind of guy you can't stand, because of his know-it-all, wisecracking ways, but then you just put up hanging around with—because, behind the bravado, he has a strange, deep well of concern for others. That he is okay openly expressing.

"Are you doing this because of today?" I asked. "Because of my mom?"

"Yup. You're not going to be here on your own."

"What if I need to be on my own?"

"Then be on your own tonight." He cracked a smile. "When your dad and Hanna get home."

I looked at the ceiling. I'd been imagining setting the strips and dots of wood on it, gluing for the most part, drilling for the heavier bits, and now my plans were shot. There was no way I'd let Connor in on this kind of work. He had no sense of finesse and would ask a million questions, mostly having to do with why I was doing this.

There was no why. Other than wanting to see what I'd sketched in my Marvels and Oddities journal come to life.

And wanting to keep my mind focused on things that didn't bring me stress.

"So, what can I do to help? Walls need another coat of paint?" He was unmoving, arms still crossed in the doorway, jaws set.

Stubbornly caring while being obtuse was his shtick.

"Let's go." I wiped the speck of paint on the back of my right wrist on my shorts.

I wasn't going to change my clothes. I was just going to get this done and over with.

Connor smiled and punched a victory fist before bounding up the stairs.

ODDITY: THE FRIENDS YOU'RE DEALT

This may be an awful thing to say, but none of the guys I hung around with in Doha before university were friends I'd choose on my own. We were kind of thrown together, and it's the law of third-culture kids, kids going to school in a country other than the one they called home, that you friend-up fast, with whatever people you're dealt. Otherwise you get overtaken by the isolation that comes from navigating a new place that you know will be temporary.

Living with your parents while they work abroad is sort of like a long vacation you're sentenced to, with the promise you'll be coming home again one day. It's not truly home, and yet you're expected to make it comfy.

Most of the other kids at DIS were children of oil industry executives from England, the US, or Australia, or professors at the many offshoot American-college campuses in Doha.

Most of them took their sentencing in Doha as a way to have tons of fun—well the tons that were available in Qatar.

Which meant each week we watched the same, limited-fare choice of movies at the theaters, sometimes over and over again. Ate at the same best burger places. Went dune buggy riding when a parent offered to take us. And hung out at the same people's houses, usually the hugest houses in our circle of friends.

For some reason, the circle I ended up with consisted of people who were loud, easily excited about movies and music, and into nothing I was into.

But they were also squeaky-clean. Meaning I didn't have to compromise anything with them—like my being a practicing Muslim. They were okay not boozing and, other than a couple who smoked once in a while, were not into drugs, either.

They were the clean crew at DIS. But that was the only way we were similar.

They say friends are the family you choose.

And yeah, I guess that's sort of true, if family is made up of people you put up with because they care about you and you them.

"Remember we thought Madison and Jacob wouldn't last?" Connor drove fast, navigating a roundabout while weaving to get to the exit lane as quickly as he could. He was roommates with Madison at UC Berkeley, having been best friends with her throughout DIS. "They did."

"That's cool."

"College on two different continents. And they did it. Well,

Madison did it. She was the one skyping Jacob every single night."
We were approaching the mall. "Did you meet anyone?"

"Nope."

"I sure did. Someone *older*." He laughed, turning the steering wheel fast to make the left turn into the parking lot. "Nancy. She's a TA. Was my TA for my intro to international economics course. And totally hot. Totally older, like four years. I turned nineteen in January, so we're legit."

I nodded, picturing Connor with an older woman, even ten years older. It was an easy thing to imagine.

"She knows I want to go into politics, and she's helping me figure it out."

"Cool."

"Hey, by the way, your friend is going to hang with us," he said, glancing at me as he waited for someone to back out of a parking spot.

"Friend?"

"At your house, your dad's party. Zee something. The girl with your little sister, with the head scarf?"

"Zayneb?"

"Yeah, Zayneb. Forgot her name. She's with the girls, and Emma Phillips—who, by the way, hasn't given up on you, according to Emma Zhang—said they'd catch the movie with us after shopping."

I nodded again, groaning inside, willing myself to not flip the sun visor mirror down and check my hair in it, check if I had paint flecks on my face.

So much for my plans for today.

So much for avoiding a fourth impression.

Exhibit A: Me in my first yoga class.

My resolution to become calmer didn't make it through even one yoga class.

Yoga was a lot of breathing carefully—"down to your toes," according to the instructor—while doing things my body had never done before, so I left to find more pleasurable things to do. Like go to the bathroom. (Before I escaped, Auntie Nandy gave me a look of triumph as she rocked on her butt with her legs almost wound around her head, in sync with the other women near her. At that moment, I'd been lying spread-eagle and defeated on the mat, so I acknowledged her prowess by whispering, "I hail your yoga mastery, Auntie Nandy, but this disco queen is going to the bathroom.")

As I turned the corner of the gym complex, the pool greeted me through a long, windowed wall, with its cheerful kidney shape and reflected-blue water. There was one middle-aged man bobbing up and down, facing a curved corner in the shallow end, as well as a woman doing laps in a black swimsuit and white cap.

I watched her for a bit and nodded. This was more like it. This was *real* exercise.

I went back to the changing room near the entrance of the fitness center and fixed my hijab, already wrapped turban style for yoga, so that it sat even tighter on my head. I was wearing leggings and a big long-sleeve tee that went almost to my knees, so it would do for swimming. Though I might have to tie a knot in my shirt once I got in the pool to keep it from riding up.

I got this.

I was going to be so zen floating in the water. Maybe even do some breathing to my toes.

Yes. The bobbing guy wasn't in the pool anymore, so it would be just me and the lap-swimming woman. Somehow the situation felt immensely more relaxing.

I wouldn't be fighting with my shirt the entire time.

If only the windowed wall weren't there, making it possible for guys to walk by and glance in, it would be utterly *perfect*.

I nodded at the woman in the pool as she took a rest to adjust her goggles, and she smiled and nodded back at me. Then she went back to her laps.

I put a toe in. The water temperature was perfect, so I dropped my entire self in and flipped onto my back.

Ah. Immediately my shoulders relaxed and my arms went limp as I stared at the diffused lights on the ceiling.

This, I thought, as I breathed down to my floating toes, *I could do each and every day.*

Every single day.

It was literally like worries were melting, disappearing into the water through those body pores of mine immersed in the pool. Before high school, I used to swim every weekday, and then it became only on vacations. And each vacation I'd make a resolution to bring the daily pool back into my life—until reality hit again via school and extracurricular life.

This was perfect.

I floated around and around, my eyes closed, water muffling my ears, feeling my way to zen, when someone nudged me. I opened my eyes to the white-capped woman by my side saying something.

After righting myself to tread water—where was I in the pool now, anyway?—I pulled on each of my ears to clear them and then turned to face her.

"Someone wants to talk to you!" she said loudly, indicating the windowed wall behind me.

Oh. It must be Auntie Nandy.

I looked, ready to smile and wave, but was greeted with a weird frozen tableau on the other side of the window. With a towel around his torso, the bobbing middle-aged man was staring at me, standing with his legs apart beside the fitness center attendant, the one who'd signed Auntie Nandy and me into the facility, who now had his arms crossed, a frown on his face.

He pointed at me and then tucked his index finger in so he was holding a thumb up, which he then pulled back in a swift motion.

"He's telling you to get out of the pool?" The woman beside me looked as perplexed as I felt. "It seems like he's saying *You. Out. Now.*"

I pointed at myself and tilted my head at the two men. *Me?*

Both the attendant and the bobbing man nodded, their frowns deepening.

"I thought it was strange when he just got out of the hot tub and marched out of here," the woman said, so low that it seemed to be almost to herself.

"Who?" I swam to the edge, worry prickling my previously relaxed limbs.

"Him. He'd been in the pool with me before you came and then moved on to the hot tub." She swam alongside me and watched as I hoisted myself up, being careful to secure my turban. "Then, when you arrived, he waited a bit and then stalked off. I wonder what that's about."

I stood up, dripping, wringing all the water I could from my shirt. "You mean he was in here the whole time?"

I thought he'd left!

I glanced around and noticed the hot tub tucked in a corner, kind of hidden by a row of short palm trees. Right.

I waved at the helpful woman and went to see what was up.

It was all about me not wearing the proper swim attire.

I listened as the fitness attendant lectured me on the pool's needs.

The pool, apparently, needed me to show my legs and arms. Caps were okay, so my turban was not a big deal, from what I surmised.

Bobbing man clutched the towel around his waist and kept bobbing his head as the attendant informed me that what I was wearing wasn't *proper swimwear*. If I wanted, I could buy *proper swimwear* at their gym shop, but they had limited choices, and I might have to go for a two-piece.

I nodded, my brain trying to work out what the exact swim-clothing rules were according to the attendant's long spiel.

"So someone's allowed to wear shorts like his?" I asked, pointing at the tips of the floral shorts showing under bobbing man's towel. Wet and hitched below his belly, they reached beyond his knees.

"That's his swimwear, yes. But you see how she's dressed?" the fitness attendant said, indicating the woman in the pool. "That's how our female swimmers dress at this facility."

"Say a woman came in shorts like his, loose, flowy, flowery, fun shorts. Then would you guys be okay with *that*?" I crossed my arms, my voice hardening. "Seems unfair if you wouldn't be okay with that. If you'd say, *Hey, you woman, show your thighs!*"

The fitness attendant stared at me. "Who's the resident that you signed in with?"

"My aunt," I said. "But why won't you answer my question? Is it okay if I show up in huge shorts like his but just a bit longer?"

Bobbing man let his towel drop as he crossed his arms.

Wait. What was I doing?

This was old Zayneb. The one who got in trouble. Who got her friends in trouble. Who may get Auntie Nandy in trouble by making a ruckus at her residence complex.

I wasn't supposed to do this anymore.

I uncrossed my arms. "Okay, okay. I get it. That's the way things are here," I said with a fake smile before forcing out, "Thanks for letting me know the rules!"

I walked away and didn't look back.

The only way was forward—into the version of Zayneb who let things just be.

Because I was asleep when she got back to the apartment from the gym, Auntie Nandy went to work not knowing a thing about what had happened at the pool.

Which was perfect. Now she didn't need to worry one bit.

I woke up to the alarm I'd set so that I'd have enough time to get ready to meet the Emmas.

I sort of knew it would take a long time to prep for hanging out with them. It wasn't so much that I was trying to be a different me as it was that I was trying to make *sense* to them.

I refuse to call it wanting to fit in with their crowd.

Besides, I liked them. They were multinational, diverse, open-minded (except for Madison), and accepted me without pause. Actually, more than that, they *saw* me. Which was different from school, where Kavi and I usually passed under the radar of the other, mostly white kids.

I wanted to continue to be seen by the Emmas and their friends.

Which means I need two whole hours to get ready.

It started with a long shower, a better shower than the one I'd had after getting back from the pool cocooned in changing room towels so I wouldn't drip everywhere. This was the kind of shower that ensured each strand of my hair was washed.

Then I emerged from the bathroom connected to my room to towel and air-dry my hair so that it would fall into its natural curls. People *not* in the know have no idea why it's *so* important to have properly dried, properly done hair when your scarf is going on top of it, but we hijabis know it's vital.

1. Your hair needs to be dried properly so that it won't get that soggy, half-dried smell that will seep out of your hijab, hitting everyone in your vicinity.

2. Your hair thoroughly dried gives it the proper volume to let your scarf sit pretty on your head.

3. Your hair needs to be happy, not drippy sad, under your hijab, or it will give you trouble later when the scarf is off at home. Happy hair means good hair.

And, I had to admit, I have good hair. I tossed it a few times and then looked in the mirror as I blew it off my face.

It's almost model hair. The one vanity of my life.

That only my friends, all girls, get to see. The only guys *allowed* to see it being members of my family.

Someday, though, I'll toss this hair in front of the one I end up with. My significant other.

I looked in the mirror at the long, dark, loose curls cascading around my face, long wispy bangs reaching into my eyes, and saw Adam's face flash in my mind.

A twinge came, unbidden.

I went back to lie down on the bed, to let my hair dry completely. To think about him.

He hasn't read your message, Zayneb. He knows you're a faker, Zayneb. He wants the real deal, just like you want the real deal in a guy, Zayneb.

Just like you want him, *Zayneb.*

I closed my eyes and imagined opening the door to Adam. Like after we were a thing, and everything was legit, with family, with everything.

I imagined opening the door to him without my hijab on, hair tousled, kind of getting in my eyes, but not so much that he couldn't see how done up those eyes were—with eye shadow, mascara, and all.

He would have been gazing at the floor when the door first opened, wearing that blue shirt I saw him in at the airport, but then his eyes would flip up and light up, and that small, consistent smile he mostly wore (before it trailed off yesterday) would spread and spread and spread, and then he would just swoop in and—

Beep beep beep. The alarm went off again.

Agh. That meant I only had thirty minutes before the Uber arrived.

As I threw on clothes, I tried to unpack my fantasizing about Adam.

I want to kiss him.

That mouth with that smile.

Agh, why was I in such *lust*? *Astaghfirullah,* Sadia would caution.

I barely knew the guy.

Well, other than Auntie Nandy telling me his background, her knowing his mom and dad. And him being seemingly a great big brother. And caring about animals. And having tons of friends who he was super quiet around but who obviously liked him a lot. And him becoming Muslim on his own so early.

Okay, that last one was a heavy one. To be that mature when you're so young.

But I didn't know *him*, the guy. What he was like personality-wise.

It was just his looks that were getting to me.

That made me want him to swoop in, from the door I'd opened in my fantasy, and wrap his arms around me as I pushed my hair away from the tight space between us so my lips could find his with urgency, his face, as it became one with mine, getting surrounded and caressed by my curly locks—

I guess it was a good thing that he wasn't reading my message.

I already had a bit of makeup on, like lip stuff, but at the Fenty pop-up Emma Domingo said we should get our faces redone as the mini-makeover lines were short.

We emerged fresh faced, me with a smidgen of color and highlight on my cheeks, and my eyes—"so big and wide and fantastic to work with" according to the makeup artist—lit up a bit, with neutral lips. My look matched the taupey-pink hijab I was wearing.

Emma Phillips checked a message on her phone. She was in white again, but this time it was white jeans and a white T-shirt. "The guys are already at the food court," she said, undoing her hair that had been tied back with an elastic while she got her makeup done. She held her phone camera up and fixed herself, pumping some volume into the back of her hair with her fingers.

My Adam hair fantasy came back to me.

I wonder if I blushed even further under the fake blush I had on.

"And, yay, Connor got *him* to come," Emma Phillips added, reading another message that had popped up, in between peering at her engorged-looking lips. She'd paid for the full-lips deal, and you could see the effect from several feet away. "Adam will be there!"

Adam was here? I flushed further. *I thought it was just us girls.*

"Well, you look perfect, then," Emma Zhang said pointedly, and I whipped my head at her, wondering how she knew about my fantasy.

But she was smiling slyly at Emma Phillips.

Emma Domingo, the one I felt the most connected to, because she was super sweet, and who had her arm laced with mine as we walked, whispered to me, "Emma P. has had a crush on Adam forever."

"No, not forever, just since sixth grade," Emma Phillips announced.

"After his mom died and he became kind of emo," Madison said.

"That's cruel." Emma Zhang shot Madison a look. "It's because he was the only one who helped Emma P. when she got picked on for her scoliosis brace."

"Emma P. had to wear a thick brace for her back all through middle school, and it was uncomfortable under her clothes, so she wore it on the outside," Emma Domingo told me. "And when kids began bullying her, Adam drew these amazing *Avatar: The Last Airbender* scenes on it. We were all into ATLA back then, so her brace became instantly cool. And then she was too."

"But he was still emo," Madison continued, grinning.

I wondered why the Emmas let Madison hang around with them. Were friends in short supply in Doha? Anyway, *I* didn't need her friendship. "Way to be insensitive. Just like with your gross, racist-as-hell Coachella clothes. Maybe grow a heart?"

The Emmas looked at me in unison. Was that a tiny bit of awe I saw in their eyes? Or shock at the disturbance I'd created?

What? She's awful, I mouthed to Emma Zhang, who nodded.

Madison ignored me, per usual, and went on. "Who says that's bad anyway? Being emo? He had a reason to be."

"The point is that's not *why* she likes him," Emma Zhang pressed. "She likes him because he's kind."

"Yeah, not like your bae Jacob, who kept calling me names throughout middle school," Emma Phillips said, staring into her phone, still combing out her hair with her fingers while we walked. "Anyway, that was a crush back then. Now we talk."

"Really? Since when?" Emma Domingo looked up eagerly. "I thought he'd dropped off the face of the earth when he went to London."

"Then he got back. He's around the corner from me, remember?" she said, as Emma Zhang side-hugged her excitedly. "But you know how he is; he's not the type to show it."

I listened to this part quietly, my face growing warmer.

Right.

Right, right, right.

MARVEL: REVELATIONS

Exhibit A: Emma Phillips and Adam.

I guess this marvel is about God.

Because He's the one who lets you know the things you didn't know before. Who allows circumstances to come into your life that make you *see*.

I'm so grateful my crush on Adam lasted exactly five days. Six if you count the airport first sighting.

Wow, Emma Phillips's crush on him lasted six *years*. And was only now coming to fruition.

She's zen. He's zen. I'm not.

That's what's important.

ADAM

TUESDAY, MARCH 12

MARVEL AND ODDITY: FRIENDS

SHE WAS SITTING AT THE NEXT TABLE OVER, ON HER PHONE, FRIES untouched in front of her. Emma Domingo was across from her, Emma Zhang next to her. They were both talking, but she wasn't.

I was at the end of a longer table parallel to hers. Connor directly in front of me, going on about Nancy, his TA, with Tsetso and Isaac beside us, then Emma Phillips and Jacob across from Madison. There was another table with a few other guys from DIS behind us.

But all I could see was her.

She wouldn't look up.

She hadn't even said salaam back after I'd salaamed her when she and the other girls had first shown up.

Maybe she hadn't heard?

"Adam, you in for the dunes this weekend?" Emma Phillips asked loudly. "Everyone else, except Tsetso, who, ahem, decided to ditch Doha early, is coming."

"I'll have to check. I don't know if my dad has stuff planned." I took another bite of my chicken shawarma sandwich.

"Okay, let me know by tomorrow then? Maybe you could

hitch a ride with my dad and me." She smiled. "You're practically next door!"

I nodded back at her and then busied myself picking up the lettuce that had fallen out of my shawarma.

Oh boy. Was it true then what Connor had told me? That Emma Phillips still had a thing for me?

Hope it's just my imagination. The way Madison looked at Emma Phillips just now, raising her eyebrows.

I'd tried for a long time to stay distant but polite with Emma Phillips.

Zayneb stood up suddenly. She bent over and whispered something to Emma Domingo and Emma Zhang. And then turned and left.

I continued eating my shawarma.

She didn't come back.

I should ask Emma Domingo or Emma Zhang if she actually left.

No, it was better this way.

ZAYNEB

TUESDAY, MARCH 12

ODDITY: IMPULSIVENESS

EXHIBIT A TO Z: THE ROOT OF EVERYTHING THAT HAS GONE WRONG in my life. Like falling for people without thinking things through. And running away from malls where they were sitting close by, because I wanted them to know how much I didn't care about Ada—I mean *them*.

It was five p.m., and Auntie Nandy wasn't back from work yet. As I looked at the food on the dining table from this morning, that I'd covered before leaving for the mall, I remembered she'd said she'd be doing errands all day.

I unraveled my hijab, hung it on the back of a dining room chair, and then methodically packed the breakfast into containers.

I went into the kitchen to put them away in the fridge, and seeing the dirty dishes stacked on the counter, I decided to do them.

I opted out of using the dishwasher. This was my chore at home, cleaning the pots and things that didn't go in the dishwasher, and, right now, I knew I needed it. I needed the familiarity.

The soapy warm water was like a balm—on my skin and deep inside me—as my arms plunged again and again into it, soaking and scrubbing dishes and cutlery and small pots. When I was done rinsing, I dunked my hands in the sink filled with warm, sudsy, murky water, to squeeze the dish sponge over and over.

Maybe this was the peace I needed, because in that water I saw a truth: *Girls like me who see and feel the pains and problems of the world don't make sense to people. So maybe we're meant to be alone, or only with people exactly like us.*

I'd thought that the Emmas and their friends made sense to me, but, as we hung out, I realized we had nothing in common.

No, this wasn't the complete truth that I saw in the murky waters, Marvels and Oddities journal.

I'm not supposed to lie to you, and here I am letting a boy come in between you and me.

I also saw the truth of Emma Phillips and Adam.

When I saw him at the food court today, looking so cutely rumpled—had those been splatters of paint on his T-shirt and cargo shorts?—with his hair up, lifted right off his head in some parts, the wrong parts, and yet also falling into his eyes, I'd taken one look at him and bolted inside.

Retreat, Zayneb. He was unattainable. Most likely taken. And supremely not interested in you. For example, see unanswered text of yours from yesterday, whereas he talked to (well, mostly listened to) everyone else around him.

That was what led me to texting him again, *Please disregard that last message thanks*, on the way home from the mall.

Because I'd wanted him to know just how much I wasn't thinking of him. So I reminded him of it. That I wasn't thinking of him.

Oof, I'm such an impulsive klutz.

I let the water drain from the sink and wiped the counters. It was time for *Little Women*, the one with Winona Ryder as Jo.

I changed into pajamas, undid my hair bun, removed my

contact lenses, put on glasses, wrapped Binky around me, cradled Squish, and pressed play on my favorite comfort movie of all time.

As Jo traipsed around being allowed to be angry when she wanted to be, and Amy threw things in the fire during one of *her* rage sessions, it hit me that maybe it was because Jo and Amy were considered cute that they got away with showing their emotions.

Like the girl on the plane coloring so happily.

Was that a factor in me not being able to just be messy me?

At the part in the movie when Jo's neighbor Laurie tried to kiss her, my Adam-and-my-hair fantasy popped right back into my head, churning my insides.

God, I had it so bad this time. I'd never felt this intensity with that brief thing I had with Yasin, Ayaan's friend.

Ayaan.

She, too, hadn't wanted to answer my texts.

She hated my guts.

I stopped the movie and closed the laptop.

Then, even though it was only seven thirty, I got under Binky, removed my glasses, and closed my eyes.

I didn't want to *think*.

Beeps from my phone woke me. It was Kavi messaging me to hop on FaceTime.

"I thought I'd do today's bulletin face-to-face. Since I miss your face," she said, her phone far enough away that I could see her sitting crisscrossed on a chair. The brick wall behind her, with its familiar posters (LIBRARIES ARE FOR EVERYONE! and WE READ BANNED BOOKS HERE!) told me she was in the school library quiet room, the exact one we hang out in when we have work to catch up on at lunchtime. The one we call our Situation Room.

I swallowed a pang of homesickness and got busy finding my glasses in Binky's folds.

As I propped my phone against the bedside lamp, Kavi peered at me. "WHOA. YOU'VE TRANSFORMED. Is that really you, Zayneb?"

I slid my glasses on, sat up on my knees, and twisted to look at myself in the mirrored cabinet door above the headboard.

My Fenty makeup was still on, subtle and flawless. My dark hair, echoing the dark frames on my glasses, lay sexy and curly around this perfection. I was in pajamas, but . . . still.

"Doha does this to you," I said, sinking back into the bed, deciding to swallow the murky-water bitterness from earlier.

I'm talking to Kavi, my best friend, acceptor of the real me, messiness and all.

I tossed my hair. "Soak in the glam, Kav."

"Tell me you're at home. That you haven't suddenly become a non-hijabi." She squinted into the screen, trying to figure out my surroundings.

"Of course not, scarf for life."

"That's my Zay! Loudly, proudly Muslim!"

"You realize that that's like saying 'long dresses for life!' or 'boyfriend jeans for life!' means 'loudly, proudly Muslim,' right? Covering your hair is just one part of believing in modesty in dressing, not the *only* part."

"Right, you periodically give me these lessons, but I guess I remain a poor victim of cultural narratives popular round these parts," Kavi drawled, accentuating her deep Southern accent that she'd almost lost after five years living in Indiana. She'd been born in Alabama. "Right. Hijab does not necessarily mean more Muslimy. It *could* mean more Muslimy, and it could mean *not* more Muslimy."

"I'm sorry, but this really interests me. This discussion. Okay if I jump in?" Someone popped their head into the frame, in front of Kavi.

It was Noemi of the blond bangs, of the lacrosse team, of the muttered "asshole" directed at Fencer.

I hadn't even known there was someone in the room with Kavi. In our room.

Noemi did a double take at my hair, having never seen me without my scarf, and then waved at me. "How does all that hair fit under your scarf?"

"It's a fine art. Which mainly involves the purchasing of the proper tools for tying it back and then stuffing it all suitably in." I swept my hair away from my face, wound it into a bun at the nape of my neck, and secured it with the scrunchie tie I had on my wrist. "Like so."

"Right, I feel so stupid." Noemi rolled her eyes. "Of course that's how you do it. It just hit me. It's like if I'd asked you how you put on a jacket over your arms or something. Or how you get socks on over toes."

I laughed. "Well, yeah, it's just like another item of clothing. To cover yourself. Like no one asks people who wear pants to school, *Why do you have to cover your legs?* No one makes a big fuss when there are mall entrance signs that say 'Shirts Required.' No one acts like *that's* oppressive."

"So, wait. If a head scarf is just another item of clothing, why is there so much controversy around it?" Noemi leaned against the back of Kavi's chair.

"Because it's come to stand as a symbol of being Muslim. And that's trouble because there are a lot of people who hate on Muslims like crazy." I shrugged and undid my hair and let it fall onto my shoulders again, looking at Noemi, wondering if she was as genuine as she appeared to be. "There's also another kind of hate from people, mostly from women who are into white feminism, who think they're helping Muslim women by finding this way of dressing oppressive. They act like if they quote unquote *free* us from our religious teachings, which they believe they've become quote unquote smart enough to figure out are oppressive, that then they're *saving* us."

I waited. Was that too much? I'd said it in a rush.

Was she going to think I was blaming her? As a white person? Well, as a white *woman*?

Impulsive-klutz me.

Again.

"Okay this is the part where I admit I used to be one of those people. I'd see these pics from around the world, of women-not-like-me, and I'd feel *so* sorry for them." Noemi sat back and propped her legs on the table in front of her. "I'd be like, *I am such a lucky person I'm not her*, when I'd see, yes, a girl or woman different from me. The Kool-Aid was full to the brim in me."

I smiled. I was warming to this Noemi, she of the blond bangs, she of the open mind.

"Do you want to know what, or I mean *who*, changed my mind?"

"Kavi?" I asked, glancing at Kavi, sitting smugly with her arms crossed. "Because you became friends with the original, authentic Kavi?"

"No, though that's been great. Hanging out with Kavi the last few days." Noemi turned and smiled at Kavi. "No, it was Fencer. Who broke me out of my white feminism like *oh snap*."

I blinked. *What in the world?*

Kavi nodded, patting Noemi on the shoulder encouragingly. "The moment has come for you, oh Noemi, to reveal to your hero, Zayneb, *her* true part in your blossoming." She leaned closer to the camera and whispered, "Your suspension was Noemi's awakening."

"My master you are, Zayneb," Noemi said, Yoda-like. "I am your Padawan."

"How?" I leaned back against the headboard, eager for Noemi to continue.

It was evident that she was an interesting person.

"For the past couple of months, I've been doing this art project on sexual assault, high-profile cases. It's called *Buried*, and it's focused on that word and how it ties in with sexual violence. Like how stories about girls getting hurt are buried, how even victims' testimonies are buried, or how they're *literally* buried, in the case of those criminals who keep their victims in cellars or dungeons to prey on them."

"Ugh."

"Like in the movie *The Lovely Bones*, which was based on a book, which was loosely based on true events. And that Austrian man who kept his daughter in a dungeon, raping her, for over *twenty years*."

I closed my eyes.

I opened them because there was silence.

"I'm sorry," Noemi said, wiping away tears. She took a breath. "So, I'm working on this project, and, in the midst of me doing a painting of the entrance to the Austrian girl's prison, built by her *father*, I remind you, Fencer gives us the handout about the buried

Turkish girl. And while I was reading it, I thought, yeah, I could use this in my project. *And then Fencer goes and makes it a Muslim problem.* I just lost it inside. *How the fuck are you saying this is a Muslim problem, to be cruel to girls, when I've just literally spent hours amassing evidence that it's a world problem, Fencer?* Then you spoke up in class and confirmed what I'd been thinking, that it's not a part of being Muslim. At that point, I knew that Fencer was an asshole, a racist, a . . . a . . . ."

"Islamophobe," Kavi helped.

"An Islamophobe." Noemi dropped her legs from the table and crossed her arms. "And then I realized I'd drunk the Kool-Aid, thinking that somehow some women were more oppressed than others due to their background."

"She came running to me. To apologize." Kavi laughed. "Because, you know, I'm a brown woman, and I stand for all brown women?"

"Well, I gotta start somewhere!" Noemi laughed too, though her eyes were still glistening from tears. "Apologies to you, too, Zayneb. Because the first time I saw you in class, I did feel sorry for you. Because of your scarf."

"Fencer? It was Fencer?" I shook my head, a smile breaking out on my face. "I can't believe *Fencer* woke you. All this time I'm burning up in class, thinking he's using his own hatred to make more Islamophobes out of the other students, get them riled up against Muslims, and then *this* happens?"

"Zayneb, hate to break it to you, but Noemi is a special case," Kavi pointed out. "Most of the other people in class just sit there like sponges. Best-case scenario is if they're tuned out, so then they're sitting there like rocks. The stuff Fencer spews just circulates around them. They don't question it."

"True." Noemi nodded. "Really true. The only reason I didn't fall for it is because I'm doing this art project."

"I don't know how I'm going to survive two and a half *more* months of Fencer." I drew my legs up and wrapped my arms around them. I couldn't even think of seeing his face again.

But I'm supposed to change myself. Like, learn to process things without overheating.

"Anyway, I just need to chill. That's why I'm here." I let go of my legs and crossed them. "I'm on my suspension vacation."

"I get you, Zayneb. You taking Fencer on like that," Noemi said. "Every time he talks in class now, it grates on my nerves. I feel like a wrecking ball, ready to smash his lesson plans."

"Wreck-it-Noemi," Kavi deadpanned.

"Well, children, don't be like me. Give peace a chance. Kumbaya and so forth," I reminded them.

"Yeah, that's not happening," Noemi said. "EatThemAlive version two is going live soon."

Kavi looked at Noemi pointedly, then witheringly, but Noemi didn't see it. Or pretended not to.

When Kavi turned to me, I gave her the same look she'd given Noemi.

"I told her about it. Because I want to keep it going," Kavi said firmly. "We need to help Ayaan. Prove that she was doing something right."

"But that'll just get everyone in more trouble!" I stared at Kavi. "One suspension, one removal from student council . . . do you want an expulsion next?"

"Zayneb, we're not involving you, so don't worry about it!" Kavi said. "Just enjoy your vacay."

She tilted her head and stuck her jaw out.

That meant not to mess with her. Kavi is the kindest friend in my life, but she can also be extremely steely.

But you only see that when you come close to her sacred truths. Like justice.

She isn't loud about it like me, but she's consistent.

Like a determined beaver chipping away at a tree, I don't doubt her ability to fell Fencer.

MARVEL: AUNTIE NANDY

Exhibit A: The swimsuit Auntie Nandy held out after immediately knocking on my door when she returned home.

"Why didn't you tell me what happened at the pool this morning?" she asked, holding a billowy, black diving suit up in front of her.

"What's that?" I'd been trying to finish watching *Little Women* and pressed pause on Jo arguing with a circle of men on a woman's right to vote and slid my headphones off.

"This is what you're going to wear to swim from now on."

"What do you mean?"

"Try it on." She beckoned me. "It took me a long time to dig it out of my closet—your mom left it here on her last visit."

"Auntie Nandy, why are you giving me this burkini?" I held it up. It was almost like the one I'd worn swimming in middle school, except my old one had two rows of purple stripes running along the sides. This one had a broad blue square extending from the neck to the waist. In the middle of the square was a brown clamshell with a pair of closed, long-lashed eyes but no mouth. Slightly strange. And sad.

"Because you love swimming. And, when I left yoga this

morning, Marc at the fitness desk told me that you needed a proper swimsuit to use the facilities." She raised her eyebrows and then walked to the bedroom door. Turning around to face me before she exited, she added, "There's your *proper* swimsuit. Completely fits the fabric requirements of swimwear suitable for a pool."

I clutched the burkini to me as it dawned on me what Auntie Nandy meant.

She wanted me to challenge the fitness center's expectation of what proper swimwear was.

She wanted me to *fight*?

She actually wanted me to challenge something?

A little spark ignited in me as I imagined Marc's face.

As I imagined tattle-telling bobbing man's face.

As I imagined the white-capped woman swimming laps who might be there again, who might high-five me for making it to the pool again.

I looked down at the burkini and saw it as a superhero outfit. One that I'd be wearing for a mission the next day.

I went into the bathroom, held it against myself, and smiled serenely at my reflection in the mirror.

"Yeah, you will do just fine," I whispered to the sad clamshell on my superhero suit.

Kavi and Noemi had #EatThemAlive, and I had a burkini ban to take down.

But, this time, I'd do it serenely, as serenely as the smile that greeted—and accepted me—in the mirror.

ADAM
TUESDAY, MARCH 12
MARVEL: STRANGERS

IN THE MIDDLE OF THE MOVIE AT VILLAGGIO MALL MY EYES clouded over.

Like they were covered with a thick layer of jelly.

I rubbed them, sure something had gotten into them, but nothing changed.

The headache, present since this morning turned drill-like, boring into the back of my eyes as I turned them to check if it was the same peripherally.

Peripheral was worse.

Like multiple knife jabs at once.

I felt nauseous with the pain.

I got up and squeezed my way past Connor, Tsetso, Jacob, and Madison, almost stumbling in the aisle before I realized I should turn on my phone for its light. I then made it halfway before remembering Connor. He would stalk me like a tiger unless I let him know what was up.

I backed up slowly, feeling my way along the aisle seat backs—not due to the dark but to my blurred vision.

"Hey, just going to the bathroom, then sitting in the back," I whispered in his general direction.

He nodded. Or at least I think it was him.

In the bathroom, after heaving emptiness and waiting for the nausea to ease up, I washed my face a few times, really rinsing my eyes out, examining them in the mirror.

There was nothing there, but it literally felt as though I were looking at my reflection through a thick layer of Vaseline.

I had to get home.

I took a taxi, one of the many assembled at the exits of the mall, praying that the door was not locked at home. That Marta, our cleaning person, had left it that way.

There was no way I could fit a key into a keyhole.

As it was, I could see shapes of things blurring by out the window, objects looming as we neared a stop, like now, at the traffic lights. I tried to concentrate on looking straight ahead, to reduce the pain that struck me every time I moved my eyes.

"Are you okay, sir?" The driver turned to look at me.

I shook my head. "I just have a headache."

"Okay, want to stop for water? Store right here. Tea or water. They'll have it."

He must have meant one of the many chai stations they have around Doha.

"No, it's okay. I just need to lie down."

"I'll get you home quickly, sir."

Maybe he could help me. Maybe I could ask him.

He doesn't know me.

"Can you wait after you drop me?" I said, hoping my voice didn't sound desperate. "I may need help with opening my door."

"Certainly I will." He nodded at me. "My name is Zahid."

"Thank you," I said, my shoulders relaxing. "I'm Adam."

I'll have help.

The front door *was* locked. Zahid used my keys and opened it for me. I turned to thank him so he could leave, but he didn't let me. Instead, he held on to my arm and led me into the sunken living room, easing me slowly down the steps.

I needed the help of his hands, as the tingling returned with a vengeance, running its fingers along my legs and arms as my eyes continued being assaulted by a thousand cuts.

I wondered briefly if I'd leaned too heavily on him as he brought me to the couch.

Grateful for him, for the cushioned welcome for my body, for reaching *home*, I lay down, afraid.

Afraid of what else was to come.

Zahid left but came back with a tall glass of water. "Drink this—maybe it is the heat. You need some hydration maybe."

I took some sips, wondering how you tell a stranger that you don't want to be left alone.

Zahid helped me up the stairs to my room, where I paid him for the ride. He wouldn't take the enormous tip I offered.

"You hurt me to give me a tip for being as I should be." He jotted down his number in case I ever needed his taxi again, then left.

I slept and slept. Whenever I woke, my eyes would fly open to check if *it* was gone, the thing covering my eyes, whether the pain had gone, but it was still the same, so finally, after the fifth time, I pulled the cover right over my head and slept more.

At one point I heard Dad opening my bedroom door, heard Hanna say, "Why is he sleeping *now*? It's seven o'clock."

"Shh, let him sleep. He's been working in the room downstairs, painting, so he must be tired."

"Are we still ordering pizza? I want—" The door closed.

I slept until the dark became light outside my window, until it was a new day. I listened for sounds to make sure Dad and Hanna had left for school.

Then I got up.

And fell.

My legs weren't legs. They were noodles.

ADAM

WEDNESDAY, MARCH 13

ODDITY: SECRETS

My legs useless, I lay crying on the floor of my room.

Not from pain, though that was still there, still boring into the back of my eyes whenever I moved them.

And I think maybe I hit my hip hard on the floor. It felt sore, bruised.

But I mostly cried because it didn't make sense.

What had just happened didn't make sense.

I cried because I couldn't see.

I didn't mean just *literally*, that my vision was affected, I meant I couldn't see what was next.

It felt like the way forward, what to do, was as clouded as my vision.

I cried for so long, I was sure hours had passed.

Then I thought of Dad and Hanna opening the door to my bedroom again.

I thought about Dad's bent head crying at prayer the other day.

Of Hanna's octopus hair bounding away with mischief.

About Stillwater, Hanna's panda, who'd become another presence in the house for her when Mom left us.

I thought about the photo of Mom swinging in our backyard in Ottawa, when we'd returned *home* for a few months. Taken a year after her MS had gotten worse, a year after Hanna had been born.

She'd been smiling wide, her light brown hair flying behind her. She'd been happy.

My arms worked, so I pulled myself forward and forward until I got to the chair by my desk. I rested my head on it, trying to figure out how to get to *help*.

Get myself to the hospital.

My phone.

Zahid's number for his taxi.

They were both on the desk, but I couldn't haul myself up.

But I could reach.

I looked at the blurry items around me. Was that my empty guitar case? Right under the bed?

I shifted myself forward until I could grasp it. And then I dragged it along with me as I inched back to the desk.

Lifting the guitar case, I banged it and swept it clumsily along the top of the desk, saying a prayer while doing so, as the case sent pencils and pens and other random things raining down.

The phone fell onto the bed, almost at the edge, and the piece of paper with Zahid's number fluttered beside me. *A miracle, alhamdulillah.*

He had written his number so big and clear I could make it out. I closed my eyes in gratitude at this, wondering if the tears prickling them again would ever wash away whatever was blurring my vision.

I held the paper tightly in my hand as I dragged myself back to the bed to get the phone.

What if it's out of battery?

Please, God, no. Please, please, no.

I spoke Zahid's number in for voice command to activate.

Another miracle: The phone wasn't out of juice.

The last miracle, the best one, happened when he picked up.

I lay there waiting for Zahid.

The kindness of a stranger.

By the time he got to me, some of the feeling in my legs had returned. I knew by the soreness in a part of my left thigh that it had hit something, maybe the leg of the desk chair, or even the floor—a soreness that I started to slowly become aware of, until the throbbing told me I could try standing up, maybe make my way back to bed.

I used the chair again and half dragged, half pulled myself to bed. It did feel like some feeling had come back into my legs, but I wasn't sure I could trust it.

I'd never forget that fall from the bed. It was like somebody had pulled the plug on the connection between my legs and me.

The sound of keys being fitted in at the front door was as sweet as music.

Zahid appeared in the doorway with one of our compound security guys, Felipe.

"What happened, man?" Felipe said, advancing to help me from the bed. Before he squatted, he fixed stray hairs back into the bun at the back of his head. "You have some kind of fall?"

"Yeah." It was true.

Between him and Zahid, I was half carried down the stairs.

"Next time buzz me. I'd have gotten the ambulance," Felipe said as we made our way out. "You're lucky I hadn't left yet. I was just about to go home. Samir is not here to take the shift after mine, so I've just been waiting."

"You know how ambulances are here," I said. "Sometimes it's easier to get a taxi."

Zahid nodded, easing me into the back of his taxi. "Thanks, sir," he said to Felipe.

I was glad Felipe was going home. He wouldn't be able to bring up what had happened with anyone at the compound.

At the hospital, once I spoke the truth, my MS truth, everything went fast, the nurses filling in the forms, ordering scans.

Zahid stayed by, asking if he should call someone for me. "What about your family? The security guy said you have a father and sister."

I hesitated before asking for my phone.

"I charged it in my car. It was at two percent," he said. "I'll dial for you."

He read the lock screen as he came over with it. "There are a lot of messages for you. Connor. Zayneb. Emma P. Connor. Emma Z. Jacob. Zayneb, again."

At any other time I would have thought he was being intrusive. But now, not one bit.

He was Zahid—the guy who'd been there.

I pressed the button to bring the phone to life.

Zayneb.

Ms. Raymond.

"Can you text Zayneb? Ask her for her aunt's number?" I sighed, leaning my head back into the examination bed. Weird that Ms. Raymond was the only one who made sense.

She'd been one of Mom's closest friends and had helped her through the illness from when it got worse until the end.

"Can. You. Give. Me. Your. Aunt's. Number?" Zahid spoke

slowly as he punched the text in. He held the phone out to display his handiwork. "Like that?"

"I can't see it," I said, groaning inside as I remembered Zayneb's message from a couple of days ago. That I'd let go unread for so long. "Wait, could you read me *Zayneb's* message first?"

"Certainly. Messages, plural. First she wrote 'Thanks for today.' With a puppy emoji. Second she wrote 'Please disregard that last message thanks.'"

"Zahid, I'm so sorry to make you do this. After this, please go back to work. I feel terrible for keeping you away from your taxi." I closed my eyes. *I need to tell Dad what's going on. You can't exploit the kindness of people you don't know.* "Can you text her back a thumbs-up emoji and write 'Great, glad you liked the saluki shelter'? And *then* text her asking for her aunt's number?"

"Yes. Done . . . and now done with the request for aunt's number," Zahid said. Then his voice dropped to a whisper. "The nurses think I'm your uncle. That's why they let me stay. So I will stay until your family comes. This is what I would want for my own nephew, you understand?"

I nodded. I wished I could see Zahid's face clearly. I thought from his voice that he was South Indian, one of the many in Doha. Maybe after this clears, after the doctors help me, I can see him again, thank him properly.

If *the doctors help me?* No. I shook my head, and Zahid came to my side.

"You need something, Adam?"

"No, just wanted to say thank you, Zahid." I held my right hand out.

"*Uncle* Zahid," he reminded me, taking my hand in both of his. He shook it, then let go as a ding sounded from my phone in his pocket. "Ah yes, your friend Zayneb wrote back. Just a number. No emoji this time."

"Can you dial it for me? Put it on speaker, please?"

It rang and rang and then went to voice mail.

Oh yeah, Ms. Raymond was probably at school teaching. "Hanging up is fine. Thanks."

A doctor came in then, clipboard in hand.

"I will try your aunt again, Adam-nephew," Zahid said, walking away. "I am outside, Doctor."

"Thanks, Uncle Zahid," I said, dropping back on the hospital bed, fear descending again.

After a round of tests—vitals, blood, X-ray—I was ordered an IV of steroids to treat the inflammations taking over my body.

As a nurse set it up, the doctor wrote on his clipboard and then addressed me. "What you're experiencing is an attack on your immune system. In order to arrest it, we're going to prescribe you a course of IV treatments for the next few days. We'll start the first treatment here now. But your subsequent treatments can be done at home with a visiting nurse or at a clinic we can recommend. It takes about an hour, but schedule time to prep, too. About an hour and a half."

The door creaked open a small increment.

"Doctor? Can I come in?" Ms. Raymond asked. "I'm his aunt."

The doctor nodded and gestured with his hand. "Your husband can come in too."

"Uncle Zahid," I said quickly, knowing Ms. Raymond would be perplexed.

She went out and brought Zahid with her.

The doctor repeated the things he'd told me, using the words "nervous system," "myelin," "attacks," "immune suppression."

"Multiple sclerosis."

"Nerve degeneration."

I kept my eyes closed throughout his entire explanation.

When he got to the part about my IV treatments, I opened them.

Ms. Raymond came over and picked my hand up. The one free of the IV needle that had just been inserted. She rubbed this hand between her own hands and spoke to the doctor. "So he can get it done at home? The IV treatments?"

I went back to closing my eyes. Dad.

Why am I still so reluctant to involve him?

"If it's suitable. You would just need a space for the nurse to come and set up the IV apparatus and for Adam to be comfortable."

"We have a large apartment, Doctor. I could take tomorrow off from work to be at home with Adam. And then it's the weekend. You said two more days of treatment, right?" She stopped rubbing my hand but continued holding it, and I felt strangely happy she did.

It made me feel like someone was going to take over now.

I wasn't on my own with this. For the first time.

I let the tears fall, surprised at the intensity of the relief washing over me.

It wasn't just my problem to figure out.

For the first time since the attack started, I had something other than pain to concentrate on.

I was also relieved, tentatively, for another reason: Did Ms. Raymond mean that I could get the treatments at *her* place?

Did she know somehow that I didn't want to involve Dad?

MARVEL: STUBBORNNESS OR, MAYBE, TENACITY

I think I've called it tenacity in my journal elsewhere. The not-letting-go of something you believe in.

I'm pretty good with that. Once I believe something is worth not letting go, I can hold on for years. Maybe even forever.

But it can also be seen as stubbornness, the unwillingness to see things in a different way from what you believe.

Is my refusal to involve Dad in my illness tenacity or stubbornness?

I like to think it's tenacity, because I have a strong reason for not telling him.

He's still having trouble dealing with Mom's death.

It will send him spiraling if he finds out about this.

I've seen that happen once before. When Hanna got a high fever when she was three and was lethargic and couldn't hold up her head, and the doctors said they couldn't rule out meningitis.

Dad went almost comatose. He wouldn't leave her side at the hospital. He took a two-week leave from work, but that was just to sit by her hospital cot, watching Hanna almost sleeplessly.

I, at eleven years old, kept things running at home until I couldn't anymore, and Marta, who'd come twice a week to clean since we'd moved to Doha, began checking in on me every day.

I don't even know if Dad realized that Marta had done that for me.

He can't handle more grief. Why would I tell him something that'll shatter him further?

My reason is ironclad, something to believe in, to not involve Dad in my MS for now.

But there's a part of me that knows I have a stubborn streak.

That once I make up my mind about something, I refuse to budge, even if it makes sense to do so.

Is it right that Ms. Raymond is being my guardian instead?

Is it right that Dad will be hurt when he finds out what I've kept from him? That I didn't want him to *care* about me?

I don't know, but I do know *this is me.*

Ms. Raymond agreed to drive me to Connor's house.

Before I left the hospital, I texted Dad that I would be staying over at Connor's, that he was having the guys over.

Then I told Connor the truth.

The long version of it.

He listened surprisingly well before saying, "Yeah, you're chilling here."

When we got to the car in the parking lot, with Ms. Raymond pushing me in the wheelchair the hospital had lent, she broke the comfortable and safe silence she'd granted me before.

"I need to know something, Adam. Before I drive you." She opened the front passenger door.

I reached for the edge of it, to get myself up. My legs were almost back to normal, back to how I knew them, but my vision continued to be blurry.

Easing myself into the seat, I waited as Ms. Raymond folded up the wheelchair and hoisted it into the trunk.

It was obvious she was going to ask about Dad, so I had to brace myself.

Then I remembered something. Two memories that I'd always tried to push away.

Two memories that merged into one.

But now I needed them, so I let them flood my brain.

I let them collide.

Memory one:

We were at our house in Ottawa. We'd come back for the summer when I was eight, would be going back to Doha at the end of it.

At our house in Ottawa, there was a door to go outdoors, and when you went through it, it was . . . the outside. There were no concrete compound walls that you had to further cross to get to the *outside* outside, like at our apartment in Doha.

Here, the rest of the world was waiting right there when we stepped out of our house.

That, to me, was freedom. And what made me feel great about being back home when I was a kid.

My grandparents lived in our house, Mom's parents. They kept our home and garden and backyard waiting for us. They kept it the same, except for the guest bedroom, permanently theirs, and the basement—where Grandpa had built the best workroom, large, clean, and organized, with the biggest table in the world (in the eyes of eight-year-old me) taking over the center, ready for any projects I wanted to do with him.

On the day of my memory, I'd been working on making a castle while Grandpa had been making something with bars on it.

"What's that, Grandpa?" I put the gray Lego roof piece in my hand down.

"It's a crib. For your sister."

Watching him push the bars into the holes he'd made on a long rectangle of wood was the moment I realized that Hanna was going to be a real person, not just something inside Mom's body, an unseen being that I was told would be my sister.

"I'm hungry." I attached the final piece to complete the roof of the castle.

"Go up and eat lunch then. Grandma went out, but she left some food on the table for you." Grandpa picked up a mallet and began banging the bars in. "If you need help, ask me, okay? Your mom's sleeping."

I went upstairs and didn't even look on the kitchen table, at what Grandma had left for me, and just went straight up to Mom and Dad's room.

I wanted French fries. Mom's French fries.

Which were the opposite of all the other French fries I'd ever eaten in my life. They weren't crispy, they weren't straight, they weren't thin.

They were soggy and lumpy and chunky and steamy.

They were so good, like a hug for your mouth.

"Mom?" I knocked lightly at first, then harder when I heard no reply. "Mom?"

"Come in, sweetie." She was sitting up in bed, under the bedspread, a book resting on her round stomach. She patted the bed beside her.

I leaned forward at the foot of the mattress, put my elbows up on it, and propped my face on the fists I'd made to cradle it. Someone, my sister, was going to come out of that stomach and sleep in the crib Grandpa was making downstairs.

"Can you make me French fries?"

"Grandma left lunch for you on the table."

"But it's not French fries."

"Maybe it is. Did you check?"

"But it wouldn't be *your* French fries."

She closed her book. "Do you want to know the secret to my French fries?"

I nodded. "Can you tell me when you make them?"

She smiled, took the bedspread off her stomach, climbed out of bed.

And almost fell to the floor, something red trickling under her.

Her face, distorted and scary, looked at me.

The moan that came from within her told me it was pain that twisted her into a mother I didn't recognize.

I sprang back, stricken, and then ran down two flights of stairs to get Grandpa.

Hanna was born that evening.

Prematurely, after a lot of pain. Pain I saw through the bars on the stairs I'd sat on while Mom and Grandpa waited for an ambulance.

I didn't ask for French fries again for a long time.

Then Mom's MS took a turn for the worse.

Memory two:

We were at our house in Ottawa. We'd come back for the summer when I was nine, would be going back to Doha at the end of it.

At our house in Ottawa, the kitchen was tiny, just two counters running parallel to each other, one bookended by a stove and a fridge, the other housing a sink. A small round table stood at the entrance.

On the day of my memory, I was in this kitchen, opening the freezer to get a Popsicle. When I closed it, Mom was standing there, leaning on her walker, smiling.

"Guess what I feel like eating," she said, opening her eyes wide, her way to let me know it was something special.

"A Popsicle?"

"No. French fries. *My* French fries." She turned the walker round and sat on it. "So, Adam, can you make them for me? If I teach you?"

I stood there for a second, pretending to work hard at unwrapping the banana Popsicle, picking at the wrapper like a scab. The seam on the plastic tore at once, and the frozen bar almost slipped out of my hands—as the image of Mom's twisted, pained face the day Hanna was born invaded my thoughts.

"Hello? Earth to Adam?" Mom tilted her head. "The best French fries in the world?"

"Okay, just putting this away. I don't need it anymore." I opened the freezer door and hid my face behind it. I twisted and wrapped the clear plastic as tight as I could around the Popsicle. Then I left the door open, a barrier between Mom and me, as I moved to the drawer beside the fridge to get a rubber band to fasten the wrapper tighter, keep it secure.

She wasn't allowed to see the tear rolling down my face.

Grandpa and Grandma had told me to make sure Mom knew I was going to be okay. Even though *Mom* wasn't going to be okay.

By the time I put that Popsicle, secured with three rubber bands, back in freezer and closed the door, Mom saw me and my face ready to learn to make the best French fries in the world.

"Before I teach you, you have to promise you'll never make them by yourself. Dad or Grandma or Grandpa or Marta has to be around."

I didn't ask her why she hadn't said, *Or I have to be around.* "What about Hanna?"

She tried to throw a dish towel at me, laughing. "Babies don't count."

"What about when I grow up and Hanna grows up and we're really old. Like ten and eighteen? I *still* can't make them by myself?" I grinned and picked up the towel and, with a hook shot, landed it back on the table where Mom had picked it up from. "What about when we're twenty and twenty-eight? Or sixty-one and sixty-nine? An old lady, an old man? I *still* can't make them?"

Mom looked away for a moment but not before I saw the edge of her mouth quiver and then turn down.

I dropped to my knees to open a cupboard door. The cupboard door that hid the potatoes. And my face.

I didn't want to make French fries. I just wanted to curl up beside Mom like I was a little kid again, not caring if I cried or not. Me not caring, nobody caring that I was crying. Nobody caring that I wasn't going to be okay.

I wasn't.

One by one, I took potatoes out and put them on the counter above my head, wordlessly.

"Okay, stop," she said, her voice husky. "Five is more than enough."

"For both of us?"

"For all of us."

I closed the cupboard door and made a face at Mom. "But I'll eat three potatoes by myself."

She *was* crying. But laughing, too. Tears and smiles. "All right, fries monster, take out more, then."

I reopened the cupboard and added five more potatoes, one by one, again.

It's okay to cry, then? Mom is crying and laughing.

I closed the door and stood up.

"Wash them well and then dry them really well," she said, her voice full again. Like her throat was tear filled too. She picked up the dish towel I'd thrown. "Use this."

I caught the checkered red-and-white cloth and hung it around my neck.

The sound of water running and potatoes being scrubbed masked the sound of Mom sobbing.

Then it hit me. Why Mom was doing this today.

No one was home. Just me and Mom.

Grandpa and Grandma had gone to Costco, a trip that took them a long time. Dad had taken Hanna for a checkup at the doctor's.

We're allowed to cry.

I let the tears fall too. I dried the potatoes with the dishcloth that had wiped away some of my tears, but not all of them.

Then I brought the clean potatoes to the table on a cutting board with a knife, and Mom showed me how to cut big fat wedges out of them.

When I was done, she grabbed my hand, looked in my eyes. "It's okay to cry a lot. But we have to get the crying done before we heat the oil. Otherwise it will splatter everywhere. When it's time to work with heat, with the hard part, we have to be ready. But get it all out now before we fry the best French fries in the world."

I got off the chair I was sitting on and tucked myself into her arms, slowly so I didn't hurt her.

It took us a long time to get ready. For the stove, for the heat, for the hard part.

I didn't know then that Mom and I would be making her fries together only a few more times that year. Before she left us.

They really were the best in the world.

She really was the best in the world.

Sitting in the car in the hospital parking lot, I told Ms. Raymond the whole thing. The collision of memories, French-fried memories.

Ms. Raymond wiped her eyes. "Adam, why did you tell me this?"

"Because I can't tell Dad," I said, settling back into the headrest and closing my eyes. "Not yet. Please, Ms. Raymond."

"Is it because you don't want to show him your pain?" Ms. Raymond started the car. "He's your parent. He'll be the best support for you. The support you need."

"I'm going to tell him. In a few days. I promise." I kept my eyes closed. "You know, it's not the right time right now. With him remembering Mom."

"I still don't understand."

"I think that's what Mom was trying to say. That there's a time for everything. The time to tell Dad is later."

"I don't know if that was what your mom was trying to tell you, but . . ." She trailed off. "I'll respect your wishes if you let me know soon that you've told him. That's the condition."

"I'll text you when I do." Relieved, I opened my eyes to the blurred shapes on the way to Connor's house.

ZAYNEB

WEDNESDAY, MARCH 13

MARVEL: VICTORIES

Exhibit A: Victory at the pool.

Auntie Nandy was supposed to come home right away after school today, but she texted to say that a last-minute meeting had come up, and that our scheduled trip to see Katara, a reconstructed traditional Qatari village, would have to wait until another day.

That was fine, I guess.

I was feeling completely good for once.

This morning had been epic. Like Marvel-movie-level epic.

Auntie Nandy and I had walked down to the fitness center, her in her "regular" swimsuit, by Marc's standards, with a thin cover-up on top, me in my burkini with the weird, sleeping clamshell on the front. The attached swim scarf, a zippered cap enclosing my hair, was up and on, goggles ready for pool use snapped on top of it.

I held my back straight, my head up, my mouth closed, trying to match Auntie Nandy's steady steps to the facility, located in the middle of the condominium complex's paved courtyard.

She opened the glass door for me, and I took a step in—with my right foot, as per Muslim custom. Maybe to make it an auspicious occasion? This showing up as my unapologetic Muslim self?

"Bismillah," I whispered.

I led the way to the check-in counter.

Marc, seated, scrolling on a tablet in front of him, looked up as I wrote my name into the facility-use binder. *Pool* I wrote in the appropriate column.

I smiled—serenely—at him.

He pushed his chair back and stood, glancing at me before searching for Auntie Nandy's face behind me. "I thought we spoke about proper swimwear yesterday."

Auntie Nandy took a step to the side and then forward, until she was at the counter herself, a big smile on her face. "Hi, Marc."

"Hi, Natasha."

"Is something the matter?"

"As I told you yesterday, your niece needs to have proper swimwear to use the pool here."

"Yes, of course!" She continued smiling. "And voila, today she is not wearing cotton leggings or a T-shirt. Instead, it's spandex, same as my swimsuit, same as yours when you swim, Marc."

"We have rules, Natasha." He put his hands on his hips. "This is a condominium complex catering to expats who like certain standards."

"Oh, no, no." Auntie Nandy said. "Don't use that on me. *I'm* an expat from two backgrounds and *both* of those backgrounds, the American and the Caribbean one, are okay with Zayneb's swimsuit. Tell me then—exactly which expats are you catering to?"

Marc stared at her.

"This *is* proper swimwear, Marc. It doesn't breach protocol in any way." Auntie Nandy picked up the pen and signed her own name into the binder. "Come on, Zayneb. Let's go swimming."

"I'll get complaints," Marc said, stepping out from behind the front desk. "We have some members who are more vocal than others."

"You mean you have some members who are more prejudiced than others." Auntie Nandy stopped walking and turned to Marc. "You can tell those members I'm very vocal too. And I'm pretty sure they wouldn't want me to take this matter out of our condo complex, would they?"

Her smile unfaltering, she waited a moment for him to answer. He went back to his chair behind the desk, shaking his head.

When we were down the hall, I turned to Auntie Nandy and high-fived her. "That, Auntie Nandy, was a work of art. You were flawless."

"Never, ever quake in the face of hate, Zayneb."

"And I can't believe you were *smiling* the whole time!" I felt like skipping to the pool in my sad clamshell burkini.

"Well, if you're speaking up for someone, why be sad about it? Or upset? Be proud of doing the right thing. Something I teach each and every student I've ever had. Celebrate!" She held the door to the pool for me.

It was empty, the water as still as a sheet of turquoise glass.

We walked to the welcoming sight.

"I love you, Auntie Nandy!" I hugged her and then pushed her in. But, as she fell laughing, she was quick enough to grab me, pull me in with her.

We swam the entire time with no one around—to bother us or question us or alert us to rules about our female bodies—and, when Auntie Nandy left to get ready for work, I floated by myself in the water, thinking.

Auntie Nandy had just been in control of the whole situation when she challenged Marc. She made it look so easy.

But then I thought about the hard parts of speaking up. About why it's so difficult to do the right thing in front of those with the power to affect your life. Say, to affect your future, your grades at school, your experience learning.

Your experience living.

I didn't want to think about it, but an image of Mr. Fencer just sitting on an empty desk, in an empty classroom, swinging his legs, grinning while he waited for me to come back to school—*while he waited to pounce on me*—appeared in my mind.

I floated and floated until the image floated away too.

I refused to be the sad clamshell on my burkini.

Today was a day for victories.

Since Auntie Nandy was going to be late again, I decided to organize myself.

After swimming, while she was at school, I'd gone to Souq Waqif, the outdoor bazaar, on my own to shop for gifts for everyone back home.

Now all of my purchases were at the entrance of my room, in a huddle of bags that the concierge had helped me carry up.

I shoved the clean laundry I'd done after returning from the pool on top of my pillows and made my bed. Then I dumped the gifts I'd bought on the white duvet.

As I was sorting them, my phone buzzed.

Emma Domingo.

Emma P. wants you to come with us to the dunes on Sunday. For her party.

Another message from her popped up as I thought about this. It's fun and fast. Dune bashing.

Mom was arriving on Sunday. It would be kind of weird if I wasn't home. But maybe it was only a part of the day?

Sounds fun. What time is it? Morning?

All day. Emma P.'s dad does this whole thing where he gets a company to set up tents in the desert with a bbq. Everyone's coming.

Maybe I can come for part of it? Because I can't go for the day. My mom's coming to Doha on Sunday.

Too bad! It's far from Doha so it'll be hard to get back.

I imagined the Emmas and the guys having fun on the dunes, doing whatever it is that people do when they're dune bashing.

I saw Adam standing a bit apart.

Then I imagined Emma P. breaking away from the rest of them to join him. They smiled at each other and then walked off into the dunes, holding hands, a sunset ahead of them.

Agh, I guess I'll have to miss it. Thanks so much for asking!

Ok, then you HAVE to come with us tomorrow to the souk.

Oops, I just went today.

Oh, come again. Please! Emma P. and Z. and Madison are getting henna done. Meet us there at one?

I thought about it. I *did* like Emma D. a lot. Even if she wasn't like my squad back home. *Ok.*

I put my phone back on the night table and saw the burkini from this morning in the pile of clean laundry. One closed eye of the clamshell peeked out from underneath pink underwear.

I pulled the swimsuit out and took it with me to the kitchen, where I'd sighted a promising-looking junk drawer yesterday.

I needed the big black Sharpie I'd seen.

I grabbed it and snapped the lid off and went back to my bedroom.

When I finished, the sleeping, sad clamshell had turned into a wide awake, widely happy, slightly high-looking clamshell.

There, this will be a sign of good things to come.

• • •

This Is What You Missed, Bulletin IV by Kavi Srinivasan, filed as FYI for Zayneb Malik:

I have nothing to tell you.

That's new. Any news about Ayaan?

The action is happening offscreen.

So there IS something happening?

Offscreen.

Off MY screen?

She sent me a speak-no-evil-monkey emoji.

Okay why send me ANYTHING at all then? Some bulletin. Some friend you are.

Exactly. Because I'm a FRIEND. I want you to enjoy yourself.

But you're excluding me. I thought we were a team. Tight.

Exactly again. You already took one for the team. So now it's our turn.

OUR turn? Who is OUR? There's the two of us. That's our team. Ayaan is our sage. She's beyond teamness.

We have new members. Noemi.

Oh.

So Kavi *was* including her in this.

I pulled up Instagram and checked Kavi's account. She had three stories I'd missed, but only one of them included Noemi. They were gawking at an open locker. The video panned the interior. It was covered, literally every inch, with stickers of a smiling white man with an Afro, sitting with a raised paintbrush in front of a painting of trees. Then we saw a quick shot of the inside of the opened locker *door*, which was covered with pictures of an angry-looking Picasso. *Noemi: Picasso on the outside, Bob Ross on the inside* was the text Kavi had added to this story.

I didn't even know what that meant. It was something artsy. That they, Noemi and Kavi, *got.*

One out of three of your Instagram stories are with Noemi?

Zay? Why are you looking at my stories in the middle of our chat?

Noemi and you?

And Ms. Margolis.

The librarian? But she's a teacher?

Noemi relies on her for art research. They're friends. She came as a package with Noemi. Listen, you already got more out of me than I wanted. Stop.

I don't like it. Not knowing what's happening. Standing by. Actually, shoved aside.

So let it be my turn now. I sat in class quietly listening to you taking on Fencer for eons, not saying anything.

It wasn't your fight.

How could you even say that? You who took on Rosie in gym class? Then the rest of the year? I'm crying.

Oh, yeah. Rosie in gym class. That's how Kavi and I met.

In second term, first day of eighth-grade gym, I'd had a cast on my left leg due to a fractured tibia, so I made my home on the bench. A thin girl with flawless dark brown skin, long, silky black hair tied in a single ponytail that hung on one side, over her left shoulder, and huge eyes, came over and asked me if I'd be okay watching her EpiPen pack—that she, with a severe peanut allergy, was supposed to wear in a pouch on her at all times but couldn't do gym properly with.

I'd been faithful to her EpiPens for the week I was benched, keeping the pack in my lap, my eyes following Kavi as she moved. I even hobbled over with it once, on my crutches, when she got knocked down during a game of basketball.

That's when I heard someone mutter, "Kebobi can't play ball."
I whipped around.

A tall girl, even taller than me, was laughing into the shoulder of a friend, her body half-turned, eyes away, the dropped comment barely traceable to her.

But I knew the way these girls worked. I'd made it my life mission to find and destroy stuff like this, from my angry-baby self onward, so I homed in on the girl like I had a whack-a-mole mallet in hand.

Because the gym teacher was close by, racist girl had already turned all the way around in her attempt to hide her bullshit.

She didn't see me limping over, stepping forward with my good leg, dragging my cast behind, crutches where I'd left them on the floor beside Kavi.

"Excuse me? Her name is Kavi."

She turned to me, sizing me up. "That's what I said."

"That's *not* what you said. It's my leg that's broken, not my ears." I moved closer, doing an awkward half step, almost losing my balance. I wanted to close the gap to look straight into her blank, blue eyes. "You called her 'kebobi.' Claim your racism."

"Oh God, what's your problem? Go back to where you came from, bench bitch." She turned away again. Her friend, short but strong-looking, snorted a laugh and crossed her arms, attempting to stare me down.

"Bitch whose ancestors stole this land, telling *me* to go back?" I looked at her friend. "You better collect her, staple up her mouth hole before I do it."

"What's going on here, girls?" Though she said "girls," the gym teacher addressed me.

I lost it inside. But knew to keep it cool on the outside, not sure what kind of teacher I was talking to. "*What's going on* is this girl here is revealing the racist she is. She called my friend Kavi over there 'kebobi.' Then told *me* to go back to where I came from."

"Ms. Larsons, I just said 'Go back to the bench.'" She blinked her eyes innocently.

"Did you call Kavi a slur, Rosie?" Ms. Larsons shifted her gaze to the racist.

"No, though I did say she can't play basketball."

"Yeah, she said 'Girl can't play ball.' Literally," Rosie's friend lied.

"She said 'Kebobi can't play ball.' Literally." I crossed my arms and turned to look at Ms. Larsons. "Otherwise I wouldn't have gotten upset. Everyone says 'Girl can't play ball' all the time in gym class. That *literally* wouldn't have gotten me angry."

"Rosie, get to the bench. For the rest of class. That's not the right attitude for playing." Ms. Larsons turned around and walked back, blowing the whistle.

She'd believed me, but I stood there fuming. *Attitude?*

The best thing that came from the whole thing was I got a true friend for life when I called Kavi my friend while talking to Ms. Larsons—and Kavi, dusted off and upright, heard.

There was a second great thing too. I kept calling out Rosie's racism, as well as other, lower-level shenanigans, in gym class, relentlessly, not caring about my gym grade.

So relentlessly that, even though she was amazingly good, she didn't make the basketball team in February, getting a rep for "poor attitude." And although her problem was bigger than that, I so loved benching her. Literally.

Now Kavi was sticking up for *me*?

Okay, but it just feels sad. That I can't know stuff.

As soon as we have something concrete, I'll alert you, okay?

I didn't reply to Kavi.

I feel sad. Thinking of you sad over there.

I didn't reply again. Because Kavi was right.

So I'm going to tell you one thing only then: Noemi found out Fencer's alias.

Ayaan found that out ages ago. @Sittingducksrevolt.

No, that was his old one. Deleted, remember?

There's a new one?

Yep. Before he got Ayaan in trouble, he scrubbed his presence, the old one.

Noemi found something else?

@StoneWraith14

Weird.

Yeah. A wraith is a ghost.

A wispy one, according to Google.

It's kind of scary. Him disappearing online to come back . . . as a ghost.

How did Noemi find out his handle?

She's super smart. Something Margolis said about this book Fencer wanted to write about gargoyles made her search everything connected to it.

That's weird luck.

Anyways, forget Fencer. Are you having fun? What are you up to?

Ya, it's low-key fun. I'm just doing whatever. My aunt's working during the day, so I just do my own thing. Like today I got gifts for you.

I miss you. I love you. I like you. More than Noemi. Way more.

I smiled. *I like you way more than Noemi too.*

A SECOND MARVEL: HUGS

Exhibit A: Auntie Nandy.

By the time Auntie Nandy got home—at eleven o'clock (must have been some serious meeting!)—the luggage I'd come to Doha with had been completely emptied and repacked with Souq Waqif gifts, my laundry was put away neatly in drawers, my Instagram was updated, my room was superclean, I'd prayed Isha and read Qur'an, and I was on my second episode of *Sweet Tooth*. I'd seen cupcakes with real-looking candy plants sprouting from them, a dollhouse cake, and unbelievable floating desserts that burst like fireworks.

After letting herself in, Auntie Nandy came right over to the couch I was sitting on, without dropping her purse or schoolbag, and hugged me. It was a supertight hug even for Auntie Nandy, who had a reputation for tight hugs. I sunk into it, surrendering willingly. In gratitude.

She held on for a long time.

"You're amazing, okay?" She let go of my shoulders and her bags, and sat down beside me.

"You are amazing too, Auntie Nandy." I wasn't surprised by the sudden hug. It was very Auntie Nandy, but today it hit the spot of sadness that I thought I'd shoved deep inside. I blinked away the sudden teary burst of emotion the hug had unleashed and got up from the sofa. "Can I get you something to eat?"

"Yes. Chips. And pop." She smiled sheepishly, kicking off her shoes. "I just want to eat a big bag of chips and drink fizzy sugar."

"What? You don't even have such stuff in the apartment. I *know*. I spent almost an hour trying to find some the other day!" I advanced to the kitchen. "I'll get you some good food. I'm sure there's something in the fridge. Remember you were cleaning out your toxins?"

"No. Go to my room. In the closet there's a big, blue plastic bin. It's not too heavy, so you can pull it out here."

I was perplexed but followed her instructions, dragging the blue Rubbermaid bin behind me to set it at her feet in the living room.

She opened it up to reveal various junk foods and cans of pop.

"Choose your poison," she announced.

I chose a bag of Doritos. She picked out a can of Pepsi and another bag of Doritos, different flavor. "Pop?" she offered, holding out a can of Pepsi.

I accepted it, slightly worried about her. "Did something happen, Auntie Nandy? Everything okay?"

"Yeah." She tore open the bag of chips. "Just taking it easy tomorrow. I decided to take a day off of work, early start to spring break."

"Oh, yay! Does that mean we can go to Katara?"

"No, Zoodles, I'll be home but busy. We'll have to do Katara another day." Auntie Nandy crunched chips and looked at me for a while, like she was considering me. "I'm sorry it hasn't been a fun trip for you so far, Zayneb."

"No, it's been good." I shrugged. I did like chilling here.

"But you've been mostly stuck in this apartment."

"No I haven't. I went to the mall, went to a shelter, went to a zoo, went swimming, went to Souq Waqif two times. Actually, it will be three times, because I'm meeting the Emmas there tomorrow." I took a swig of my Pepsi. "That's a lot of stuff!"

Auntie Nandy sat up. "When are you going to the souk tomorrow?"

"One o'clock."

"Perfect. I have a meeting at that time. If you get back home from the souk by four, I can see if we can go somewhere fun together in the evening. Maybe go eat dinner on the Pearl."

"Oh, that would be amazing!" The Pearl was this man-made island with a gorgeous waterfront all the way around it. Mom was always showing me pictures that Auntie Nandy would post, eating at different fancy restaurants or shopping at high-end boutiques there.

"I'll take you to my favorite French restaurant." She crunched more chips and laughed. "But today, let's eat good ol'-fashioned junk. Just don't tell your mom, okay?"

I nodded and put my head on her shoulder and turned up the volume on *Sweet Tooth*, intent on recharging myself with more of Auntie Nandy's warmth.

ODDITY: JEALOUSY, THE TINY KIND

Exhibit A: Kavi doing stuff with Noemi.

I lay in bed, and it wouldn't leave me. That feeling of fear mixed with sadness.

I should have known they were getting tight when Noemi had shown up in our—Kavi's and my—Situation Room at the library.

When I get back home after this Doha trip, they'll have even more stories—not just on Instagram—between them, more stuff I wasn't a part of, and maybe more stuff I won't understand. An image of them laughing together, while I stood by, flashed in my head.

Like the inside art joke about Noemi's locker.

I didn't get it.

I didn't like it.

· · ·

I don't like that other thing either, but it isn't in any sense close to what I'm feeling about Kavi and Noemi—of course and completely.

In fact, if I think about it, it's the exact opposite of Kavi and Noemi.

Noemi is the one infringing on me and Kavi.

But in the second case, *I'm* the interloper.

I'm the one who thought of the possibility of us two when there was already a pair there.

Adam and Emma Phillips.

Wow.

I need to retreat all the way to the old me. The one who doesn't get so hot and bothered by stupid stuff like this.

I'm someone who gets consumed by stuff. It engulfs me, wraps me up in its embrace, and doesn't let me be until I've deal with it.

I sat up in bed.

I don't *like* getting consumed by things like jealousy and . . . lust.

Yet I *want* to get consumed. Because I like winning. I like things getting dealt with.

Like the high I got when Auntie Nandy took on Marc and won.

Maybe I need something to take on all the time. That I can actually *win*.

That's actually good to win. Because it isn't just for me.

"Winning" Adam, or even Kavi, isn't going to make the world a better place. And it involves their feelings.

Yeah, let people be however they want to be, Zayneb. Your high can come from something else.

I smiled. Today was supposed to be for victories, and this was another one.

I'm going to be me.

I'm not going to back down from Fencer. I'm going to out him myself.

Kavi and Noemi can do all they want over there. Find information, help Ayaan, become friends, fall more for each other, whatever.

I have everything I need right here in Doha: *@StoneWraith14*.

And the ability to investigate online deep into the night.

ADAM

THURSDAY, MARCH 14

ODDITY: JUSTIFIED ENDS

I WOKE UP TO THE UNUSUAL SCENARIO OF ACTUAL *VOICE* CALLS—
two of them—happening simultaneously. My phone, on the
dresser, was ringing as Connor stood by my bed, nudging me
awake, holding out his phone. He'd opted to sleep on the floor of
the guest room I stayed in, in case I needed anything.

His arm was now across his stomach, holding the top of the
sleeping bag that was encasing his legs. He must have hopped over
with it like some kind of weird, bouncy caterpillar.

*I can see the colors of the plaid lining the sleeping bag. Red, green,
and white.*

I blinked hard. My vision was clearing.

I wasn't seeing through a dense layer of jelly.

Instead, things were only slightly blurry.

I felt an immense wave of gratitude rising inside.

"It's Ms. Raymond on here. And . . ." Connor paused and,
after I'd taken his phone, hopped over to the dresser to glance at
my phone. He continued, "Your sister, Hanna, on your phone.
She's calling on FaceTime."

I muted Ms. Raymond's call and shook my head, the euphoria backing up. "No, don't pick up. I'll call her later. When I'm more ready."

"She's sending angry emojis."

I shook my head again and unmuted the phone. "Hi, Ms. Raymond?"

"How are you, Adam?"

"Better. My vision's much better. Feeling better too. I'm still in bed, though."

"I'm glad you're feeling better and resting. I've been thinking about you all night," she said. "I'm also readying everything for you to get your IV here. I was thinking, I can come pick you up around twelve thirty? The nurse is scheduled to come by at one thirty. I thought if you got here early, you'll have time to get comfortable, get ready."

"Sure. Though Connor told me he'd drop me, so I don't think you need to worry about picking me up. That okay, Connor?" I asked, as Connor settled back into his spot on the floor, bunching a pillow before placing his head on it.

I can see each polka dot on the pillow. Brown and pink.

"Yep." He nodded, then lifted and bent his arms into upside-down Vs to cradle his head. He looked at the ceiling. "We're hanging out at the souk for lunch, so it's on my way."

"Yeah, he'll drop me. He's going to Souq Waqif."

"That's the other thing. I didn't know how you'd feel if Zayneb, my niece, was home while you got your treatment, but I found out she'll be out, at the souk as well. So no worries on that front."

That *had* entered my brain briefly. But I hadn't let it bother me too much, because, really, if she saw me with an IV drip, she would be just another stranger who knew I had MS.

She must be hanging around with the DIS crew a lot. To be going to the souk with them today.

Must be going dune bashing with them this weekend, too.

I didn't need perfect vision to imagine her eyes widening at the beauty of the desert. At the way the dunes rippled, visual echoes of one another as far as the eye could see, varying shades of orangey brown.

She'd be moved. And have fun. With everyone.

The euphoria deflated further.

"Okay, I'll be at your place at one then." I paused. "Thanks again, Ms. Raymond."

I wanted to say more to her but not now.

Connor's a caring guy, but he wouldn't get that I wanted to say, *Thanks for filling in for Mom like only her best friend would.*

I succumbed to FaceTiming Hanna, first checking my actual face in the phone's camera. Checking if she'd be able to tell something was going on with me.

I looked sort of normal, only slightly puffier.

"WHERE ARE YOU, ADAM?" She'd been sitting at the kitchen table when she answered, but with a jolt, she stood up with her hands on her hips, wearing a frown under front bangs that were more askew than usual. I could see the edges of Still-water on the chair beside her. "THIS IS NOT FAIR! YOU'RE ALWAYS WITH YOUR FRIENDS AND NOT YOUR FAMILY. YOU'RE. BEING. MEAN!"

Connor chuckled from the floor.

"Whoa, I'm coming home. Around three o'clock, maybe four," I reassured her.

She sat back down. "Then can we go to the new exhibit?"

"What exhibit?"

"The one I told you about! The Rare Jewels of an Empire exhibit? At the museum?"

I remembered. She'd talked about it the day I arrived. When I gave her the azurite.

She'd said she wanted to check the display and then go shopping at the museum shop to add the special rocks connected to the exhibit to her rock collection.

"Oh, yeah. Okay. But not today." I scanned my brain. I had to come up with something. "Let's go Sunday."

My treatments will be done by then, and I will have had one extra day to rest. *Maybe I'll feel better enough to walk around the Museum of Islamic Art?*

"Why can't we go *today*? I thought you were coming to Doha to visit *me*. Do things with *me*. And to do things with Dad, too, cause he wants to come to the exhibit too! At least *he* agreed to it!" She stood back up, her hands finding their way to her hips again.

But then she sat down abruptly, grabbing Stillwater into her lap. I could see her face beginning to crumble.

Hanna rarely cried, so I was surprised. "Hanna? I can't go today, but it's not because of my friends. Hey, don't cry."

She buried her face into the top of Stillwater's black-and-murky-white head. He stared at me un-panda-like, with weighty disapproval, loyalty to Hanna his first duty.

Connor stood up and dropped his sleeping bag, revealing Pikachu boxers, with Poké Balls down the front. I frowned at the sight.

"Gift from Nancy, my ex-TA," he whispered. "My hot girlfriend, Nancy?"

I frowned again and looked back at Stillwater. Hanna's face had completely disappeared from view.

Connor came and knelt down by the bed, behind my phone.

"So I don't scare her," he said quietly to me. "With my Pokémon boxers. Play along, buddy."

He then raised his voice, off camera. "Hey, Adam, what are you doing, man? Why you on your phone? I thought you were going to hang with us? We're going to Souq Waqif this afternoon."

I tilted my head. I didn't know where this was going. "Nah, I can't."

"Why? You've been in Doha almost a week, and we never see you, man. You've been working on that room downstairs in your house all the time."

The top of Hanna's head emerged a tiny bit from Stillwater's fur.

Whatever it was that Connor was doing—it was working. "Listen, I gotta finish that room. It's like this thing my mom made with me a long time ago, a house and garden in a jar. This is like that but different, too, because it's bigger. It's a world in a room."

Hanna's head lifted a bit more, and, from the floor by the bed, Connor made a confused face. He had no idea what I was talking about.

But Hanna did.

"That's why I'm so busy, man. I gotta find the right bits, make the right pieces, gotta go to Al Rawnaq, the different store locations to find special parts." *Which I have done this trip, so it isn't completely a lie.*

Connor nodded. "Oh, you mean that store with the stuff to make things? Like paint and stuff? Kind of like a hardware store?"

"Yeah, I'm trying to finish it up over spring break. The room . . . it's going to be amazing."

"But what about us? Your friends, man? When're we gonna see you?"

"Well, not this weekend, for sure."

"What? We're going dune bashing this weekend. You *can't* miss that!"

"Oh, wait. Let me check something." I looked back at the screen. I could see the entirety of Hanna's eyes now, atop Stillwater's head. "Hey, Hanna, are we going to the museum on Sunday? You, me, and Dad?"

She nodded. I smiled. "Nope, sorry, Connor. I've got plans on Sunday. The Special Empire Rocks exhibit to see."

At this affront, Hanna's entire face emerged until her chin rested on Stillwater, squishing his brow fur into his eyes so much, he looked like an angry panda. "It's *not* called Special Empire Rocks. It's the *Rare Jewels* of an Empire exhibit!"

"Yeah, Adam, the *Rare Jewels* of an Empire exhibit!" Connor stood up, swallowing a laugh.

He disappeared into the bathroom.

He was pretty cool.

I spent the rest of the morning sitting by Connor as he gamed, answering his questions about my diagnosis in between the intense rounds of battle onscreen.

After the phone call with Hanna, I'd made it to his room with pretty steady steps.

With this and Hanna's sadness being diffused, the euphoria had returned.

I knew the doctor had said it would take a few days for the symptoms of my attack to potentially clear, and that one or two would continue reoccurring, even after the rounds of steroids, but I felt better.

Mostly because there was a way to deal with it.

And maybe because more people, people who weren't strangers, knew about it.

The nurse asked if I was comfortable before she inserted the needle for the IV drip.

I answered yes truthfully.

Ms. Raymond has been in the same apartment for as long as she's been in Doha, and I'd been over to visit it with Mom many times.

Sitting in the black leather club chair, the one that was always diagonally placed—in between the sofa and the sliding door to the balcony—was comfortable.

On our visits, while Mom and Ms. Raymond chatted at the dining table adjacent to the living room, I'd sit in this chair and draw in my sketchbook or play on my PSP or read comics.

Always from this exact chair.

Now I relaxed into the soft leather as the needle went in.

I was grateful that Ms. Raymond had left me alone to it. I think she was in the kitchen.

She'd said that she would be going to the gym. "I'll give you your space. But I'll be back before you leave. And I promise I won't fuss over you."

I couldn't believe I'd been upset to see her when I first landed in Doha.

I mean, I knew *why* I was.

She was completely connected to Mom, completely connected to her disease, to her last days of life.

Seeing her had been like seeing Mom's casket again.

"Okay, so I'm going down." Ms. Raymond came over to the living room, carrying plates. "I cut some fruit for you, Adam, for after, and for you, too, Annabelle."

The nurse nodded her thanks as Ms. Raymond set the two plates of mangoes and strawberries on the coffee table.

After Ms. Raymond left, Annabelle settled into the corner of the sofa and opened a paperback book. "You okay?"

"Yes, thanks." I nodded to reassure her.

"You want to watch TV?"

"No. But thanks." I was actually sketching. Without a sketchbook.

In my mind, I was working out the rest of the transformation of the room I was fixing up at home. The world within a room.

The room holding the marvels and oddities of life.

When I got to the part of conjuring slices of wood to evoke blades of grass, the front door opened.

Zayneb walked in.

She didn't see me at first.

She appeared exactly as she had the first time I'd seen her, at Heathrow Airport, completely absorbed by her phone. When she let go of the door and it swung shut behind her, she even used both her thumbs to tap nonstop into her device, like before.

Like when I got my first impression of her: busy, beautiful, brilliantly blue.

After briefly waiting, staring at her phone, she slid a hand under the front of her hijab, under her chin, and began sliding it off.

As it moved up, and a small slit lay across her eyes, she saw me.

She yanked her scarf back down, a look of shock on the face that remerged from in between the folds of fabric. "Oh my God!"

A dark curl of hair dropped in front of her face. I looked away.

"Hello," Annabelle said from the couch. "You are related to Ms. Raymond?"

"I'm her niece."

When I lifted my gaze back, she was looking directly at Annabelle.

"Hello," Annabelle said again. "I'm Annabelle."

"Hi?" She glanced at me and then looked away again, blowing up at her curl and then flushing when she tried to stuff it back up and it wouldn't cooperate.

I shifted my gaze again.

She's got curly hair?

How long is it?

Ugh. I switched off my stupid brain and whispered to Annabelle, "The remote?"

She passed it to me, still staring at Zayneb.

When I turned the TV on, Cardi B's "I Like It" blasted out, making us jump.

I flicked it off. Silence showed up again.

"Your aunt told you that your cousin Adam was coming here, yeah?" Annabelle pressed gently. "To get his treatments?"

"No, actually. No." She stopped fighting the curl and looked down the hall to her right. "I'm just going to drop my stuff in my room and come back, okay?"

She didn't come back out of her room.

And I was okay with it.

Her showing up like this, then completely getting blindsided by me sitting here IVed, with Annabelle casually on the sofa, two strangers in her aunt's living room, must have been awkward. Maybe even scary.

I couldn't wait for the treatment to be over. To get out of here, go back home and rest, see Hanna.

See Dad.

I groaned and let my head sink into the headrest of the chair. *Dad*.

Zayneb walked back, her scarf securely fastened now, and I straightened up again.

Her head scarf was blue with white polka dots.

Her standard smile was back on her face.

"So, hi again." She beamed at Annabelle.

I closed my eyes. God, she was . . . cute.

"Um, Adam?" It was Zayneb's voice, soft. "Are you okay?"

I opened my eyes to find her seated on the two-seater couch across from me, her phone on the arm beside her. "Yeah. I mean, other than the steroids dripping into my blood to stop my body from attacking itself, yeah, I'm fine."

"What happened?" She leaned forward. "What do you mean your body's attacking itself?"

Annabelle looked from me to Zayneb, confusion on her face.

"I have multiple sclerosis."

Zayneb pulled back, her eyes large. "MS? Isn't that what your . . ." She wouldn't go on.

"My mom had it too, yes." I tried to smile and then added gently, "Remember my mom is an okay topic?"

And here we were talking about the real *taboo topic: my diagnosis.*

"I remember." She lifted her legs up and tucked them under her and then pulled at the hem of the shirt she was wearing. "Isn't this supposed to be happening at a hospital?"

Her head now swiveling between Zayneb and me, Annabelle looked even more confused. She thought we were cousins, having been told that Ms. Raymond was my aunt, so she was probably wondering why we were so out of touch.

Well, even cousins can keep secrets from each other.

"IV treatments for MS attacks can take place at home if the patient prefers," Annabelle explained carefully, in a voice clearly communicating she was unsure of what was going on with us.

"Or at aunts' houses," I added, raising my eyebrows at Zayneb, the moment Annabelle's gaze left my face.

Zayneb nodded, bestowing me with a thumbs-up as soon as Annabelle looked away from *her*. "Even at cousins' houses."

Annabelle settled back and nodded. Maybe more satisfied with the state of things now, she picked up a mango slice with one hand and her book with the other.

"I thought you were going to the souk? With the DIS bunch?" I asked Zayneb, genuinely curious. What made her come back home?

She picked at her hem before answering. "I kinda had a late night."

I waited.

"So when I got to the souk, I was just exhausted. And when the others were getting their henna done, I came back home." She looked at me, at the IV pump. "I actually didn't like the way one of them was treating the henna artist, kind of bossing her around. So I guess I got angry and left?"

I didn't say anything, because a smile was growing on Zayneb's face, and I wanted to let it grow without stop.

"Like, I had exactly two hours of sleep last night, because I was working on a project, so I felt kind of unpredictable. I was afraid I'd scream a lecture about Cultural Appropriation While Hating on People from the Culture You're Pretending to Be." She laughed. "I'm messy like that."

I smiled. And picked up my phone.

She was here, across from me, almost the exact distance as we were in the airport waiting area when I first saw her.

At that moment, a week ago, I had a secret I couldn't share.

And now here it was, out in full view of the girl in the brilliant blue hijab.

I was sitting in her aunt's living room, and Zayneb knew my diagnosis, and she was sharing her day and laughing like everything was okay.

Thanks. For being chill. About me being here and just in general.

She picked up her phone from the arm of the sofa. *Of course. But I don't get it? Why are we pretending to be cousins?*

Hey do you want to come with me and Hanna and my Dad to the Museum of Islamic Art on Sunday? If I'm up to it?

Is that that beautiful building sticking out into the water? That structure made of cubes?

Yup. Designed by the one and only I. M. Pei.

But isn't Sunday the dune-bashing thing? That you're going to? With Emma P.?

I looked at her, searched for a sly smile, a laugh, something. But she didn't lift her gaze from her phone, just closed her eyes and shook her head, her smile frozen.

Wait, did Emma P. tell her something too? Like she'd told Connor and Madison?

No. Hanna wants to go to an exhibit at MIA.

Pausing, I thought for a minute.

If Emma P. *had* said something about me and her, I had to set it right with Zayneb.

I couldn't let her think—

Emma P. does her own stuff. Nothing to do with me. Nothing.

Was that clear enough?

I'm not into that. I mean I am, but not with Emma P. Not with anyone.

Wait, now she's going to think—

I mean I COULD be into someone. Someone I liked.

Oh yeah, Adam, way to go. Full steam ahead, instead of pushing pause.

I didn't dare glance up to see what effect my textual diarrhea was having on her. *It must be the medication, my extreme impulsiveness. A side effect. Or maybe the remains of the euphoria from this morning.*

Okay, I'll come with you guys to the museum.

Then we both looked up from our phones at that same moment, and, you know what?

Marvelously what?

Fifth impressions are the absolute best.

Her eyes were as wide as her smile.

I don't remember what Ms. Raymond said to me when she got back to the apartment. Or the particulars of how I got home after.

The only thing I remember is the trail of questions Zayneb and I texted each other back and forth—her mostly about how I was feeling, about my diagnosis, about MS; me about how she liked her Doha visit so far.

The clearest feeling I remember is this: the way that it felt like the space between us folded and folded, and kept folding until the distance shrank, until we made sense to each other.

Exhibit A: A super philosophical song.

I woke up to Auntie Nandy singing loudly from the kitchen, a song about joy and fun and seasons in the sun. But even though it had such happy words in it, it was an unbelievably mournful-sounding thing.

Oh yeah, it was the weekend.

Adam is coming over again.

It was to get his treatment, yeah, but he was going to be here, in my vicinity, again.

And then on Sunday, we're going to the museum.

Not dune-bashing with Emma P.

I turned onto my back and smiled at the ceiling.

A curl of hair fell into my eyes.

I flipped on my side again, snuggled into the pillow, more hair covering my face, and, as Auntie Nandy sang on about skinned hearts and knees, saying good-bye, and more seasons in the sun, I thought about him.

. . .

I couldn't imagine carrying what he'd carried with him all the way here from London, from last fall.

I marveled at his sense of calm and quietness. That he held something so hard inside for so long without bursting.

A small part of my heart hurt so much just thinking of what that must have felt like.

Did he ever feel the need for someone to share some of it, some of the heaviness of knowing he had the same disease that his mom had? Did he ever wish someone would reach out and hold the weight with him?

That small, hurting part of my heart spoke up inside, wanting to offer itself to share the heaviness with him.

"Ridiculous," I whispered, quelling it. *You're going back home; he's going back to school. You're both leaving Doha.*

And then my arms began a disturbance.

They wanted to be that part of me that reached out to him. To envelop him. To say he'll be okay.

I turned on my back again and wrapped those arms around myself, tucking my hands tight against me to hold the ache inside, closing my eyes as Auntie Nandy kept singing of good-byes.

I have eight more days in Doha, so the only thing I can do is help Adam in the ways I'm able to. The halal ways.

I untucked my hands to clear the hair off my face and sat up.

As I got out of bed, I blew that one lone curl off my forehead. Begone, sexy-hair fantasies.

"Sylvia loved the song I was just singing. 'Seasons in the Sun,'" Auntie Nandy said, her big breakfast spread out in front of her. She raised a fork. "Adam's mom."

"Oh. But it's so incredibly sad sounding." I picked up a slice of cucumber and rotated it. "Like my heart hurt listening to you."

"*She* didn't think it was sad. She used to sing it whenever someone got something Sylvia wanted, like a position at school or an opportunity she was trying for."

I stared at Auntie Nandy. *Whut?* "But that's still something sad. To sing it when she didn't get something?"

"No, no. Wait. I'm not explaining it properly." Auntie Nandy put her knife and fork down. "Okay, let me tell you of the time when Sylvia wanted to display her artwork at an exhibition at Katara, the village I was going to take you to."

"We're still going, right?" I put the cucumber slice in my mouth. "To Katara?"

"Yes, for sure. But anyway, Sylvia didn't get chosen to exhibit her work. Instead, the junior high art teacher at DIS, Vernon, was accepted. And that was an example of when she would get into her 'Seasons in the Sun' mentality. Because, the way she explained it, it wasn't *her* season at that moment; it was Vernon's turn to shine. She believed in such a world, where everyone got a turn, a season in the sun." Auntie Nandy picked up her cutlery again. "She was a beautiful soul like that."

"Oh, wow." That *was* deep. To think you were one of many who deserved great things. To be so unbelievably gracious, graceful. No wonder Adam's face lit up whenever he spoke of his mom. "You can tell Adam loved her so much. He gets happy when she's mentioned."

"Yeah. He's got a lot of his mom in him. That sense of balance, a way of thinking bigger." Auntie Nandy resumed eating. "I like that you guys are friends."

"Well, I'm leaving soon." I swallowed the cucumber, but it was hard to make it go down my throat. "So, yeah."

Auntie Nandy paused eating again and glanced at me.

That glance held a lot of unspoken questions, so I quickly shoved it aside by changing topics. "Can we start planning stuff? Mom's getting here Sunday night!"

"Sure, make a list, and we'll maximize our days now that I'm off too."

I got up from the chair, tapping on my phone as if I were starting a list, but what I was really doing, as I walked to my room, was looking up the lyrics to "Seasons in the Sun."

It *was* incredibly sad.

After setting up Adam's IV, Annabelle sat at the same spot as yesterday and picked up her book, *More Unsolved Mysteries*.

Auntie Nandy sat on the other end of the sofa, closer to Adam, turning on the TV, looking for something for us to watch.

Adam and I sat across from each other again.

And, as the opening credits of *Black Panther* began, and we stole glances at each other in turns, I realized something: *I don't want this season in Doha to end.*

My arms and heart and the rest of me wanted to be curled and squished beside him in that chair he was sitting in.

Get on FaceTime, I messaged Kavi. *A situation is happening.*

I looked at the clock. Oops, she was in class.

Well, there were only seven minutes left before senior lunch hour. *I may be in love. With a guy.*

A message popped up right away. I'm texting from Fencer's class. If he catches me I might get suspended too. WHO?

I refused to add anything more. No way Fencer was going to get me, Ayaan, *and* my Kavi.

I didn't have to wait long.

"TELL ME EVERYTHING." Kavi was walking down the crowded halls, earbuds in. "I didn't even wait for Noemi, okay? I fled. TELL ME."

I could tell she'd just left Fencer's class.

"I'm going to wait till you get to the Situation Room." I watched her walking toward the sunken foyer area, across from which were the windows of the library. She opened the blue door that said LIBRARIES BRING LIFE TO LIFE! and walked through the turnstiles, waving at someone.

"Wait, say hello to Ms. Margolis." She turned her phone and brought it closer to the library counter.

Ms. Margolis, a pencil in her ear, peered at me. "Zayneb?"

Oh yeah, I wasn't wearing hijab. "Yeah, it's me. Sorry, don't have my scarf on."

"How are you?" She looked at me carefully.

"I'm good. It's nice to see you." I waved.

"It's wonderful to see you as well." She waved back. "Now go talk to Kavi. She misses you intensely."

Kavi turned the phone back to herself and, after she'd walked far enough away from Ms. Margolis, whispered, "I'm so sorry. I forgot you didn't have your hijab on."

I didn't say anything and just covered the camera on my phone with a hand. "Just tell me when you get to the Situation Room. Then I will reveal everything, including myself."

"Okay, dish!" The brick wall was behind her. She was safely in our room in the library.

I took my hand away from the camera lens. "It's . . . Adam."

"Who's Adam?"

I scrolled through my phone and found the first picture with the Emmas and him, by the water at his house, the one she'd seen before, and sent it to her again.

"Oh wow, I remember. This guy? So cute. Okay, be in love." She flashed a thumbs-up. "I definitely understand!"

"No, this is . . . different."

Kavi leaned back, raising her eyebrows. "What do you mean?"

"I mean, I think he likes me back."

"Of course he would! You're awesome!"

"No, I mean, as in he seriously likes me back." I thought about how he'd left the apartment today.

He'd said, "For the first time in a long time, I'm feeling absolutely good."

Annabelle had nodded, rolling the IV machine to the door. "The treatment will do that for you. Some people feel it right away. You just need to continue your appointments with your neurologist in London."

When Annabelle turned around to put her shoes on, and Auntie Nandy went to her bedroom to get car keys to drive him back home, he said, "I'm feeling good for other reasons too."

Without exchanging glances, I knew what he was talking about.

I'd looked calm on the surface, but fireworks had exploded inside.

"Oh wow, you're really feeling it. Your face is like rippling. I've never seen it like this," Kavi said, leaning forward to examine me so close, her face took up the entire screen. Then, as she sat down, she zoomed out again. "But wait. You said you don't believe in dating. How does this work?"

"It doesn't, actually. Work, I mean." I lay back in bed and lifted the phone high above me so Kavi could see the pitiful state I was in.

"This has been me for most of today. Lying here, tossing and turning."

"Inflamed by passion? Tormented by desire? Horny?"

"Ew, but yeah, kind of." I didn't admit to her how much that was true. "See, that's why Islam tells us horny ones to lower our gaze around people, not look at them like you're eating them with your eyes."

"Zayneb, did you eat him with your eyes?" Kavi giggled. "Because you look like you've got a stomachache from overeating."

"Astaghfirullah. That's been me all day, saying astaghfirullah." I groaned. "And the worst thing is that he's *Muslim*, too."

Kavi sat up in the chair, her big eyes activated with interest. "But that's amazing, isn't it? He'll *get* you. How Muslim you are, because, girl, you and Ayaan are super Muslim."

"No, it's terrible that he's Muslim. Because if he wasn't, it wouldn't have made sense in my head, and I would be over it. Because then maybe he would have asked me out, and I could have been like, *Nope, that's not me, I don't go out with dudes alone.* Bam, done with." I groaned again. "Kavi, help me."

"I don't get it. What about you and Yasin? When you guys were talking to each other?"

"That was nothing. And his parents knew my parents, so it would have been legit, if things had developed."

"Make it legit, then. If he likes you as much as you like him." Kavi shrugged. "There's always a solution, remember?"

I pulled myself up to lean on the headboard and put my glasses back on. *Is that even possible?*

It's weird.

But could it be possible?

"Kavi, I'm scared about how much I *crave* him." I blinked at her sadly. "Like, it's intense."

"Tell me why, then. Other than the physical reasons, because, yeah, I see that." She tilted her head, her face serious now. "But don't tell me that's the *only* reason?"

"No, no way. Like, yeah, there's this part of me that's excited about him liking me back. Excited that, hey, this guy I thought was cute on first sight likes me, too! That's there, yeah, and that's purely physical," I admitted. "But then . . . if I'd been around him and he had turned out to be a douchebag, even with those looks, I would have slammed the door shut super fast."

"So you like him because he's cute, likes you back, and is *not* a douchebag? Zay, not good enough reasons to twist yourself like this."

I didn't tell her that I wanted to be there for him. That he had something going on that was huge and that I didn't want him to go through it by himself, or, I mean, with the DIS crew, who didn't know about it—except for Connor.

But MS was his truth to tell.

I lay down again. "I like him because he's gentle and kind and considerate and has this sense of confidence without being in your face about it, and he's super thoughtful; his little sister adores him; so do his friends at the international school he went to. But then he's kind of alone. I can see that. It oozes out of him." I sat up, something dawning on me. "Like, when we were talking about Hogwarts houses the first day I hung out with his friends, all of them said he was in a house by himself, because he didn't even fit in half houses, or quarter houses. Like how I'm part Gryffindor and part Slytherin, and you're three-quarters Ravenclaw and one-quarter Hufflepuff? He's houseless."

Kavi frowned. "You like him because *you feel sorry for him*? Sorry, I don't want to dump on you, but I'm not feeling this. Falling for someone is *not* a social justice cause."

She didn't get it. And I couldn't explain it over FaceTime. I crossed my legs and pulled my hair back into a bun, securing it with a scrunchie, ready to switch topics, ready to shut down my Adam-ache. "Okay, listen, Kavi—let's change subjects. Give me a bulletin."

She relaxed her frown. "You wouldn't believe what Noemi did. She volunteered to present her analysis to the class. Remember, the one about the Turkish girl buried alive?"

"Yeah?"

"She did an analysis comparing the incident to Austrian culture—Christian, European culture—linking it to the girl kept in a dungeon by her father for decades." Kavi smiled huge. "Fencer *lost* it."

"PLEASE TELL ME MORE," I begged, conjuring an image of Fencer with his own racist methods thrown in his face like a fluffy creamy pie.

"Basically, he gave a BS rant about how that was an isolated case and she was generalizing about a sensational news story and how that was shoddy analysis, not senior-year-level work at all, blah blah blah. He was saying all this shit calmly, but his face was on fire. So Noemi just did this thing where she kept smiling while he kept getting redder and redder, and then, right before she went and sat down, after he'd done his whole you're-a-bad-student spiel, she said to the class, 'And, to sum up my presentation, that, boys and girls, is why you don't generalize.' Mic drop."

Okay, I'm moving toward officially liking Noemi. "I wish I'd been there. Just so Fencer could see me enjoying the entire thing, and then giving her a standing ovation at the end."

"Well, here's the awful thing. For some reason, you did enter the picture, right after Noemi's presentation. Before the next student went up, Fencer came over and told me that you had to turn in the analysis too. That he'd e-mailed you a copy of the assignment and article, and that it was due by the end of today. Or you'd lose ten percent of your grade." Kavi shrugged her shoulders. "I'm sorry, but maybe Noemi triggered him into remembering to shit on you again."

I drew my laptop to me and logged into my school account. There it was, an e-mail from the fiend, from four days ago.

GIRL BURIED ALIVE IN HONOR KILLING Analysis was the subject line.

"No problem," I said to Kavi. "I'll just follow Noemi's brilliance and compare it to American *culture*, heh-heh. Lord knows I can find enough dirt."

"That's what I did too. But I wasn't brave enough to present it like Noemi." Kavi's face suddenly lit up as she looked beyond her phone's camera. "Speak of the devil and she shows up."

Noemi? In *our* room again?

"Hey, I'm going to have to say see you later to finish this thing for Fencer. Bye, Kav." I waved, reaching to end the call.

"Bye, Zay. Wait!" Kavi shouted. "If he makes sense, he makes sense. Adam. Okay?"

I nodded, pretty sure she was saying that because she didn't want me to get upset about Noemi.

Auntie Nandy wouldn't let me cut out dinner at the French restaurant on the Pearl, even though I'd told her about the homework I had to do ("EXCUSE MY LANGUAGE, BUT THAT DICK OF A TEACHER OF YOURS IS NOT GOING TO RUIN MY FRIDAY!" was her response), so we went and ate (me, gratin dauphinois, her, boeuf bourguignon), and then she drove me to a café that she said I could work in while she met with a friend.

The friend turned out to be Adam's dad.

With an iced coffee by my laptop, and glasses on, I pretended to be completely absorbed in my homework, but I couldn't stop myself from glancing over once in a while. They were near the entrance of the café, almost at an angle so that I couldn't see either of their faces, but I could tell that Auntie Nandy was the one doing most of the talking.

She wouldn't be revealing all, would she? About Adam?

He was planning on talking to his dad this weekend. *I've gotta let at least three days pass after the date of Mom's death,* he'd texted.

Wait, *weird*. Auntie Nandy was laughing. Here in the café.

Her back was shaking the way it does when she guffaws.

I stood and made my way to the counter, as though I wanted to order something else. After studying the menu for a few seconds, I let my gaze fall on Auntie Nandy.

She *wasn't* laughing. She was sobbing.

Adam's dad was too.

In my urgency to get away, I almost ran back to my table in the corner.

As a result of not getting any work done at the café, due to a mind racing with wondering about what exactly Auntie Nandy was talking to Adam's dad about, I stayed up on returning to the apartment to finish my analysis of GIRL BURIED ALIVE IN HONOR KILLING.

Springdale was eight hours behind Doha, so because I sent my analysis in right before twelve a.m.—with the subject line *COMMUNITY COVERS UP RAPES BY FOOTBALL PLAYERS Analysis*—I made the end-of-school-day, end-of-term deadline.

• • •

At one a.m., as I was climbing into bed, the best thing happened.

Ayaan texted me. All right. I still love you.

I clipped my hair up into a bun and smiled at the message in my lap. *My heart is floating in the air right now.*

I'm sorry for not answering your texts. And your crying faces. And the million broken hearts you sent.

My heart is swelling and pulsing, covered with a zillion golden beams of pure light.

Z, can we cut the drama. Enough of that happening in real life.

But what am I, if not drama?

I don't want to leave Porter, graduate, with Fencer still here.

Ok, I'll stop shakespearing. Listening.

I also want to be reinstated on student council. I worked damn hard for that.

At your service. Tell me what to do.

Kavi and that other girl found out he has a new online name. @StoneWraith14. Kavi and Noemi.

Right. I need you to sleuth @StoneWraith14 from over there.

I tried to do a lot of sleuthing already. And failed.

Different countries have different firewalls. Including here at home. You'll have access to sites and information we can't get in the US.

I sat up completely in bed. *What do you mean?*

I mean there are certain things I can't see that you can. That you can find for us.

Are you talking about censorship?

Yup, I know this from traveling. It's not just China that does it.

So I can see things here in Doha that you can't over there in Springdale?

And I can see things here that you can't in Doha.

Whoa. But I couldn't find anything on @StoneWraith14.

That's because you weren't looking in the right places. Fencer is very tight online with British Islamophobes. I'm guessing he's got some internet tunneling service to pretend he's in the UK.

I'm getting excited. Like I've been asked to join a secret spy mission of international significance.

I'll send you the list of sites I want you to check for his presence. The ones I've tracked links to but can't access.

I'M ON IT.

For the first time in a long time, I went to sleep completely happy.

And that's why today I've recorded no oddity.

ADAM

SATURDAY, MARCH 16

MARVEL: *ENERGY*

ENERGY AFTER RESTING IN MY OWN BED. WITH DAD AND HANNA in the house.

Energized that my vision is better, that there is nothing disconnecting my legs from me right now.

Energized with the knowledge I'll be seeing Zayneb tomorrow, and we aren't complete strangers anymore.

With hopes that maybe we can be on our way to something more.

EXHIBIT A: WHAT I FOUND ON THE BREAKFAST TABLE.

I woke up to Auntie Nandy's rendition of "Wild World."

Finally, a seventies song I knew *all* the words to. The singer, Cat Stevens, had become Muslim—in the seventies too—so any time one of his songs came on the radio, Mom and Dad would point it out.

"'Oh, baby, baby, it's a wild world!'" I sang along with Auntie Nandy, who was fixing breakfast. I brought the first plates she'd assembled on the kitchen counter to the dining table.

A stuffed toy blue bird was sitting in the middle of the table.

"Do you recognize it?" Auntie Nandy came up behind me. "It was in the box I found your mom's burkini in. You left it here when you visited Doha last."

"Oh my God. It's my Angry Bird, the Blues!" I picked it up. "I was obsessed with collecting all of them when I was a kid, and this was my favorite. Do you want to know why?"

"Because it's the angriest?"

"No, because look." I undid a zipper at the bottom of its stomach and flipped it inside out. Three smaller plush birds emerged.

"The Blues has the power of *three* birds. It's like a surprise attack in the video game! When you strike it midlaunch, *boom*, three birds shoot out of the one, and *bang*, the enemy's setup gets mangled."

"So it's like a Trojan horse?"

"In a different way." I hugged the Blues to me as I walked back to the bedroom. "I'm taking this home with me. Thanks for keeping it."

I sealed the three birds into one again and set it down beside Squish on the night table. They looked like an odd couple together—one, pristine, with colorful plush elements, including feathers, and the other . . . well, Squish.

As we were getting ready to go to the Corniche, the waterfront promenade that edged the coast in Doha, where the city met the waters of the Arabian Gulf, Mom called.

She had news that gave me pause: Dad left to go to Pakistan today, having gotten more information about Daadi's death.

For the first time in a while my grandmother's face held still in my head for a long moment. But when I blinked again, into *Mom's* face on Skype, Daadi was gone from my mind's eye.

"Was it something important, the news about Daadi?" I asked after Mom told me a bunch of hows, including *how* Dad had learned there was new information and *how* he'd left from Chicago and other particulars—other than the news itself.

"No, don't worry," she answered. "Have fun in Doha," she added with a clearly disturbed expression.

"But why did Dad have to leave so suddenly?" I asked.

"It wasn't sudden. He knew he'd have to go when there were things to do." Then she said bye, because she was prepping for her own trip to Doha.

Basically, she didn't want me to know whatever it was that she and Dad knew.

So, as soon as I got home from the Corniche, I called Sadia—my sister who always tells me the truth.

I also wanted to talk to her about Adam.

Exhibit B: My sister, a part of my power pack.

Sadia is the closest one to Daadi's personality in our family, so as soon as she picked up and said, "My Zu-zu!" just like Daadi used to call me (except Daadi said "meri Zu-zu"), I teared up.

Because Sadia was at her fiancé's parents' place and said she couldn't talk long, I asked her point-blank, "Why did Dad suddenly leave for Pakistan?"

"I don't know. Really." She looked earnestly at me, her eyes wide and free of all secrets.

But she's always like that. Pure Hufflepuff.

So I tried again. "Did you find out any other information?"

"No, I'm in the dark too. Mom said that Dad got a call that they wanted him to fill some paperwork now that new information had come up about Daadi's death." Sadia peered at me, her usually smiley, long mouth turned down. She shook her head and exclaimed, "Zu-Zu, take a deep breath. Please. It will be okay."

"Okay." I actually did do as she asked, taking a breath and letting it out slowly. *I mean, what else can it be? It's already horrendous, her dying like that. In a car accident.*

I closed my eyes.

"Tell me about Doha," Sadia instructed. "I talked to Auntie Nandy the other day when I called for you, but I want to hear from you."

"It's good." I opened my eyes and looked at the calm beauty of my sister's face. She was back to smiling—encouragingly now, so I burst out with it. "I met a guy. A Muslim guy. Who I really like. Don't laugh, okay?"

"Why would I laugh?"

"I don't know." It felt different to talk to Sadia about Adam than it had talking to Kavi. It felt like talking to my parents about it. Like it was making it serious.

When nothing had even happened.

"But I really like him. I mean, from what I know of him so far." I didn't look into the phone, at her eyes, pretending instead to clean my glasses.

"Is he cute?"

"Yeah, of course." I put my glasses back on, sure she'd understand that part. Because, masha'Allah, he was *very* cute.

"Ha-ha, *of course*, she says."

"I'll send you a picture."

"I'm going to play Mom and Dad for a sec, okay?" Sadia stroked her chin like Dad stroked his beard, and I laughed at how oddly like Dad she *did* look. "Does he appear to have the same values as you do? Same commitment to the deen?"

"Yes, actually maybe more than I do." While Adam and I both did our prayers (he'd told me that when he got his IV done yesterday, it was the first Friday prayers at the mosque, the first jumah, he'd missed in a long time), *he'd* also attended Islamic classes every week when he was in London. *I* didn't, only going to Muslim conferences and camps sometimes.

"Now I'm Mom." Sadia tilted her head and looked at me carefully like Mom did when she wanted to know stuff. "Does he treat his family well? Is he family minded?"

"Oh for sure." I nodded my head vigorously. "Like, his sister is special to him. And his mom, though she passed away."

"By the way, you *are* going to tell Mom and Dad, right?"

"Yeah, I mean soon." I made a face, imagining telling them. "How would I even do it?"

"Can I? You know I'm good at that stuff." She laughed. "Remember when I told them about Yasin?"

"Oh God. This guy is the *opposite* of Yasin." I perked up. She had actually done a good job of breaking the Yasin news. "Can you tell them, then? His mom was one of Auntie Nandy's best friends, if they want to know more. But only say I met Adam—not that there's anything major going on."

"Okay, I will. *My* love is calling me now." She turned and laughed at Jamil, her fiancé, offscreen. Then she leaned in and whispered, "Take it from me—you want someone who's good to his family like Jamil is. And here's one more thing I want to leave you with. From Mom, Dad, and me: Make sure that you make the beginning of whatever you begin beautiful. Make it right by Mom and Dad. Make it right according to our deen. The beginning of something can determine the beauty of the entire thing, okay? So no alone times or coming closer than you should be, okay? That's how Jamil and I did it, and, alhamdulillah, it's been good for us. You know that."

I nodded my head at the same advice I'd heard tons of times—from everywhere: my family, the Muslim community, the mosque.

It was easy to nod to, but I wondered if it was such an easy thing to do.

"WE CAN'T GO TO THE GIFT SHOP UNTIL THE END," HANNA announced as soon as we stepped into the museum's hushed, light-filled foyer. "That's my rule."

"Okay, what about my phone, Mr. Mellon? Can I keep that on me to take pictures?" I joked, walking slowly, setting each foot down deliberately to keep myself balanced, glad Dad had opted to not come with us.

He'd apologized profusely for having to prep for a last-minute interview committee meeting to replace his deputy head of school. Hanna had crossed her arms, upset at first, but then succumbed to patting Dad's head, saying, "It's okay," when she saw the stack of files he had to look through, his eyes already tired-seeming.

But I said, *Alhamdulillah, hallelujah, oh yeah,* right away. Quietly, inside myself.

Dad wasn't here to see my first foray out after my MS scare.

I could explain away the unsteadiness on my feet to Hanna ("hurt myself" was enough), but that feeble excuse wouldn't have worked on him.

Hanna skipped ahead until she got to the center of the lobby, where a marble staircase split into a pair of winding ones that met on the second story. She dipped her head right back on her neck to look up at the ceiling and then, still staring up, took her iPad out of the turquoise-sequined cross-body purse she wore.

"My other rule is that you can take pictures of everything and anything that's beautiful as much as you want so that you can remember this trip forever and ever," she said when I reached her. She showed me ten photos that she'd just taken of the magnificent alcove ceiling above the staircase. At the center of the multilayered design was a star-shaped window to the sky. "See, my field trip rules are better than Mr. Mellon's!"

"Nice. Oh, wait. Remember I asked you if it's okay if a friend came on our field trip?"

"You mean Zayneb? She's not a friend!" Hanna said. "She's like a cousin. Because Dad told me Ms. Raymond was Mom's best friend, so that makes her our *aunt* for all time. Anyone related to her is our cousin."

I nodded gravely while laughing inside, thinking of having to pretend to be cousins with Zayneb just a couple of days ago. "Yeah, so we have to wait for Zayneb, our cousin, at the fountain."

I couldn't wait to see her again.

Since we knew that we were okay with each other.

More than okay, hopefully.

Hanna took a few more pictures while I walked to the dark stone fountain that commanded the space behind the staircase. In an echo of the museum's stunning ceiling, the water was contained within two niches, a star inside an octagon. Arranged neatly around the fountain, again with geometric precision, were square, white café tables, as well as neat pairs of white couches with low tables between them.

I took a seat at one of the tables and looked out the tall windows at the water, Doha Bay, which almost completely surrounded the museum.

This place, this perfect space, is my favorite spot in the whole city.

It connects me to Dad and makes me understand why Doha is our home now.

After Mom passed away, Dad found it hard to work from his home office on Saturday afternoons, like he'd always done.

For a while he shifted from room to room but then would end up staring into space or reading or watching something, with Hanna strapped into either a bouncy swing or a baby seat fitted with brightly colored, dangling toys bobbing above her head.

And me? I disappeared.

Because we had school the next day, the deal with Mom on Saturdays had been that if I got my homework done early, I could play an extra hour of video games on top of the hour she usually let me have each day.

As Dad began flitting between rooms, when he went back to work after grievance leave, and things got back on schedule at home, I'd game for exactly two hours, shut in my room.

At first.

And then, after two weeks, with no one to check on me, I'd game for a bit more, then a bit more, then more, until I fell asleep with the controller in my hand.

That's when Dad began taking us out on Saturdays, whether homework was done or not. We went to different touristy spots around Doha, and he'd let me explore while he kept an eye on Hanna.

The one place I'd ask to go back to again and again was the Museum of Islamic Art.

There was a big playground outside that was fun—for Hanna *and* me, because it had equipment designed for different ages. Even a bungee trampoline that I was into and a kiddie carousel that preoccupied Hanna as she grew into toddlerhood. There were also bike rentals, and, during the cooler months, Dad would bring a tiny helmet and a portable bike seat for Hanna, and we'd ride around the horseshoe path edging the bay, looking out at the water and the skyline of cutting-edge architecture situated across it.

Then one day we went into the museum itself after our bike ride, to get a snack at the café, and, when we got to our table with our drinks and cookies, Dad discovered that Hanna had fallen asleep in the bike seat he'd been carrying her in.

We looked at each other, shocked.

Until that point Hanna had been a no-sleep kid. Except when she'd drop at the end of the day, usually sometime between seven and ten o'clock, with no telling when her tiny form would be found curled up sleeping somewhere in the house.

This didn't mean she was hyperactive—because she wasn't— just into doing things all the time. Sometimes quiet things, sometimes loud things, sometimes staring at an ant colony for hours while pretending to write about it in a "secret" notebook.

She was just not into saying good-bye to the day because day-life was her friend.

But here she was, at three years old, sleeping at four o'clock at the Museum of Islamic Art.

Dad put a hand on her forehead. "She's okay. No fever."

He gently put her upright seat into a chair between us. She continued sleeping.

I passed Dad his drink from the tray I'd been holding and

placed the plate of chocolate chip cookies at the center of the table. He stared at Hanna as he took a sip of his coffee.

"Huh. I've never seen this." He reached for a cookie and looked at me, stumped. "There's a first for everything, I guess."

I nodded. "Maybe it was because she went on the carousel *and* rode on the bike."

"Yes, that could be it. It was a double-fun day for her." Dad smiled. He lifted both his hands up in the air like Hanna did when she got excited. "Doubah fuun, she'd say."

"No, she'd say doubah doubah fuun fuun," I clarified, dunking my warm cookie in the cold glass of milk in front of me. "She says the things she likes two times."

"You're right. Especially if she liked each of them two times as much," he said, laughing and nodding, popping the last of his cookie into his mouth. When he finished chewing, he asked, "What about you? Did you think it was doubah fun?"

"Yeah." I gave a thumbs-up. "Because this time I bounced back up the highest ever when I landed my somersault. On the trampoline."

"Ah, wish I'd seen." He split his second cookie and held out half. "I already had one too many."

I took it and dunked it into my crumb-filled milk. "Dad, can we do this every week? The bungee trampoline and bike riding? And the carousel and riding for Hanna?"

"Hmm." He considered it and looked around at the café. It was quiet but also busy. Some people were talking in groups, others were working on their own or with company, laptops out. "But then we'll end up going back home later, and then homework becomes later. My work becomes later too. Hanna becomes later. Speaking of which, we have to get a move on. Both of you need to take your baths, too."

I made a face and drank the rest of my milk. Hanna's cookie

remained on the plate so I slid a napkin toward me and folded and creased it and kept folding it like origami paper until I had a little envelope. I slipped the cookie in and enclosed it safely with a final napkin fold. "What about Hanna's milk?"

"I'll ask for it in a to-go cup. Watch Hanna?" Dad got up and took the glass of milk with him.

Instead of watching Hanna, I watched Dad.

The way he bowed slightly and put a hand to his heart when he almost bumped into a custodian wiping tables.

He'd been teaching me about Islam for almost a year, and for a while I'd wanted to tell him *I* wanted to do the things he did too. Go to the mosque or prayer rooms at malls or other places when it was prayer time, instead of watching Hanna outside like I did. Go to jumah on Fridays, instead of staying home with Marta.

I also wanted to fast for Ramadan like he had done for the first time that year, and then I wanted to break the fasts with him, when he'd close his eyes after taking that first bite of a date, saying a prayer of gratitude.

I also wanted to hold my hand to my heart like him, like he just did now, like he did whenever he said salaam, peace, to someone, closing his eyes again, like he was grateful for that, too.

He had told me a long time ago that what he liked best about being Muslim was the peace to be found in it.

Maybe that's why he touched his heart. Because the peace was there.

When he came back to the table, I burst out with it. "Dad, can I be Muslim too? Now?"

He put Hanna's cup of milk on the table, then sat down. "Why?"

I was going to say because I want to go to the places you go to and do the things you do and say the words you say and touch my heart the same way, but then I looked up at the staircase behind Dad. The one that split into two and then met again up higher, under a light coming straight down on it from even higher, from the sky itself. "Because I want to have peace too. Like you."

He sat back. "I actually don't have peace, Adam."

"You don't?" Surprised, I slumped down on the table.

"No." He sighed. "But I look for it."

"But then didn't you say you like being Muslim because there's peace in it?"

"Well, I *like* looking for it, for the peace in things. That's why I'm a Muslim. It's someone who knows there's more to life than just going through it, letting things happen. I make sense of everything, that there's more to it than just me and my worries, knowing it's all connected."

"Like the sky? And the world and everything in it?"

"Yup, everything. Bad and good, sad and happy. All connected to God."

"I like that too. I believe that too." I lifted my head from the table and said, "So can I?"

"Yes, you can." He smiled. "You can seek peace with me."

After I became Muslim, the Friday of that same week at the mosque, we began going to the museum every Saturday, me bringing my homework, Dad bringing his head-of-school work, and, after having doubah fuun time with Hanna and her falling asleep, we would eat a snack, chat a bit, and then do our work at the café, across from each other.

Those Saturdays helped Dad find peace after Mom's death.

And they helped me find Dad.

And Hanna find sleep.

• • •

"Our cousin is here!" Hanna said, coming over to the fountain with Zayneb.

I stood up.

She had on the same brilliant blue hijab I'd first seen her in, but this time her face wasn't taken over by the frown she'd worn while reading her phone at the airport.

Today it was lit by a smile, which became happier when she saw me.

"Assalamu alaikum," I said, touching my hand to my heart, to quell the thrill of seeing her—more than due to the peace in my heart.

In reality, it was the opposite of peace in there. Excitement central would be a better way to describe it.

"Walaikum musalam!" she answered, infusing the greeting with bubbly energy. She looked at Hanna. "I heard there's an awesome exhibit we've just *got* to see."

"That's right, the *Rare Jewels* of an Empire." I gestured for her and Hanna to go ahead, and, when they did, I took a step to test myself, to check my abilities once more. This had become my way now whenever I started moving again after being stationary— ever since that fall off my bed, shocking more my mind and my confidence than my body. "I don't know the specific empire we're talking about, but have no fear; we have an expert with us. Hanna Chen, future gemologist."

"It's the Mungal empire," Hanna told Zayneb, walking beside her, iPad out.

"The Mongol or the Mughal?" Zayneb asked.

"M-U-G-H-A-L," Hanna spelled out from her iPad.

"The Mughals of India. So I know I'm going to love this. It's

205

part of my cultural background," she said, slowing her stride to include me, to let me catch up. "My father's family is from Pakistan, which was part of the Indian subcontinent, and of course under Mughal rule."

I nodded, remembering some of Dad's history lessons. "And your mom is Caribbean, obviously. Like Ms. Raymond."

"My mom's parents are Trinidadian and Guyanese, so yeah, West Indian. Which, I guess, means that *that* part of my family was also part of the Mughal Empire. Because they originally came from the Indian subcontinent." She beamed. "I actually really like learning about my heritage. Because we don't learn much of it at school back home. Mostly just Greek and Roman cultures. And Egyptian, sometimes."

"You know, one side of my Dad's family, generations past, migrated as laborers to Jamaica from China, decades ago. He's been trying to get information on them for a while. He's also into history in a big way." I paused when we got to the stairs.

"I thought he was supposed to come today?" Zayneb stopped too and looked at the stairs. Hanna was already at the landing where the staircase split into two sides.

She held up her iPad and snapped a picture of us and then exclaimed, "Cousins forever!"

Zayneb and I looked at each other and laughed.

"I promise I didn't tell her that," I said, shaking my head, hoping I wasn't turning red. *Hanna.* "My dad had a last-minute thing come up at school. Hey, I'm going to take the elevator, just over there. Mind going up with Hanna?"

"No problem!" She waved and proceeded to the stairs. "Meet you at the rare jewels?"

I nodded as Hanna bounded up and Zayneb began climbing.

• • •

In the elevator alone, I tried to tell myself not to think about what was happening right now.

Here was a girl I was interested in, way more than any other girl I'd met before. Actually, way more than any other *person* I'd met before.

Who had something, a spark, who showed an interest in things, who was confidently alive, and here we were having to split up because I couldn't walk with her.

Adam, this may not be the time to begin anything.

And there it was, the voice of reason, of pragmatism, that ruled my life, that I didn't want to listen to today.

Not the right time for love, it whispered again as the elevator doors opened.

I tested a tentative step out and then sped up, holding on to the wall, to leave that crippling voice behind in the elevator.

We were meant to meet.

I believe that there's a connection between the things that happen to us, beyond ourselves. Like Dad taught me to believe.

And I've believed this way for seven years.

Zayneb and I were meant to cross paths. I want to get to know her, keep her showing up in my life.

This was the script I used to replace the thoughts I didn't want inside anymore.

I want to keep her showing up in my life was in my head as I entered the darkened exhibit hall and saw the back of that blue hijab, under a spotlight, in front of a display.

She turned, face full of life, eyes dancing with excitement, and I thought, *Yeah, she's a marvel meant to be in my life.*

ZAYNEB

SUNDAY, MARCH 17

MARVEL: ADAM . . . AND HIS SOUL

Exhibit A: Him, at the museum.

One of the reasons Ayaan said she loves being Muslim is because it makes her feel like a natural feminist. "Like, hello? Our queen Khadija didn't wait for the man she had her eye on to *ask* her, to get on his knees. Nope. Instead, she said, *I like you, oh employee of mine. Will you marry me?* And then, after they hitched, she just kept her job as his boss. *Mad respect.*"

She was talking about the prophet Muhammad. How he was proposed to by his boss, Khadija.

Those were the two I kept thinking about as we moved through the museum, with Hanna flitting around and between us and the other museum visitors like a butterfly, excitedly "landing" on a display of jewelry every once in a while to stare at the stones and pearls, read the caption sometimes, and then, *always*, take a picture.

I was thinking of Ayaan and the prophet Muhammad. And a third person too: Adam.

How Ayaan would just say, *Tell* him. *That* you're *interested in getting to know him seriously. Make a move, advance like our queen.*

Like you're supposed to. Be the boss you're meant to be, Zayneb.

I was thinking of how the prophet Muhammad was a soft, beautiful soul, who didn't get bothered that a woman had asked him, didn't get bothered that she was his boss.

How Adam had that kind of a soul.

I could tell from the way he loved his mother to the way he treated his sister.

Like, right now he was calling Hanna over to a display case. When she arrived, iPad held out ready to snap, he bent over so that he was at her level and then told her quietly about whatever precious thing they were looking at.

I hung back, my facial expressions blocked by a pillar display housing a bejeweled sword sheath, unnamed feelings eating me up inside and most probably spilling out on my face.

My parents have always been pretty relaxed when it comes to relationships. As long as we're in a group or in public and observe certain boundaries, it's okay for my siblings and me to be on friendly terms with anyone. They have no interest in setting us up or arranging marriages or, the best, making harsh statements like *Stay away from boys!* My sister, Sadia, met Jamil on her own at college, and my brother, Mansoor, has been talking to the same person, Hodan, forever, since they met in middle school, and everyone knows where *that* is headed. I mean, it was great for my parents that they knew Hodan from the mosque and that she was related to Ayaan's family, which immediately gave her another layer of legitimacy.

Because they've told me I'm free to meet someone who shares my values, whether they know the person or not, on that front, I know that they'd be completely fine if I told them that I'd met a boy in Doha. Like Sadia had been okay with it.

But I didn't know what to do with all this.

I mean, I knew he liked me. And vice versa, to the hundredth power, if we're talking mathematically.

But what did that exactly . . . mean?

The "certain boundaries" my parents had coached Sadia, Mansoor, and me about were physical ones. Touching leads to kissing leads to sexing.

Which they (and every sermon at the mosque regarding this topic) had warned us about—especially that being alone with someone you had the hots for and who also had the hots for you could lead to *touching and kissing and sexing.*

Until Adam, I hadn't understood this.

"This is my favorite necklace." As we exited the exhibit, Hanna extended her iPad to show me a picture of a heavy-looking choker filled with rubies, emeralds, and pearls, which appeared to cover the entire neck and part of the shoulders of the mannequin head it sat on. "Adam said I have a good eye. Because this one took a lot of crafting to make."

I peered at it. "I love it. Especially the rubies and emeralds, the way they're stuck inside the gold."

Adam glanced over at the image. "Yeah, some of these are stones, but the parts inside the gold are like enameling. We just read a bit about it back there."

"It's called meenakari, and Adam says we're going to try to do it at home," Hanna said. "Like, an easy version."

We came out of the hallway onto the landing of the central museum staircase, into a burst of light.

I looked up at the amazing ceiling with a star-shaped skylight.

"This is my favorite place in Doha, the museum. Actually, one of my favorite places on earth." Adam joined me in gazing up. "I love things that inspire me to try my hand at making stuff."

"Adam is a maker," Hanna said, breezing by us, going back to her favorite activity of skipping around snapping pictures. "He's making a world in a room at our house. You should see it!"

Adam laughed and straightened his head to look right at me. "No, you shouldn't. Because there's nothing there yet. It's a work in progress."

He was just a few inches taller than me, and, maybe because of that, when he looked at me, we were almost eye to eye. It made me look anywhere but at him. Mostly because—cringe—I was afraid he'd see the feelings on my face. I examined the huge circular light fixture suspended just ahead of us. "What else do you make?"

He turned to look at the fixture too. "All sorts of things. Whatever gets my interest at the moment."

"Wait. Was the last thing you made the rock-collection box for Hanna?" I stole a glance. Oops, it happened to be at the same time he did.

"I heard my name!" She flew by us, snapping a picture of us.

I'd have to get that girl to send me those pics she took of Adam and me.

Adam nodded. "Yeah, but I've started another project since."

"The world room? That Ha—" I paused as Hanna made her way around us again. "That your sister talked about?"

"And something else. A special project that I started just this morning. Before I came here."

After a quick glance at each other, we both turned to the light fixture once more. It was super intricate, the designs on it.

Wait. What was in that look he just gave me? Is he making something, a special project, having to do with me?

211

Stop, I told myself. *Be realistic.*

I cleared my throat. "So, when are you going back? To London?"

He became quiet.

I waited a bit before facing him.

He wasn't looking ahead, at the light, but down at the floor. "I'm not. Going back to school. That's something else I have to talk to my dad about. I officially de-enrolled from university before I flew here."

Then he lifted his head, ran his fingers through his hair, and gazed up again. All the way up at the ceiling.

He doesn't look sad.

"What are you going to do?" I couldn't imagine it. Dropping out of school. Handling so many unknowns.

"I'm going to make things." He smiled. "The thing is, I've got a bit of money that my mom left for . . . 'fun,' she called it. She wanted me to have a gap year before university, but I never took it. So I guess I will now. I may even go spend some time with my grandparents in Canada. Dad's side in Vancouver, Mom's in Ottawa."

My heart lit up. *That's kind of close to Indiana. Close to Springdale.* Well, closer than Doha and London, at least.

"Are you guys coming? I want to see the other exhibits too, not just stand here." Hanna materialized right in front of us, ever-present iPad clutched to her chest.

A bit of annoyance crept into me. At her antics.

I was glad I didn't have a little sister or brother.

Adam must have seen something on my face, because he laughed and said, "She's been a great big sister to me all these years. On top of being a little sister."

He paused, watched her opening the door for us with an exaggerated flourish, and then added, "I guess she's had to be all sorts of things."

Oh. Yeah.

I hadn't thought about how growing up without a mother must have affected her.

And made Adam and her tight in a way I couldn't understand.

Like Daadi's death in October had dimmed some of the lights inside me and made me clingy, to even a blanket my grandmother had knit for me.

We followed Hanna into another exhibit hall, both Adam and me quiet. We drifted from artifact to artifact, sometimes the three of us together, sometimes separately.

And then I glanced to my left and saw it.

The Marvels of Creation and Oddities of Existence.

That was the caption under a framed double-page spread with Arabic writing and pictures of trees and plants.

THE INSPIRATION FOR MY JOURNAL WAS STARING AT ME.

AN INTERLUDE

Here, one must take the reins of the story from both Adam and Zayneb. Their observations of the events that unfolded next differ so vastly that it's hard to understand what actually happened if we rely solely on them.

To find the truth and present it clearly, one has to wade through two vats full of emotions and perceptions—i.e., their journals—to collect and clutch at those stray facts, proven to be facts as they showed up in *both* journals.

These mutual bits were then combined with the feelings for each other they'd admitted to themselves up until this point, and thus I present the following to you.

Reading the caption below the glass-enclosed thirteenth-century manuscript, Zayneb let out a small "oh."

Adam came to stand beside her.

They stared at *The Marvels of Creation and Oddities of Existence* folios.

Adam wondered if he should bring up that he knew she had a Marvels and Oddities journal just like him. Wondered whether that would sound slightly stalkerish, or whether it was cute. Or perhaps even romantic?

The truth remained that he *had* previously wanted it to come up naturally, and here it was now right in front of them.

Zayneb wondered if this—being presented with the *real* Marvels and Oddities—was a cosmic moment of significance in her life. The universe, or, in fact, the creator of it, sending her a message. That her life was on the right course.

And then her phone buzzed.

An e-mail from Fencer.

The subject line read *Analysis assignment = D- for extensive use of false equivalencies.*

Zayneb stared at the notification and then swore.

It was a muttered swear, quiet in its volume but strong in its impact. On Adam.

He tilted his head at her (in her journal, she recorded this tilt as being "judgy") and asked, "Whoa. Everything okay?"

She said, "No. My beeping"—as Adam recorded in *his* journal—"social studies teacher just gave me my first D ever."

"That stinks." He tried to think of something to say to make her feel better. "Can you do the assignment over?"

She shook her head. "I can't. He's like a crazy Islamophobe who hates on us Muslims."

Adam was taken aback. At this fact and the intensity of the way she pronounced it. He thought he glimpsed a . . . Was that a snarl on her face?

"Can you go to your principal? Speak up? If this teacher is treating you unfairly?"

Zayneb surprised herself by grimacing at Adam. At him using the word "if." She was surprised both that he had said "*if* this teacher is treating you unfairly"—as if she wouldn't know whether someone was treating her unfairly—and that she had made a face at him so openly.

But he was in the wrong to use "if" so effortlessly, so she held the grimace and exploded with "It's because of the principal I'm here in Doha for two weeks!"

Adam put his right hand in his pant pocket and pinched the seams inside, something he did when he was getting worried.

Zayneb's expressions were getting him worried.

He'd never seen anger completely taking over someone's face as it was now, plainly and frankly, in front of him.

"I *spoke up*, as you said, in the stupid teacher's class, and then, yes, I took my frustration out by doodling a simple knife, BUT I WAS GOING TO ADD THE FORK, and then I got suspended for one week!" She walked ahead for a bit then paced back. "That's why I'm here in Doha!"

Her voice was loud.

He looked around, wondering if the other visitors were getting as alarmed as he was. Luckily, the family nearby had exhibit headphones over their ears as they stood in front of a video on Islamic calligraphy through the ages.

"Whoa. Okay, do you want to sit on that bench over there to talk about it or even go to the café downstairs?"

She marched to the bench and took a seat. Then she stood up, agitated, wanting him to understand the depth of her predicament. "He got me suspended. Got my friend removed from student council and now just gave me a D for dishing up the same BS he teaches in class."

Adam walked over to the bench and sat down at one end. He was confused about how to proceed.

Pragmatism, his old friend, poked him. Ah, yes.

He'd take it logically and find out why she was suspended. "So you got suspended for speaking up in class?"

"No, for drawing a knife."

"Okay. Can I ask why you drew a knife?"

"To accompany the hashtag EatThemAlive, which is this movement to get racists removed from their jobs. Which we plan on doing to Fencer, my teacher." She sat down at the other end of the bench. "STILL plan on doing to him. Get his racist ass fired."

Adam blinked at the *Marvels of Creation and Oddities of Existence* display right across from them. "Because he hates on Muslims?"

"Yes, completely for that reason." She lifted her phone and scrolled through it. "Like, look at this gross article he passed out in class just last week."

Adam reached for it and drew a breath at the title. GIRL BURIED ALIVE IN HONOR KILLING.

He flicked through, reading slowly. When finished, he lowered the phone "Whoa."

That irritated her, the "whoa," the third one he'd muttered in the span of a few minutes.

It sounded too much like the reaction of her classmates to that buried-girl article.

She stared at him. *Wait, what are his views on issues like these anyway?*

Like, did he even have any of the same values she did?

"Could you stop saying 'whoa' like that? It's kind of annoying."

He looked at her. She found him annoying?

"WHY ARE YOU GUYS JUST SITTING HERE?" Hanna stalked over to them. "I went ahead to the ceramics room and thought you were behind me and almost went to the science room. But you guys are just taking a rest here?"

Zayneb turned to her. "Yeah, we are. Because we're old. And your elders. Have a little respect, 'kay?"

Adam raised his eyebrows and took his hand out of his pocket. He wasn't worried anymore.

He was getting tired.

And he wanted to get Hanna away from Zayneb. "Hanna, do you mind just waiting in the ceramics area? Zayneb's kinda upset at something right now."

Looking crestfallen, Hanna walked away, glancing back at Zayneb a few times.

"She's got nothing to do with your teacher," Adam said quietly.

Zayneb, guilt flowering within at the way Hanna looked back at her over and over, with a mixture of shock and shame, felt her anger quelling.

She was about justice. And this, what she'd just done to a little kid, wasn't very just. "You're right. I'll apologize to her."

Adam sat up. That was refreshing to hear. *She'll apologize to Hanna.*

And she seemed to have calmed down. "Well, I'm sorry that you got suspended. That your teacher is a terrible person."

He looked at her face and saw that it was true—she *had* calmed. A bit.

A frown knitted her brow, though. "I can't sit still when things are wrong. I need to do something about it. Or I can't rest."

"Well, we are what we want."

Now Zayneb tilted her head at *him*. (In his journal, he recorded this tilt as being "in disbelief.") "What does that mean?" she asked.

"It means whatever we want in life is what defines our existence."

"Okay, so what do you want?" *It must be something super peaceful, chill, zen,* Zayneb thought. If he was as good as he appeared.

"I want peace. I want to see it in the things around me, natural and not, but mostly natural. The marvels of creation." He nodded at the manuscript displayed in front of them. "I want to examine how the wonders around me are connected, find peace through that. What about you? What do you want?"

He smiled encouragingly, and the frown she wore softened, because his smile was that open.

She also felt satisfied about being right about him. About his wants being so chill. *Peace.*

But the truth was there couldn't be peace without—

She took a breath. "I want justice. And I want it now. For everyone."

His smile grew as though he liked hearing that, and she, for the first time in a long while, had a sudden, beautiful thought: *He likes me for the way I really am.*

So she went on. "And sometimes I feel like I'm the only person who feels this want so strongly. Because I'm the only one in class speaking up. The only one in my family, that's for sure, who cares this much. Who goes on marches and writes stuff and just gives a care."

"Maybe they do in their own way." Zayneb had softened so much that he went on. "Maybe *everyone* does. Care about justice on some level."

Her brows activated and began their approach to each other again. "What do you mean? Do you mean, *everyone* everyone? Like, even Fencer?"

"Well, he gave out the article about this girl killed by her family. Maybe he wants justice for her?"

Zayneb shook her head, aghast. "No, he was trying to get the class riled up about Muslims. He was *using* the Turkish girl, not expressing care for her. You don't even know Fencer. And I just can't believe you're giving a real-life Islamophobe excuses."

"Whoa," he said. And the second it came out of his mouth, he regretted it intensely, like he had regretted few things in his eighteen years.

Adam leaned back, stumped on how to proceed. Her voice had become loud again, and the family, who'd removed their headphones, turned in unison to look at Zayneb.

He had to explain himself.

"I'm not giving him excuses. It's just something I thought about while reading the article." Adam refused to put his right hand in his pocket, refused to worry about what Zayneb was doing or its effect on those around them. "I just wanted justice for her, for the girl buried alive. That's a terrible tragedy."

Zayneb stood stock-still, mouth agape. "You're falling for Fencer's tricks, and you're not even sitting there in his class?"

"It's still an injustice, isn't it? A girl getting buried for talking to boys? Or for anything at all? Maybe that's what made your teacher upset."

"Of course it's an injustice. That's not what's going on here, though. I'm talking about Fencer's behavior here." She bent to get her phone from where she'd left it on the bench. "Okay, time for me to exit."

He watched her scrolling and typing and, for some reason, couldn't stop himself from adding, "Why do *you* get to decide what injustices to call out and what not to call out?"

"Oh my God, you're the one who should get a D for false equivalence!" she exclaimed, shaking her head. "Adam, it's been good knowing you for a week, but I guess we don't make sense in any way. We're too different, and . . ."

It was Adam's turn to stay still, sure he was holding his breath as he waited for her to finish.

"We're from two different worlds. You and your friends don't make sense to me." She glanced down at her phone. "You don't get my deal, and I don't get yours. Like you being chicken to tell your dad about your MS. My Uber is here, so I'm out of here."

She walked off.

And Adam?

He sat down.

Put his head in his hands and refused to look up at the visitors milling around, glancing gingerly over at him once in a while.

He also refused to look at that manuscript.

The one he'd thought bound them together in some kind of out-of-this-world way.

Ha.

ODDITY: *A RELATIONSHIP THAT ENDED BEFORE IT EVEN BEGAN.*

MARVEL: *THIS TOO WILL PASS. LIFE GOES ON, EVEN IF LOVE DOESN'T.*

ADAM

SUNDAY, MARCH 17

ODDITY: ZAYNEB . . . AND THE TRUTH

ZAYNEB WAS NOT WHO SHE WAS IN MY MIND.

Before, I'd thought that the more impressions you got of someone you liked, the less projecting would be happening. That you wouldn't see them according to how you *wanted* to.

I hadn't realized that, in this case, I'd been hoodwinking myself all along, though.

Because I'd just fallen for her so quickly.

On the ride home, with Hanna super quiet beside me, even though she had a velvet bag full of new rocks for her collection from the museum shop, I realized I'd escaped someone who wasn't who I thought they were.

Zayneb was the only marvel I'd observed and recorded that turned out not to be a real one.

Bullet dodged, Adam.

You don't get my deal, and I don't get yours. Like you being chicken to tell your dad about your MS.

I couldn't get Zayneb's words out of my head as I helped Dad with dinner that evening, him chopping up vegetables for a salad, me taking the packaging off a frozen lasagna, getting it ready for the oven.

Zayneb didn't know anything about it, anything about me. *At all.*

Just like I hadn't known anything about *her* true self.

I slid the foil tray into the preheated oven. Then closed the door and turned to Dad. "Do you have time to talk?"

I wasn't scared of any of it.

"For sure." Running the edge of his knife along the cutting board, he slid the red peppers he'd just cut into a wooden bowl already full of lettuce and cucumber. He put the board back down, lay the knife on top of it, and looked at me. "Do you want to talk here or go into the living room?"

I didn't want it to be monumental, this talk. The kitchen was okay, because it was just us two here in a no-fuss space.

But then Hanna was in her room, arranging her rocks, and could enter at any moment soundlessly.

Telling *her* about my MS had to be done in a special way.

"The patio? I can put a timer for the lasagna on my phone, and we'll know when to call Hanna for dinner."

Dad nodded and picked up wooden salad tongs and put them into the bowl. He carried it with him to the kitchen table and placed it in the middle of its glass surface.

Was it my imagination, or was there some weariness to his actions after I'd asked him for a talk?

Just follow him to the patio and speak, I coached myself.

After clearing an ottoman of Hanna's skipping rope and scooting it over, Dad pulled his lawn chair closer to mine, facing the water and sky, already dark.

"Should we turn on more lights?" he asked. When I shook my head, he adjusted his seat so that it leaned back before sitting down and putting his feet up on the ottoman.

Then he crossed his fingers on top of his stomach and sighed. "Adam, tell me."

The sigh threw me off. I glanced at him. He was looking at his fingers. "I'm ready to hear it. Our committee interview for a new deputy head is at the end of the week. I didn't need to prep for it today, the third day of spring break. I mean, I pulled the files to try to bury myself in work. But I was in fact prepping for you to talk to me."

He looked at me then, and the patio light was strong enough for a revelation: His face looked more tired than ever before. And aged. Like suddenly, overnight, he'd become the middle-aged dad he was, not the fit, young-looking one my friends joked was really my older brother.

It was his mouth. The edges looked slacker, weaker.

I almost bolted inside. "What do you know?"

I didn't ask *how do you know.* Because I knew how.

I guess Ms. Raymond had done what an adult would do.

Maybe what someone who loved Mom would do.

"I know you have something to tell me, and that I have to be strong to hear it. That's it." Dad looked away, toward the water, but his eyes were closed. "I'm here for you in whatever way you want me to be."

"Even if it's hard?" I concentrated on the tiny white triangle sails of the boats docked in the curve of a far-off shore. "Because it's hard."

"I'm ready."

"In November, I was diagnosed." I paused. "With MS. Like Mom."

Dad was silent, and so I turned to him. His eyes were open, looking straight ahead. Maybe he, too, was looking at those sails.

"And then I stopped going to classes early this year. Because I couldn't concentrate. My mind was going miles a minute trying to figure out next steps, what it meant, just processing it. So I just took all of it out of my mind—my diagnosis, school, everything—and made stuff." I paused to smile, trying to make it light. "You should see the Boba Fett helmet I made for you, Dad. Ryan, that friend I told you about? He's gonna send all my stuff back here, back home, including the helmet. Because I quit university."

At some point during my verbal vomit, he'd closed his eyes again.

I stood up. "Listen, it's going to be okay. I had an attack, my second one, the first being just the nonstop tingling that got me to the hospital in the first place to get diagnosed, and, yes, my second one was a lot worse, but it was treated. And it can be treated, Dad."

He spoke. "Was that the day you were sleeping all day?"

"Yeah, then I got my treatments at the hospital and Ms. Raymond's."

"Adam. Why didn't you tell me?"

"Because it was the anniversary of Mom's passing. You're always down that week."

"Why didn't you tell me in November?" He was staring at me, wanting an answer, demanding one with the unflinching steadiness of his eyes on my face. "It hurts me that you had to bear this on your own. That I couldn't help you."

I sat back down.

"You and Hanna are the world to me. Every day I think about whether I'm doing right by you. That's all I want."

"I know, Dad."

"The thing you don't know, or maybe don't seem to *believe*, Adam, is that I can help you. That I want to."

"But it was hard for you with Mom. I thought you'd get triggered. Just not be able to take it."

"Yes, okay, you're right. Mom's death was hard. It devastated me. But that was only because it progressed so fast at the end. It wasn't the MS that got to me. She'd had it since she was in her twenties, when I met her, and it went into remission for so long, especially after she had you. We'd read that pregnancy does that, almost makes the disease disappear." He shifted and sighed. "I was on a high that everything was getting better for her. And then, after Hanna, it was swift. I didn't have time to prepare."

"I get it." *Dare I say it?* I spoke gently so he wouldn't think I was trying to be rude. "But, Dad, that was a while ago. A long time ago."

He didn't speak. I didn't either. The silence stretched until I wondered if he'd fallen asleep, but I couldn't bring myself to check.

I switched from sail watching to observing the sky. It was sprinkled with hundreds of stars, and suddenly I remembered the night Zayneb was here, blowing bubbles with that secret smile.

I couldn't believe my mind jumped to her so fast.

You don't get my deal, and I don't get yours. Like you being chicken to tell your dad about your MS.

Beside me, Dad started heaving, pounding sobs taking over his body.

I immediately got up, made my way to his side.

He wiped his eyes with the bottom of his T-shirt and spoke through his tears. "What I can't get over with Mom's death is *not* her death; it's how I wish I could have helped her more. I don't feel like I did enough."

"Dad, you were there for Mom. I remember so clearly. You were unbelievable, with your support." He really was. So much that, in my head, I couldn't see Mom at the end of her life without seeing Dad somewhere in the background, ready to help, ready to do something. And everything.

"You know how I like to research?" He wiped his eyes again and looked at me.

I nodded, kneeling to put my arm around his shoulder.

"I've now learned that there is so much out there that I wish we could have at least tried, instead of sitting back and watching Mom's MS progress."

"But you did what you could with what you knew then."

"But that information was available then, too. I just never looked for it." He let the tears fall again.

I let him cry, and me a bit too. "But, Dad, you yourself taught me not to look back. Just forward and ask for guidance moving on, forgiveness for the past."

He took a breath and swallowed before putting an arm out to me. "You're right, but I still haven't learned to take my own advice."

"That's okay."

"Look at me, crying about the past, when you've got something to face in the present." He gripped my shoulder. "But I promise you: You'll never face it alone. As long as I'm alive."

"And as long as Hanna's alive." I swallowed and smiled. "I guess that's why I came back home."

"You did right. In leaving school. And I'm so glad you have something to focus on too, with your making things and your workshop. You're going to be okay. I'll be here to make sure of it."

The timer on my phone went off, and I thought about the

lasagna and the salad waiting already. And Hanna coming down, holding her newly arranged rock-collection display case, most probably. "I'm just glad to be home."

We both stood, and, though it was the first thing on my mind, Dad reached for a hug before I did. When we broke apart, he smiled. "I can't wait to see my Boba Fett helmet, so tell your friend to send it over right away."

As I silenced the timer and we made our way to the patio doors, I had a sudden thought. *Ms. Raymond is the best.*

Without her prepping Dad, I don't know if it would have gone like it had.

ZAYNEB
SUNDAY, MARCH 17
ODDITY: ADAM

EXHIBIT A: AT THE MUSEUM, WHEN HE SHOWED ME WHO HE WAS.

Someone with zero awareness of what was going on in the world.

I pushed his care for Hanna out of my head.

I pushed his struggles with his diagnosis out of my head too.

I pushed him completely out of my head.

As soon as I let myself into the apartment, I texted Kavi. Talk? On FT?

Auntie Nandy, who'd been sitting on the couch, immediately got up and walked swiftly by me to her bedroom, her phone stuck to an ear.

She closed her door tight.

What's that all about?

Walking into the living room, I undid my hijab and threw it at the big couch.

It landed on the arm of the single chair.

An image of Adam, hooked up to the IV machine, presented

itself in my head. I calmly walked over to the chair, the Adam chair, and sat in it, to claim it back.

Why wasn't Kavi replying? I checked Instagram and saw I'd missed the latest story from her.

A shot of an arrow pointing at an inbox with an e-mail from SAIC. A shot of her face overjoyed. A shot of Noemi, grinning big, beside her, then one of Nhu making a surprised O with her mouth.

Kavi got into SAIC?

I FaceTimed her. It rang and rang, so I hung up and tried again.

At the third try, she picked up, but with only audio. Audio of yelling. "ZAY!"

"CONGRATULATIONS! Oh my God!" I burst. "Your number one choice!"

"Thanks! I'm doing a mini celebration!" she shouted again, and I suddenly noticed the noise around her. "Waiting for you to come home for the real one!"

"I'm so proud of you! I knew you'd get in!"

"Sorry, wait. I can't hear you fully! Let me get to a better spot!"

"What're you doing? I mean, where are you?"

"It's a VR adventure place, MAZETOWN! So cool! We gotta take you when you get here!" It became quieter. She stopped yelling. "I just stepped outside. It's like crazy loud in there. We finished eating, so we're getting ready to go on the Galápagos tour. Zay, we have to get suited up and everything, so we can dive and swim with the sharks and sea turtles. I'm going to be in heaven!"

Kavi loves marine life. Her entire portfolio to get into art school was sea creatures done in different mediums.

"Have tons of fun." I pulled my legs onto the couch and smiled, happy for her. "Mazetown. Must be a new place. Never heard of it before."

"No, it's not in Springdale. Noemi drove us to Indianapolis. Me, Nhu, and Ayaan."

"Oh wow. Are you guys staying there?"

"Yeah, we got a cheap hotel room."

"Cool! Have fun," I repeated, my mind incapable of thinking up anything more exciting to say, being too busy conjuring up images of Kavi, Nhu, Ayaan, and Noemi laughing in unison—in the car, in the hotel room, at Mazetown, whatever that place looked like.

"We miss you so much!" Kavi said. "We were doing this-is-what-Zay-would-say so often that Noemi just started saying it for you. The stuff you'd say."

"So she's being me?"

"In a fun way. She's good at improv."

As I considered this, my phone pinged nonstop.

Picture messages from HannaChen.

"Well, you better get back. To get ready for the Galápagos," I said. "Tell everyone hi for me."

"Hey, what about you? Any word from UChicago?"

I shook my head, forgetting that it was only audio.

I'd begun looking through the pictures Hanna sent me. "No. Talk to you later, Kav."

Many were fuzzy, but even those stopped my breath.

I've never seen myself so happy in photos before.

It could have been the fact that they were impromptu pictures, and I hadn't had time to arrange my camera-ready smile. Which was just slight turnups of the corners of my closed mouth, like a *there, are you satisfied with my smile* smile.

But these were different. My mouth was open and turned up naturally, and my eyes joined the smile, scrunching up with joy.

And then Adam.

His face could be used in a picture dictionary for the word "eager."

Boy, were we ever fools.

I sent five blue heart and five blue gem emojis in reply to HannaChen. And added, *Thanks. Sorry for my rude self today.*

I thought for a bit, then added, *Cousin.*

She replied with a single, simple puppy emoji.

I'd decided not to ruin Kavi's fun by unloading both the Adam and the D-from-Fencer situations, so that meant I was a mess inside. Full of churning emotions, mostly anger and frustration. With a lot of worried wonderings as to my next steps.

I needed to vent. But without venting verbally.

I went to Auntie Nandy's room to ask her if I could soak in the Jacuzzi in her bathroom. When I'd first arrived at her place, she'd shown me the vast array of fizzy bath bombs and bottles of scented salts and collection of candles that lined the edge of the Jacuzzi. "You must help me deplete these while you're here. You'd better be in here soaking!"

As I drew near her door, I didn't hear anything.

Then: "She'll understand! She's eighteen, not seven!"

I put my ear to the door.

"Just go. I'll talk to Zayneb. Only return when Rashaad is okay. It must be terrible for him."

Rashaad? Dad?

Was Auntie Nandy talking to Mom? About Pakistan?

I knocked.

"Wait. I have to go. I'll take care of it. Stay safe. Love you, Leesh."

Leesh was Auntie Nandy's nickname for Alisha. Mom.

The door opened. Auntie Nandy tried to smile, but it came off weird, with her forehead wrinkled by a frown.

"Can I use your Jacuzzi?" I asked, wondering if I should just outright say I heard something.

"Yes, yes you can." She opened the door wider. "If you're okay with me being here? That was your mom on the phone."

I paused my steps to her bathroom. "Is her flight okay?"

"Yeah, but . . . Okay, why don't you get ready for your soak and we'll talk?" She went to her walk-in closet and bent to open a bottom drawer. A kimono-like bathrobe, silky and subdued in mint green and gray, emerged from it. "You can use this."

"Thanks." I took it with me to the bathroom, undressed, and put it on while the water ran. I selected a random bath bomb and threw it in and watched it erupt. The door was ajar, so I called out, "Auntie Nandy, what were you talking to Mom about? Her flight comes in at nine, right?"

Auntie Nandy showed up at the door. "No, her plans changed."

I stopped watching the fizzing action in the water and faced her. "What? Why?"

"Your mom is meeting your dad in Pakistan. She just landed in Doha, but then is flying on to Islamabad in a few hours. But we'll go to the airport, because she wants to see you. Talk to you."

"Why is she going there too? What happened?"

"Darling, why don't you sit down on the bed?" She came into the bathroom and turned the water off. "You can do your soak later."

I obeyed her and went toward the bed.

ODDITY: WORTHLESS LIVES

With her arm around me, she told me everything Mom had told her. That they'd found out exactly how Daadi had died in October.

The day when she'd gone to enjoy a wedding in the mountains the way she had when she was a young child—which meant traveling out of her familiar city.

A drone strike. A missed target. Collateral damage.

A wedding caravan of cars and buses dispersed, shredded, gaping holes, gaping wounds, missing body parts, missing bodies.

Daadi had wanted to sit in one of the cars, as the bus with the family members—the one vehicle that had survived the attack—scared her with its speed and rickety way of moving.

The report Dad went to learn about had all the details.

My hands went to my face, and I cried without stopping.

Auntie Nandy put both arms around me and kept whispering that I was a beautiful soul and that my grandmother had gone on to the next life and that she was at peace, and so were Dad and Mom now that they knew what had happened to Daadi, but I kept crying.

Because it came back to me again, like it had in the fall, that I'd never see her face or feel her hands again.

Because it hurt that, with the way things were in the world, my grandmother's life and her hands, her love, didn't count as much.

It hurt that some lives were worth *less*.

After talking to Sadia and Mansoor on Skype, ten minutes where we each took turns consoling one another while resharing memories, Auntie Nandy drove me to the airport.

234

Mom had a short layover, so we were going to see her in the transit area, across a barrier.

On the first sight of her, of her smallness, her white trim hijab, the worry in her eyes, I began to sob. She reached out to me, and I slumped into her arms.

The rhythmic way she stroked the back of my head for a long while was the balm I didn't know I needed. I laid a kiss on her cheek before I broke away to let Auntie Nandy hug her.

On releasing her sister, Mom turned to me. "Sweetie, I'll be back. I'm going for a few days, and then I planned my trip so that I have a couple of days here before we go back home together."

"Mom, how did they know it was really Daadi? That she died that way?"

"There are records that an organization that tracks civilian drone deaths collects. It just took a long while to get all the information." Mom reached out to me again, putting her hands on my arms to hold me steady, to look into my eyes. "She's at peace. Remember to make duas for her, darling."

I nodded, but I couldn't get Daadi, a certain look of hers, out of my mind. The one Mansoor and Sadia and I had talked about. That encouraging face she'd do when she wanted you to try a food she'd made that you weren't sure about, how full of love that face was.

And her hands again. This time I saw one of them holding out a slice of mango, during the times she'd feed me by hand, even after I'd grown up.

Mom's light brown eyes explored my face with care. "You look tired. Have you been sleeping?"

I nodded again and put an arm through Auntie Nandy's arm. "Yeah, I have. Auntie Nandy's been taking good care of me."

"And will continue to. Don't worry, Leesh. Go take care of

what needs to be done. Zayneb is going to rest a bit, maybe swim a bit?" Auntie Nandy raised her eyebrows to me and, when I said yes, went on. "And see more of Doha."

"And pray for Daadi," I added, reaching for Mom again. She wrapped her arms around me. "Is Dad okay?"

"Well, he's obviously shaken. I'm going to help him settle things, finish the process of closing up Daadi's house there." Mom spoke softly. "We're also going to fill out all the papers and make sure her death has been recorded as a victim of war, make sure it's on the record."

"It doesn't seem like anyone will care," I said.

Mom glanced at Auntie Nandy before putting a hand in her purse. "I've got some mail for you."

She held out some envelopes. I noticed a UChicago label on one of them.

I didn't get in to UChicago.

But today, it didn't matter.

In October I'd been in English class discussing *Hamlet* when I was called down to the office, where Mom told me to get my things, that I was going home, that something had happened to Daadi.

Now I knew what that *something* was.

I wanted to know *everything* that had happened to my grandmother, so when I got back from the airport, I went online and spent all night researching.

I found facts I'd never been told.

Facts that I'd never learned as we sat discussing *Hamlet*.

Millions of victims of our recent wars in Iraq, Afghanistan, Pakistan, Somalia, and Yemen.

Drone strikes that have killed countless innocent civilians—people picking crops in the field, lining up to buy bread, going to school.

Going to weddings.

With each new fact learned, I felt Daadi's hand as she sat stroking my hair while I did my homework in front of the Pakistani dramas she'd watch. I saw her hands knitting the cozy items she'd make me each fall, and Binky long before that. I saw her hands holding my face in greeting when I came in after school, the love in them melting away whatever pains school had thrown at me, and then those same hands kneading and breaking dough to make me a fresh, flaky roti, my favorite after-school snack.

I ached for those hands and couldn't stop the tears that dripped onto my laptop.

ADAM

MONDAY, MARCH 18

ODDITY: GETTING THE TRUTH OUT

CONNOR CAME OVER ON MONDAY AFTERNOON, BUT NOT ON HIS own. Jacob, Madison, Isaac, Emma P., and Emma Z. turned up too, with a box of ice cream sandwiches. We ended up sitting outside on the patio so that Hanna could feel like she was hanging with us, skipping rope, riding her bike along the boardwalk, or just doing stuff on the lawn.

Once he knew I'd told Dad, and it was okay for him to tell the others, Connor had done a message blast about my diagnosis, so now I fielded what felt like a hundred questions. Questions politely asked and thoughtfully spaced apart between bites of quickly melting ice cream, but still kind of wearying.

Emma Z. brought up returning to university, and I didn't say anything.

Which I thought would get everyone more inquisitive, but thankfully they started giving their own stories of going back to school after the break.

"I'm leaving tomorrow," Emma P. said, scrunching her ice cream wrapper into a ball.

The others chimed in, offering their own dates of departure, many of them leaving Doha tomorrow as well. In a few days, it would be just me left here. With Hanna and Dad, yay.

But alone with my MS.

I was in this weird space of wanting not to be alone and wanting not to be crowded, either.

I just wanted the right mix of being with someone I connected to, who cared, but also let me be.

I spun my trash, folded small, between my fingers. Just origami folding that plain white wrapper into a perfect tiny square while listening to everyone talk about my illness had been therapeutic.

I twirled it to not think of the future. Of loneliness.

When things fell silent, but not awkward silent, Emma P. looked at Connor, then at me, and then back at Connor, before speaking. "That's why we came by today, Adam. We couldn't leave without saying good-bye. Without seeing you."

"I'll be here when you guys come back." I waved at Hanna as she rode by, trying not to show my discomfort at edging close to the topic of Me, Alone. "And hopefully everyone will come back to Doha? For the summer?"

"Let's take a pic," Connor said, standing up, holding a plastic bag out to collect everyone's trash. "Hey, can your sis take our picture?"

I nodded, thankful for the change in conversation. "Yeah, Hanna's pretty good at clicking. Lots of practice."

"Hanna!" Connor advanced to the stairs leading to the boardwalk, to get her attention.

Madison and Jacob got up and walked to one of the big white rocks on the lawn, with Isaac following, taking photos of them with his phone. I'd heard Madison and Jacob had an account called Long-Distance Love where they posted their miss-you picture postcards to each other.

Emma Z. unfolded herself from the canvas chair she'd been curled in, stretched, and wandered away.

Seeing what had just happened, I scratched my elbow.

They'd left Emma P. and me with empty patio furniture.

"Adam, I hope you know that finding out about your MS . . . how much it affected all of us," she began. "I cried so much when I heard last night. But Connor told us not to badger you with messages."

I continued scratching, nodding to acknowledge her thoughtfulness.

"The thing is, I want to be there for you. If you need anything, just let me know, okay?" She pulled her legs up and crossed them on the ottoman she was sitting on. "I mean, I'll be far away, but in terms of emotional support, you know?"

"Thanks."

"You were always there for me, and I'll never forget that. I still have the *Airbender* back brace." She smiled and then lowered her voice to a whisper. "Don't tell anyone, but I took it with me to school in Chicago. It's in my dorm right now."

I laughed. "Well, it took me two weeks to finish. I hope it's framed somewhere."

She laughed too. Then blurted, "Adam, you know I'd keep whatever you made me, right?"

I went back to scratching my elbow. This situation was painful. But she was looking at me for a response. "Yeah."

"I don't know how to say this, but it's been a long time coming, and now I feel like I can't go back without saying it. That you're important to me."

"You guys are important to me, too."

"Just to rest my mind, is there someone else for you?" She

spoke softly and slowly, like she was trying to make it less painful for me, and for her. For us, I guess.

I was about to quickly blurt, *No, no there isn't anyone, but I don't want anyone now*, just to stop this thing before it started, but then . . . it would keep something open.

In Emma P.'s eyes it would mean that there could be a chance.

But while Emma P. was someone kind and fun, she wasn't the someone for me. She wasn't the someone I *chose*.

She was part of the friend family I'd been dealt.

I hesitated, trying to select my words carefully.

And then Zayneb, sitting at the back of the plane, a light above her head, came to me.

Wait. Yeah, there *had* been someone else starting to put roots in my heart. And even though it lasted only until yesterday afternoon, after which the roots froze cold, their remnants were still there.

I could call them to mind.

Because this was an emergency situation.

"This is hard to say, Emma, but yeah, there is someone." I stopped scratching. "I met her right before getting back to Doha."

"Oh," she said, her voice even softer.

And then there was nothing, no more words from her, or questions, nobody else around to break the silence. No elbow scratching from me either.

Just her face clouding fast in disappointment and me trying not to see it.

Then, after a long, long pause, she uncrossed her legs, dropped them, and leaned forward so she was at the edge of the ottoman, her hands clutching the cushion on either side of her, as though she were going to launch herself out of it. "Okay, I guess. I guess I should be happy to know the truth."

I didn't know what to say.

Because it wasn't the truth.

As an act of solidarity with me and my diagnosis, everyone in the group, including Emma D., who'd dropped by while we were gathering for the photo, after visiting a friend, and even Tsetso, who was already back at university in France, posted the group picture of us on all our socials, with no message accompanying it.

We posted it right then and there, at the exact same time, everyone back at our spots on the patio, Connor passing around bags of chips he'd rummaged from the kitchen.

It was one of those pictures that was frame worthy, that would be talked about when we grew up, that already felt nostalgic.

I looked at it and whispered a prayer of gratitude.

Gratitude for the fact that I *did* have this special family of friends.

In the photo, we were settled on the sunshine-filled lawn, looking up, sitting in a semicircle around one of the big white rocks. Hanna had stood on top of it to take our picture with her iPad, after a vigorous debate with Connor as to whose device had the better camera.

I'm in the middle, Jacob on one side of me, with Madison and Isaac beside him, Connor on the other side of me, and then Emma Z., Emma D., and Emma P. We were all smiling up into the camera. But Emma P. and me?

Our smiles were forced.

"Your sister takes great pictures, Adam," Emma D. said, motioning Hanna over. "This is awesome, Hanna. Thanks."

"*See* Adam? I *am* a great photographer!" Hanna crossed her arms at me before flouncing over to sit on the arm of my chair.

"I didn't say you weren't."

"You deleted the pictures I sent you from the museum yesterday. The ones with Zayneb."

I stared at her.

Hanna laughed. "I saw you deleting them last night! From my bedroom window!"

She scooted away, back to her bike.

Oh God. She's such a sneak. Her bedroom window faces the patio. Where I'd been sitting last night after dinner, while Dad read to Hanna in her room.

She must have used that telescope she keeps at her window.

Everyone looked at me, some more pointedly than others.

I avoided Emma P.'s face.

"I was with Zayneb before I came here." Emma D. picked up a chip from the pile in her palm. "She found out more information on how her grandmother passed away."

Inna lillahi wa inna ilayhi rajioon. The prayer came immediately to me. *To God we belong and to God we return.*

"That sucks," Connor said, passing the bag of chips my way, along with an inquisitive glance.

He was checking my reaction on hearing about Zayneb. So I gave him a sincere one. "I hope Zayneb's okay."

"She is. But it was really terrible. Her grandmother died months back in Pakistan, and they only found out now that it was in—get this—a drone strike. Her family'd never known." Emma D. shook her head and rubbed her palms together to get rid of chip crumbs. "She's so down. And yeah, angry. Like anyone would be."

Emma P. spoke. "That's awful. We should do something for her."

"Oh, yeah, maybe we can stop by her place? She was just in bed when I left her." Emma D. perked up. "We can take some food or something? Ms. Raymond would probably like that, for us to see her."

"Who's in?" Emma P. looked around.

Madison, Jacob, Isaac, and Connor bowed out, having other things to do. Emma Z. said, "Of course!"

Emma P. turned to me, and I tried not to see too much in her gaze, but it was there, that slight *Is this the girl you met who you told me about?* That *aha!* curiosity.

"I can't," I said. "Dad promised Hanna some stuff later this afternoon, after which we're going to sit her down to tell her about my MS."

She nodded, satisfied.

I couldn't help adding something. "But can you tell Zayneb I'll do a dua for her grandmother today, with my dad? A prayer?"

She nodded again.

When everyone left, I went down to the workroom, bringing along one of the folding chairs from the patio. I set it in the middle of the empty, half-painted room and sat on it to gaze around, to envision everything again.

My ideas were half-formed, but I knew what I wanted. I wanted a reminder of the good things in life, the marvels of the world, for these to flood whoever walked into the room. Filled with lights and shapes and sudden little details that were hidden until they weren't, until you came upon them at the right time.

I dipped my head back and stared at the ceiling.

The sky atop was a brilliant blue, like Hanna's azurite . . . like Zayneb's scarf.

I stood and folded the chair to take it out of the room.

Maybe I'd finish painting everything.

But the ladder, leaning in a corner, only reminded me of Tuesday, and then the thoughts came tumbling back.

What if I get another attack? When I'm on my own?

Dad made it a point to check on me every few hours, and I was okay with that, but what about when he went back to work?

We had an appointment with a neurologist this week, but that didn't mean it would be smooth sailing after.

It didn't mean I could get my life sorted out again.

But I *could* sort the pieces I'd started working on for the room. The thin blades of wood, the flattened bottle caps I'd scraped the paint off of and then drilled with patterned holes to let light through, that I was going to use in homage to the geometry found in nature—I could sort these little bits of art I'd collected.

On the table in the hall outside the room, I laid out the pieces by the parts of the room they went to in my installation: ceiling, floor, left wall, right wall, far wall, and entrance wall.

I sorted and tried not to think about anything else.

The thing about making things is that it soothes every part of me. And connects everything in me too.

It's the thing that gets me up in the morning.

What if I didn't have that anymore? What if I couldn't *get up in the morning to make anything?*

I put down the box of LED light tape I'd been holding in my hand. Back in the box and not in the section of the table I'd designated for ceiling items.

Since the news was out about my MS, out with Dad, my friends, and soon with Hanna, it emerged in the real world.

Like a boggart from Harry Potter's world, it took shape in front of me. Unmoving, but relentlessly forcing itself into my thoughts.

My MS, it was real now.

I didn't want to climb the ladder to finish painting the room.

I was scared to.

I wasn't part of any Hogwarts houses, because there wasn't a house for people who'd rather tuck away, overwhelmed with fear.

Hanna came thundering down the stairs in her turbaned hijab and sunglasses, and the boggart disappeared. "Dad is calling you to pray Asr! And then can we play Monopoly? Dad said yes!"

"Sure." I left the table.

"When are you going to start the world in a room? Like the house in a jar?" Hanna fingered one of the bottle caps and then slid her sunglasses up onto her turban to examine the pattern of holes on it.

"Soon." I went to the stairs.

"Oh, I love it! Is this a goose?" Hanna picked up the small Canada goose I'd begun whittling yesterday. "It so perfect. Like Mom's goose she made."

She hugged it to her heart.

I nodded. "You can have it when I'm done."

"WHAT! It's for me?" Hanna came over and threw her arms around me. "Thanks, Adam. I knew it was good to choose you for a topic for my Weekly Reflection journal this week. Mr. Mellon told us to choose something that made us proud. I chose you."

We went up the stairs together. "Mr. Mellon gave you home-work for spring break?"

"Yeah, can you believe it?" She led the way to the prayer mats spread in Dad's study. Dad was sitting at his desk, reading the Qur'an, so Hanna lowered her voice. "But we won't talk about it. Because there's someone here who'll say it's a conflict of interest if I talk about how mean that is, to give kids homework when they're supposed to be having fun."

When Asr prayer was done, I brought up Zayneb's grandmother, and Dad said some duas for her soul to reach the highest of heavens, for her soul to be reunited with God.

As I said ameen, I tried not to think of Zayneb in tears.

"Why'd you delete Zayneb's pictures?" Hanna asked as we were putting away the prayer mats after Dad had left. "If you want us to pray for her grandmother?"

"What do you mean?"

"I mean you looked like you were mad at her, deleting her pictures like that. But now you're caring about her."

"I'm caring about her *grandmother*."

"Because you care about *her*, right?"

I shook my head. "Listen, nosy, you'd better get the Monopoly game set up before I change my mind about playing."

She unwound her hijab and stuffed it into the basket of prayer mats. "Just remember, she's our cuz. And that she said sorry to me after I sent her the pictures. And Dad said *he'd* set up the Monopoly board! That's where he went."

She left the room.

I pulled out my phone.

I *hadn't* deleted the photos of Zayneb and me at the museum. Without looking at them, I'd dumped them in a random album. In case Hanna asked me later if I'd received them and looked in my phone, a thing she did randomly.

Finding the series of photos, I scrolled through them.

I paused on a picture that Hanna had taken as a selfie of me and her. Zayneb was in the background, smiling at our backs. But in the next selfie, same spot, with her in the background again, she was frowning at a display she was reading.

Maybe what drew me to Zayneb was the same thing that made me stay away from her.

She wasn't like a steady heartbeat. She had a heart that moved and rose and fell as things affected her.

I flipped to another picture. There it was again.

She was really frowning in this one, by a display of ornaments worn by the lower classes and slaves.

She was alive with passions, so alive that they exploded out of her, plain to see, loud and proud, not hidden. Like mine were.

Something flooded through me; maybe it was impulsiveness; maybe it was desire; maybe it was even *physical* desire at seeing her face so vividly like this, where I could look at it unhindered by anyone. I don't know what it was, but it felt exciting.

It felt exciting to be connected to someone so full of life.

And maybe it was because of the dua I'd just made to pull me out of this sunken feeling, but I gave in to the desire.

I wanted it wrapped around me, to be a part of it.

I didn't press pause on what was coursing through me, because it felt real.

I kicked pragmatism aside and went for it. Went for her.

No matter the outcome.

Zayneb, I'm sorry to hear about your grandmother. My dad and I (and Hanna) prayed for her.

Zayneb, I can't figure out what happened yesterday between us. But there's one thing I CAN figure out and that's how much I don't know. How I don't know what you went through at school. With your teacher. I don't know about the extent of the Islamophobia you've faced. I don't know what it feels like to be you. But here's another thing: I DO want to know.

I paused and then added But if you don't want me to know, I get that, too.

I followed up the message with a picture.

It was the one with both of us on the landing of the museum stairs, looking up at the ceiling.

The light's shining down on us, and we look sort of magical.

Hanna's random photo clicks were the best.

Almost as good as her heart.

FIVE MINUTES AFTER AUNTIE NANDY LEFT FOR THE GYM, I HEARD
a knock on the apartment door. I didn't have time to scarf up, so I
hooded myself with Binky, pulling the blanket off my bed, draping
it onto my head with the rest of its length dragging down my back
and onto the tiled floor behind me, its width wrapped around my
pajama shorts. Whoever it was at the door would get a jolt at my
ghostlike appearance.

I didn't give a shit.

I opened the door to the Emmas.

We stared at one another for a few seconds, me at their mourn-
ful expressions and appearances—Emma Z. holding a plastic bag
of what looked like take-out containers, Emma P. clutching a bou-
quet of flowers, and Emma D., empty-handed but back again—
and them staring at my white-shrouded self.

I turned and led the way to the living room.

"We're so sorry to hear about your grandmother," Emma P.
said, placing the flowers on the dining table.

"This is for whenever you feel up to eating." Emma Z. placed
the bag of food beside the flowers. "Whenever."

I nodded from the corner of the big sofa I'd already settled into, cocooned in my blanket. Emma D. joined me, taking a seat to my left. Emma P. proceeded to Adam's—the club chair—and Emma Z. sat on the two-seater.

"You guys know she died in October, right?" I asked. "That's when they killed her."

They nodded.

"And you know who did it, right?" I asked. "*We* did. Because we're okay with bombing other countries."

They nodded again.

"I'm really angry. Then get sad. Then angry. It just doesn't stop."

"Are there some special prayers you can say? Or things you can do?" Emma Z. said. "To help?"

"There *are* things. And I've said them." I sighed and pulled the bedspread around me tighter.

"Is that something special you have to wear when someone passes?" Emma P. indicated my blanketed self with her hands rotating in the air.

"This? No, it's my blanket." I dropped it from my head so that it fell back and showed my pajama top. "I'm wearing pajamas. And I didn't know if you guys were *guys*, so I used my bedspread as a scarf."

"Oh, sorry!" Emma P. looked embarrassed. "I just thought . . . I don't know what I thought."

"It's okay."

"Your hair is nice," Emma P. said, rotating her hands again, this time a bit higher to indicate the messy hair escaping from a quick, high bun I'd wound it in.

We sat silently for a while.

Then I got up, emerging completely from the white blanket, and went to the kitchen. "You guys want drinks?"

There was nothing in the fridge.

I came back to the living room empty-handed. "Well, there doesn't seem to be any if you did want some."

"Hey, we're okay. We just wanted to make sure *you* were going to be okay," Emma D. said. "Where's Ms. Raymond?"

"Gym." I remembered Auntie Nandy's stash of junk food. "Wait. I got something."

I dragged the big blue bin into the dining room and pried the lid off. "There's stuff in here."

They stayed seated. "Zayneb, it's okay. We're good," said Emma D.

"Pop? Chips? Chocolate?" I held up different items. "It's all in here. If I don't feed you, I'll feel my dad's disapproval all the way from Pakistan. It's a Muslim thing."

"We just came from Adam's house and had a ton of junk there," Emma Z. said.

"Aha, Twizzlers!" I lifted the bag high like it was a trophy, then peered back into the bin, as I'd caught sight of the edge of a box that had become dislodged. I dunked my hand in.

Cigarettes. *Auntie Nandy smokes? Or did?*

I didn't pull it out, just moved it, but when I did, a bottle covered in a plastic bag, wound tight with rubber bands, came free from underneath.

Emma D. got up. "Okay, let's break out the Twizzlers, then."

I tossed the package to her and took out a few cans of pop and passed those to Emma Z., and then dragged the box back to Auntie Nandy's bedroom, into her closet.

Had to hide the bin of sin quickly.

But before I tucked it into its spot on the floor, under her row of pants folded on hangers, I examined the plastic bundle by taking off the rubber bands and undoing it.

Yup, booze.

Auntie Nandy wasn't Muslim—so why did she have to hide it?

It took me a while to reassemble everything back to its place so she wouldn't suspect a thing, and by the time I got back, the Emmas were chewing on Twizzlers.

When I sat back on my blanket, Emma D. passed me the package, and I took one out. I looked at the shiny red twisted candy for a moment. "I want to make someone pay for my grandmother's death."

I didn't need to look up to know they'd traded glances with one another.

"But does that actually make the world a better place?" Emma P. ventured. "Like, doesn't that just make more problems?"

"Sorry not sorry to say this to you, Emma P., but that's what people who don't feel the pain of injustice say." I bit into the Twizzler and gave her a stare, chewing fast. "Like, why are we supposed to just take it? Innocent people getting killed?"

This time they didn't trade glances but shifted uncomfortably in unison. Then Emma Z. spoke. "I don't think that's what Emma P. was trying to say, Zayneb. I think she's trying to say that the better people should do better. Right, Emma?"

Emma P. nodded, nibbling on her Twizzler.

"But are we better people? Is it being better just to look away? Or post a few words of outrage online? What's so BETTER about that?" I put the rest of my Twizzler on the arm of the sofa. It was plasticky and felt like lead going down my throat. "Isn't it better to stop it for good?"

253

"We went on a march before. In London. It was our junior-year trip and we were in Hyde Park and there was a march to remember the victims of war and we joined," Emma D. said.

"And the shoes to remember Palestinian victims? In Brussels?" Emma Z. asked Emma D., sitting up. She turned to me, eagerly. "Last year, on our senior trip, we went to Belgium, and we saw all these shoes, over four thousand, laid out to remember Palestinian lives lost in the last decade. That's the kind of *better* we mean."

"But did those things make a difference? NO." I stood up and paced, something Kavi pointed out I do when I get an energy spurt. "I've been reading a lot since last night about drones and war. The biggest global protest event in history occurred when we were babies, February fifteenth, 2003. People in over sixty countries, almost fifteen million people around the world, including a huge march in Rome that made the Guinness World Records, protested the invasion of Iraq. The protest was monumental. Unmatched before and since. But GUESS WHAT? The invasion still happened. And guess what? Overreach from that war, which lasts to this day, killed my grandmother!"

I slumped back into the blanket I'd shed and re-cocooned myself, including shielding my face, sure it was burning up in pain and anger.

"It's true we have to do more. But not through violent actions." Emma Z. spoke quietly. "Because that would just continue violence."

I pulled the folds apart in front of my mouth so they could hear me. "I'm not a violent person. I'm not advocating violence. But I *am* an angry person. I'm advocating for more people to get angry. Get moved."

"Well, I'm going to be honest," Emma D. said. "Until I met

you, I didn't think about it much. War and justice, things like that. Now I will."

"Same," Emma Z. agreed.

"Me too," Emma P. said. "I'm going back to Northwestern, and I'm going to join the antiwar club."

I poked my head out of the blanket. "You go to Northwestern? That's on my list. Just got rejected from UChicago, so not sure I'll get in. My sis goes to UChicago, and I was going to live with her."

"Oh, I hope you get in! Ill show you around, no problem. And we can hang out together." Emma P. looked excited. Genuinely excited.

I let go of how tightly I was holding on to Binky as I felt some of myself relaxing.

I looked at their kind faces, reassessing, and I realized something.

They weren't the enemy. Their ignorance was bothersome, but they weren't the enemy.

"Thanks for offering to help, Emma P." I sighed and gave away holding on to my security blanket and then undid and rewound my hair bun. "And thanks, guys, for coming. And eating Twizzlers with me. You guys have been one of the best parts of visiting Doha, you know?"

Emma Z. blew a kiss my way. "We love you, too. So much that we did a search-and-destroy mission." She looked at Emma P. "You tell her, because it was your idea."

"When we were at Madison's place the other day, Emma Z. and I stole her Coachella headdress and destroyed it," Emma P. announced proudly. She raised her eyebrows at Emma D., who looked confused. "We didn't tell you, because we didn't want it to be on your Hufflepuff conscience. It involved some methods we Ravenclaws and Slytherins are familiar and comfortable with."

I beamed at the Emmas. Who . . . maybe were becoming *my* Emmas?

"Zayneb, you have to keep in touch with us. Emma P. and I are leaving tomorrow. She's staying with me on the East Coast before going back to Chicago," Emma Z. said. She smiled at Emma P. before turning to Emma D. "Wish *you* were coming."

"One day!" Emma D. turned to me. "I leave for Toronto on Tuesday. It wasn't even spring break there. I just skipped classes."

"She's Canadian, like Adam," Emma P. informed me. Was it my imagination, or did she widen her eyes at his name? At me?

There was an awkward silence.

Emma Z. leaned forward. "So, did you meet Adam here in Doha or before? Asking because he's so quiet but, you know, befriends people fast."

"Technically before Doha." I tried not to whip my head to look at Emma P. Her interest in my answer was practically palpable, the way she made small, jittery movements on my right. "We met on the plane over here."

"Oh my God, that's so cute," Emma D. blurted, before becoming subdued again, maybe on account of Emma P.'s feelings. "How? He just came up to you?"

I thought about it. Seeing him—okay, *supercute* him—advancing down the aisle of the airplane, the way we locked eyes immediately after those first couple of times we saw each other in the waiting area. I remembered the jolt of pure happiness that went through my body when he'd said salaam to me on the plane. First, because he'd been one of those guys who actually salaamed a girl, instead of acting like we didn't exist, and second, because the cute guy I'd noticed *had actually been Muslim*. Which is a pure sort of *rare.* "Yeah, he did just come up to me. Because he knew I was Muslim, because of my hijab, I guess."

Emma Z. sat back and glanced at Emma P., who began twisting a lock of her long brown hair.

I turned to look at Emma P. "But it's nothing like that, okay? We're just friends. Or cousins, as Hanna calls us. You know my aunt and his mom were best friends, right?"

She nodded, relief lighting her face, causing her to let go of her hair. "Oh yeah, I forgot. And yeah, that's okay." She looked at the other girls and shrugged her shoulders. "It's okay, because Adam is not into me. He told me clearly, just today in fact. He's into someone else, he said. Someone he met before he came to Doha."

"We just wondered if it was you that he was talking about, ha-ha." Emma Z. laughed. "But obviously it wasn't."

I just stared at them.

Because obviously it was.

I decided to write Kavi a long e-mail about what had happened to Daadi. Out of everyone, she, my best friend, would understand my sadness the most.

I needed to set it down in words before I spoke to her in person.

In the middle of composing the e-mail, tears streaming down my face as I thought of how happy Daadi must have felt to get into that car headed for a traditional village wedding, right in the middle of that grief, a message from Adam came in.

Zayneb, I'm sorry to hear about your grandmother. My dad and I (and Hanna) prayed for her.

Zayneb, I can't figure out what happened yesterday between us. But there's one thing I CAN figure out and that's how much I don't know. How I don't know what you went through at school. With your teacher. I don't know about the extent of Islamophobia you've faced. I don't know what it feels like to be you. But here's another thing: I DO want to know. But if you don't want me to know, I get that, too.

I lifted up the edge of my pajama T-shirt to wipe away my tears and then enlarged the picture of us he sent right after this message. It was the same one I'd favorited yesterday when Hanna had first sent it, making a mental note to crop Adam out.

I sniffed and went back to my e-mail to Kavi. When I finished, I pressed send without rereading it. Kavi needed to hear my uncensored, unedited thoughts.

Then I went back to what had become my favorite pastime since last night: research.

I now know more about drone warfare than I ever have, more than most topics I was interested in previously. I know that every US president increased the military's drone program, no matter what political party he belonged to.

Everyone had blood on their hands.

But I couldn't find the answer to one thing I'd been searching for: What made the public okay with it? With accepting the killing of innocent people?

The answer came in the evening, when my sister, Sadia, messaged me an old picture of Daadi and me on the first day of second grade.

My grandmother was holding my hand, about to walk me to school.

She was dressed in a loud pink-and-green shalwar kameez, a long scarf wound around her head.

She was different-looking, but the same, too. Same, like a lot of the other people killed *over there*.

Maybe she looked too Muslim. And people thought it was okay if some Muslims got killed, because so many Muslims were weird anyway, like Fencer believed.

Like, if you believed Muslims were the type of people who buried girls alive, you would be okay with them being dealt with.

My grandmother in her pink-and-green suit with a covered head, holding my hand tenderly, looked into my eyes now and told me the truth:

Islamophobia is the thing keeping it okay to kill people like us without repercussions.

Then, with this realization, I fell asleep, exhausted.

Auntie Nandy was sitting at the edge of my bed when I woke up. "I'm sorry to be sitting here like this, but do you want to eat something with me? It's past dinnertime."

I nodded, my eyes on the ceiling. "The Emmas bought some food. It's on the table."

"Zayneb, I couldn't help seeing your phone when I came and sat down, and there are a few messages from Adam." Auntie Nandy cleared her throat. "Totally didn't read them. Just thought you should know."

I nodded again, too heart tired to care whether Auntie Nandy had seen them, or about Adam messaging me.

She left the room to set up dinner, and I stepped into the shower and into a decision.

I'm not going to let up on Fencer.

I don't care if they expel me.

Because that isn't worse than having my grandmother taken from me.

• • •

"Are you okay going out tomorrow?" Auntie Nandy passed me the tray of sushi rolls.

I took two and said, "Where?"

"Well, there's a concert happening at Katara. Again, if you're up to it, we can go earlier, look around, then sit for the concert. It's the Qatar Philharmonic Orchestra, but, because it's spring break and Katara will be full of kids, they're playing popular movie soundtracks."

"Okay."

"Some friends of mine will be meeting up there for the symphony part, but we'll be on our own to wander Katara," she assured me.

"I'm fine with anything," I said, mixing wasabi into my soy sauce puddle.

"Maybe it will be good for you to go out. Just feel the air."

I kept swirling the wasabi with my chopsticks, staring at it instead of Auntie Nandy's face. "Did Mom tell you why I was suspended?"

"Yes, that you drew something that the school thought was threatening."

"There's more to it." And then I told her. About #EatThemAlive. Everything about Fencer. And Mom and Dad wanting me to lie low.

And how it felt like Fencer and his kind had killed Daadi. "Am I reaching, Auntie Nandy? Am I crazy? For wanting my grandmother not to have died? Not to have died like *that*?" I began sobbing, covering my face.

I felt Auntie Nandy's arms around me, then heard her voice. "You're not crazy; you're in pain. You have a right to feel pain. And you know what?" She paused and waited for me to move my hands away from my face before she reached up and lifted my chin until I looked at her. "You have every right to want justice."

"But then why do Mom and Dad act like I can't feel this?"

"They just want to protect you from the consequences you'll get for fighting for justice. Because there *will* be consequences when you shake the world." She pulled out the chair closest to me and sat in it. "But here's a secret: If you plot and plan wisely, the consequences are less unexpected."

"You mean to plot quietly? My friend Ayaan did that, and she, too, got in trouble."

"You plot so quietly that no one knows anything, then you spring, armed with the facts, like I did with Marc at the pool." She reached across to her plate and picked up a sushi roll and popped it into her mouth, chewing fast before speaking again. "I'm going to say something really radical now. That you have to promise you won't tell your mom came from me."

I paused, a roll on its way into my own mouth. "I promise."

"If everyone listened to their parents who feared the consequences of fighting for justice, this world would be a more awful place than it is now."

"It's already an awful place."

"Imagine if it were even worse? If Nelson Mandela had feared the consequences of fighting against apartheid? If Malcolm X and Rosa Parks and Martin Luther King had?"

"If their parents had held them back?"

"No, if they'd *listened* to their parents, or anyone else for that matter, holding them back." Auntie Nandy turned to face me fully. "That itch in your heart for justice was put there by God. Your bravery, too. Don't let anyone squash it—it's like squashing the source of it."

I leaned over and hugged her.

She made me feel proud of my angry self.
But yeah, I had to learn to be quietly angry.
Spring without a roar.
And spring I will.
Insha'Allah.

إن شاء الله

MARVEL: ANGER

> *You cut me*
> *Now I sit, sharpening my blade*
> *One day I will loom, a shadow no more*
> *Silence your hate, leave it shredded*
> *Strewn around your feet*
> *The only sign I've roared my pain:*
> *You*
> *Cut*
> *Down.*

I sent this poem to Kavi too, with the subject line *I've started writing poetry.*

Kavi called and cried with me. She, too, had felt Daadi's loving hands.

As I was going to bed, I finally looked at the new messages from Adam.

> We prayed again for your grandmother, at Maghrib.

Then: Hope we can clear this up before you leave.

Then: I swear I'm not trying to bother you, just not leave it like this between us.

Then: I've never met anyone like you before.

Then finally: It's like we were meant to meet, but then I ruined it somehow. I'm sorry.

Lying on my pillow, I shook my head.

Because *he* didn't ruin it somehow.

The circumstances of our lives did.

ADAM

TUESDAY, MARCH 19

ODDITY: *IMAGINING THE FUTURE*

THE EXPERIENCES OF MS PATIENTS VARY CONSIDERABLY. SOME degenerate fast and furious. Some take a general, slow decline. Some experience symptoms sporadically.

Mine seems to be the latter. And that makes me fearful.

Maybe it's because mine is at the beginning stages, but it's like waiting for the ax to drop, the other shoe to fall, the tension of not knowing where you'll be, ability-wise, the next day, next week, next month.

It's stressful. And right now it immobilizes me.

I lay in bed, staring at the ceiling beams, thoughts gathering at the back of my head, some telling me to get up and get downstairs to work on the room while I could, to use my hands to bring it to life.

And then there were other thoughts, cautioning me to preserve myself, to not make a movement, to wait for the inevitable.

For the first time in a long time, I wanted someone to talk me out of these crippling thoughts.

I glanced at my phone and saw that Zayneb hadn't replied to any of my messages.

I wanted her around.

Her straight-shooting talk would be welcome now. And the way she said things so resolutely.

I needed that sense of bravado.

I also wanted to just *see* her.

I sighed and scrolled through my messages to find Connor.
Hey, you up to anything?

Just about to play. League of Legends.

You want to play here?

You ok?

Yeah.

I'll be there in a bit.

Connor brought his gaming laptop and set it up in my room.

I'd attempted to make myself look less pitiful. So I was sitting up, still in bed, and scrolling mindlessly on my phone.

Connor tried my desk chair out, giving it a spin. "Wait, let me see if Jacob's getting online. We've been playing together. Duo."

He put his phone on speaker and dialed. Madison picked up, groggy sounding. "Hello? Connor?"

"Hey, where's Jacob?"

"In the shower."

"Tell him to give me a call. You guys have plans today?"

"No, just hanging out. We're at the Hyatt. You know how Jacob's parents don't like us staying over at each other's?"

"Oh, right."

"So we're spending the last days in Doha together at the Hyatt." She laughed. "They think we already flew back to college. Think we left last night."

"You guys are baaaad."

"Hey, *my* parents know."

"Okay, then forget about telling your man to call me. I was just checking if he was getting online for League." Connor hovered his finger over his phone to end the call. "Bye, talk later, have fun in that room." He laughed before hanging up.

I looked at the guitar on the floor by the bedroom door. The one I'd made sure to bring to Doha because Hanna had wanted me to play at her birthday, coming up in a few days, but that I hadn't touched except to check its journeying condition. "Pass me my guitar, by the door?"

"I don't know how those guys do it, Madison and Jacob. The way they can't see each other when they're at school, different countries, and then they can't *see* each other, if you know what I mean, when they're together here, either. Summer's going to be brutal for them, when everyone goes back home. Jacob's family to Spain and Madison's to Australia." Connor handed me the guitar and sat back down in my chair. He laughed wildly. "And now they're banging for all its worth."

"Okay, relax." I strummed a few notes.

"Why? It's one of the best parts of life, man." He turned to his laptop and activated it from sleep.

"Didn't say anything about it."

"You told Emma P. you weren't into her, huh?" He tilted his head to consider me. "That there's someone else?"

I began to play the opening notes of "Seasons in the Sun," Mom's favorite song. Then paused. "Yeah."

"Who's the someone else? Because you told me there wasn't anyone else."

"I wasn't sure she liked me, too. I'm still not sure." I picked up the chords again from where I'd left off.

"What's she like? I don't know her anyway, so fill me in completely."

I played a bit more, then stopped. "She's sure about herself, who she is as a person, and just cares about stuff. And is an activist. And cute."

"And is she Gryffindor and Slytherin and Muslim?" Connor twirled in the chair and faced me. "The Zee person. Forgot her name again."

"Zayneb."

"Oh man, I thought so from the moment I saw you look at her at your dad's party!" he said, snapping his hand at me, excited he'd gotten it right. "You were a goner from then."

I shrugged in acceptance. Maybe I was.

"What's holding you back? Is she available?"

"Yeah. I mean, I don't know. We're just talking to each other. Me more than her."

"Why isn't she falling for Adam, the wonder kid?" Something dawned on his face. "Wait. It's not because you've got MS, right? That she's not into you?"

"No. Okay, stop. You're making a story in your head. She's mourning her grandmother. Change the subject."

"Forgive me. I just don't want you to stay a virgin all your life, dude."

"Ass."

"You're lucky I'm turning the crass down, 'cause I like you. Only 'cause you used to save my math grade all the time."

He laughed and turned to his game.

I finished playing "Seasons in the Sun."

. . .

After a couple of hours of him gaming while throwing out song challenges for me to play on the guitar, he packed up to leave.

I made myself walk downstairs with him, walk him to the door. And then out the door too.

I sat on one of the pair of white rocks right at the entrance to our pathway and just looked at the back of his car as he drove away, down the avenue of sprawling white houses, "Spanish villa" type houses, as Zayneb had called ours.

The sky Connor drove off toward was a vivid, distinct blue, and I stared at it, wondering if I noticed everything blue suddenly because of the blue scarves she wore. Zayneb.

I wondered what was under the scarf.

What she was like, completely at home, somewhere.

I could almost imagine it, but it was like a dream that you wake up and try to remember but only have the wispy fringes of.

Like a face that you've seen so much—but when you try to conjure it to hold in your head, it's too ethereal to stay still and clear.

Maybe it was Connor bringing up sex before, about Madison and Jacob, them in their hotel room, but I couldn't stop thinking about her.

I went inside and back to bed.

Hanna had been at her friend's house down the street, but the minute she got back home, I knew it. My door was closed, locked, so she knocked a pattern on it, politely—first. I knew it would get incessant soon, so I immediately called out to get her to stop. "Yeah?"

"Can you open this thing?"

"What is it?"

"I wanted to see if you're okay. Because, you know. The MS thing."

Dad and I had talked to her last night about it. And though she'd reached for Stillwater *and* one of Mom's photos while listening, she'd been surprisingly strong on hearing the news.

But then the checking on me started. Like this morning when she woke up, then before she went to her friend's, and . . . now.

I sighed. "I'm okay."

"Can you open it?"

"Hanna, I'm okay. I'll come down soon."

"How soon?"

"Soon soon."

"Okay, I'm waiting then."

She left and I sighed again.

Maybe she *was* spoiled.

Or maybe she just cared too much.

There are two ways to see everything, I guess.

Maybe lately I've been seeing things only in one way. Only in the hopeless, helpless way.

I grabbed my Marvels and Oddities journal off my desk and flipped through it.

Yeah, sure enough, everything had become oddities.

I went back farther and saw that I'd always been a marvel-heavy observer.

Maybe that's how I'd kept myself afloat, all those years.

Everyone told Dad that he was "lucky" that I was so "good." How he'd done a "good" job, given the circumstances.

Of Mom passing away.

And being in another country.

And converting to a new religion as a family.

What they'd meant was that I was easy to handle, didn't talk back or push limits.

But maybe it wasn't that I was just good or that Dad had done a good job.

Maybe it had been this journal.

This way of noticing that even during the suckiest moments in life there was something marvelous to be seen, heard, touched. Or just a tiny awe felt in the heart.

Maybe it was going out of my way to try to notice something, this noticing, that had saved me all along.

And now I couldn't see anything good.

Because I had stopped trying.

Before I went down to show Hanna I was okay, I picked up a pen and wrote three marvels to make up for the ones I'd missed the last few days.

MARVEL ONE: CONNOR

Yeah, Connor. Because when he'd thrown out random songs for me to play on the guitar, he interspersed them with repeated requests of "Leaves from the Vine." From *Avatar: The Last Airbender*.

Because it was the first song that I'd ever learned.

The first one I picked up a guitar for.

He knew this and remembered it, and it was like the *I love you, man* that I'd needed today.

MARVEL TWO: HANNA

Because the minute she got home, she came up to check on me.

MARVEL THREE: BLUE SKIES

What I meant was Zayneb, because that sky had reminded me of her so fast, and now she was still in my head.

ZAYNEB
TUESDAY, MARCH 19
ODDITY . . . AND MARVEL: PLOTTERS

KATARA TURNED OUT TO BE MAGICAL. WE ARRIVED AT THE GOLDEN hour, with the sun setting, and it was like stepping back in time, into another world, pristine and protected.

The first thing we saw was the dazzling mosque, covered with geometric designs and calligraphy in dark and light blues, interspersed with gold.

Two pigeon towers stood in front of it. I couldn't stop staring at the birds going in and out of the holes that ran up and down the tall, clay, conelike structures, with wooden perches sticking out in a pattern.

Auntie Nandy took my hand and led me to a bench, and we sat there for a long time, watching.

Something about it was like floating in the pool. So I let go.

We spent time wandering around the cultural village completely constructed to look like cities from another era, especially the cities of the Muslim golden ages in Baghdad, Timbuktu, and Spain, with small galleries and cafés and petite museums and restaurants and symmetrical gardens.

It was like we'd left *our* era.

It felt like a sanctuary.

"I love this," I said to Auntie Nandy, indicating the water flowing in neat streams at the edges of the buildings, where the foundation met the paved stone path, the sound providing just the right amount of melody, soothing and calm. "Can we sit here, too?"

"Of course." Auntie Nandy pointed at a bench. "We'll need to be at the amphitheater in fifteen minutes, so we've got a bit of time."

Once we sat, I leaned on Auntie Nandy, and she put her arm around me.

"You know you and I are alike, right?" Auntie Nandy asked. "You got your can't-be-a-bystander genes from me."

I nodded. "Yeah, I figured that."

"That means I can be firm in what I'm about to say, Zayneb, and you have to listen to me like it's *you* telling you. Okay?" She waited until I agreed before continuing, her voice solemn. "You need to have a way to take care of yourself. A way to recharge. Otherwise the world will get you down so fast, you won't be able to hold your head up. I learned this the hard way."

"I know how to take care of myself, Auntie Nandy. I'm about to go to college."

"I mean, like this. Like sitting here listening to the water. Like looking at the birds earlier. Like sitting in a tub with fizzy bath bombs."

I couldn't stop myself. "But not like smoking, right? Or boozing? From the bin?"

She tilted her head to try to look at me. After catching that first glimpse of her expression, I kept my Slytherin head securely down against her and my mouth clenched tight in an attempt not to laugh.

273

"Zayneb. Did you go through my stuff? Without me?"

"It was an accident. I was trying to be a good host to the Emmas."

"Oh no, did they see?" Auntie Nandy let go of me, and I looked up, worried she was angry at me.

"No, no, don't worry—they didn't," I assured her quickly. "Nobody looked in the bin except me."

She sighed and put her hands in the pockets of the dress she was wearing. "Actually, I'm glad you're bringing that up. It goes with my point; you need to find healthy ways to center yourself. Otherwise, you'll dip into the bin too much."

"I'm sorry, Auntie Nandy, for looking too deeply into it, into the bin." I hugged her to emphasize my apology. "I call it the bin of sin."

She laughed. "True, that it is. I try to keep myself away from that bin of sin. Sometimes I lapse. But you'd better *never*."

"My bin of sin would have a ton of macarons and cream puffs. Only French pastries."

"Well, isn't that snobby." She stood up. "Let's get going? It's a bit of a walk to the amphitheater."

As the sun descended, the sky turned yellowish-pinkish-purplish blue.

It was such a breathtaking walk to the open-air concert that I arrived with a bit of space opened in my heart.

We got spots directly across from the stage, not too high up, with Auntie Nandy's friends, three teachers from DIS, just in front of us.

Auntie Nandy pointed out how we could see the water far off in the distance, behind the stage, as she put her purse on the bench beside her. "Can I borrow your bag too?"

"Why?" I passed it to her.

"Saving some seats for a few more friends coming." She set my purse down. "They're on the way over from the mosque. The one we saw when we first entered Katara. So it may take them a while."

The friends arrived just as the orchestra began the second song, "Can You Feel the Love Tonight" from *The Lion King*.

I looked to my left and into the eyes of Adam, following his sister and his dad, as they made their way to their spots beside us.

As the song ended, I looked toward my purse, on the other side of Auntie Nandy, and when I glanced up, Adam smiled at me.

I'm not going to lie.

It set something fluttering in me.

Maybe it was because he was dressed differently. A black polo shirt and jeans.

A black polo shirt with a collar.

I reached over and brought my purse to me, brought my phone to me.

He'd already messaged me.

Now I'll get to say sorry in person.

As "Let It Go" began, I tilted myself to make sure Auntie Nandy couldn't see my phone.

Maybe I will too.

May I suggest something?

Yes?

Let it go.

I leaned back to look at him from behind Auntie Nandy's and Hanna's and his dad's heads, to groan at his corniness.

But *he* had leaned forward to look at me.

Then we switched and missed each other again.

Auntie Nandy looked at me. But it was with a Slytherin-like smile.

"Did you plot this in some way? Him being here?" I whispered to her.

"Shh, people are trying to listen," she said, the sly smile lingering on her face. "Little kids are singing and dancing. And some kids are falling in love."

"Auntie Nandy, stop," I whispered again, making the mistake of looking his way.

He shot me another smile.

I'd never seen him look so happy.

He was bursting with it, and it suited him so well.

In all ways.

The things I'd read about MS flooded my brain just then.

Because I hadn't only been researching drones and warfare.

I'd also been reading about Adam's disease.

How it didn't need to be a death sentence.

And while I was reading, I'd been itching to tell him what I'd found.

He needed to know, he needed to see that there was hope ahead, so I smiled back at him.

And he sent me a rose emoji.

We sat through the *Star Wars* theme, and then he got up and left the amphitheater.

I waited for a while. Then I did too.

MARVEL: ZAYNEB . . . I MEAN, WATER

That first day in Doha, when you were over at my house, I'd wanted to show you the night sky above the water.

But I didn't get to.

Now I can.

There's a beach right in front of the theater.

In the lightly breezy night air, I waited outside the amphitheater.

It was just me and a few stragglers lining up for tickets, and I realized something.

Maybe she'd be reluctant to follow me because she might not be sure that I knew the protocol. Of us interacting.

Btw, I'll follow the rules. Like, we won't be alone. My dad's taking Hanna to play on the beach too.

And I'll never touch you. Of course.

I paused. Until you give me permission, I mean. Until your family does. Until everyone does, I mean.

As I cringed at the awkwardness of the message, someone cleared their throat nearby. "I know you'd follow the rules, Adam."

To look up to see her standing there—beaming, beautiful

face framed by a teal scarf, vibrant against the cream color of the amphitheater—felt like a dream that I could hold on to in vivid detail. "Hi. Salaam. Zayneb."

"Walaikum musalam." She smiled again and looked down the wide, shallow steps to the left of her, leading to the beach part of Katara. "This enchanting sky and the water?"

"This way." I began going down the stairs, then paused midway and turned to her, standing a few steps above me. "Hey, I'm really sorry about the way our trip to the museum went. I just wanted to say that first. I didn't pause to think about what you could have been going through with your teacher."

She stopped too and shrugged. "Maybe I wasn't seeing straight either, because I was so caught up with being upset. And I had this weird feeling about my dad going to Pakistan. I'm sorry too. For yelling at you. So sorry, Adam. Like you wouldn't believe."

"That family? At the exhibit next to us? They acted like we were a museum display too." I laughed, and her laughter joined easily with mine.

It was an amazing sound.

We continued the descent in perfect silence.

At the bottom of the stairs we emerged onto a paved ramp, and at the end of that, after we rounded a corner, the beach stretched before us, lit with lights lining a path cutting through the sand, as well as lights along the edges behind us, where the sand met the paved walkway fronting restaurants.

I was right, we wouldn't be alone. Clusters of families and friends were grouped here and there, either sitting on the beach or on the benches along the boardwalk behind it.

The colorful street-food carts on the boardwalk caught my gaze. "Wait here? There's something I gotta get you."

She nodded and turned to look at the dark water, twinkling with the lights of numerous boats moored in the distance.

When I returned with two steaming cups of karak and two hot chapatis, balanced on a flimsy, folded cardboard tray, Zayneb was sitting on one of the brightly colored beach chairs dotting the beach. But it was right next to a family.

"Here, this spot is for you." She took a towel off one of the chairs beside hers and hung it on the back of it. "There aren't any empty seats around. I was looking for a pair for us, and these kind people just told me to take two of theirs. That they were using their blanket, too."

"Thanks." I passed her one of the teas before sitting down. "I remember you saying you were a tea person. This is something everyone visiting Doha has got to try. Karak. And chapati."

I passed her the flatbread, rolled in white paper.

She took the lid off the tea and let the steam warm her face, eyes closed. "Mmm, chai. Smells amazing. Thanks." She opened her eyes and smiled at me before unrolling her chapati to rip a small piece off. "I'm suddenly ravenous."

"Oh man, look at those waves." I bit into the toasty flatbread as I watched the water lapping the shore with foam-speckled edges.

The chapati was unbelievably fresh, having been made right in front of my eyes, the flaky, grilled part on the surface leading the way to the soft, steamy dough underneath.

So good.

I turned to Zayneb to see what she thought.

She was crying.

"I don't get how I'm supposed to move on from my grandmother being murdered." Her chapati lay uneaten as Zayneb finished telling me about her grandmother's death. How the bread had reminded her of her daadi preparing this after-school snack for her every single day during the months she lived with them. "Like, I'm a person who feels things strongly. And I don't know how to deal with my feelings. The way society tells me to. Which is mostly to ignore them."

I wanted to console her, and it took my all not to reach out to her. I don't know for what . . . to wipe those tears? Because I wanted them gone. "Maybe you're *not* supposed to deal with them in that way. The way you're told to. Maybe you're meant to be the person you are."

"That's exactly what Auntie Nandy told me. That I'm supposed to feel things, then shake the world. Smartly." She picked up her chapati, broke another piece off, and put it in her mouth. "I just don't like the alone part of it."

"You don't have to be alone. I . . . can be there too." I took the lid off my tea. "I'm not a shouter, but I'm a helper. And I'd love to help you, Zayneb. Because you care about the right things."

"You're making me cry again." She covered her face, then drew apart her hands to peek at me, laughing through the tears. "Or maybe it's the chapati. Maybe I can't eat fresh chapati or roti or fresh bread ever again, because I'll cry. Maybe I'll be a breadless woman for the rest of my life. But . . ." Smiling, she let out a sad sob. "I just love bread so very very much."

"Wait. Maybe you can try chewing the chapati with the hot karak. Maybe it will change the sensation, the feeling that you're eating the bread your grandma made."

She took a sip and chewed, the lights on the beach reflecting the dried tears still glistening on her moving cheeks. "Now I'm making a roti slushie in my mouth. To erase a sacred memory. Kinda ewww. And sad."

"Look at the water, too. To make a new visual connection. Or . . ." I shrugged and smiled. "You *can* continue looking at me."

"Astaghfirullah. I thought we were following the rules. You should be telling me to lower my gaze, brother," she said, shaking her finger at me, a smile on her face. "And where's your dad? If my sister, Sadia, were here, she'd say we weren't following the rules."

I looked behind us and, not seeing Dad, texted him.

"Okay, let's both look at the water then." I laughed and watched the waves some more. "Did I ever tell you the minute I saw the water, I was interested in it? In London? At the airport?"

"What color was the water?"

"It was deep blue. Azurite colored, like the rock I'd bought for Hanna."

"Was that why you'd noticed the water? Because of its blue hijab?"

"Yeah. That's exactly why. But also because the water was so busy. Like nonstop busy. So busy all her luggage fell over."

"The water was dealing with online hate. The water was being mobbed by ruthless sharks."

"I want to know all about the water. *Every*thing about it. 'Cause I . . . like the water. A lot." I didn't turn to her.

"Because you're thirsty? Because you've never drunk water? Ever?" Her words were rippled with the hint of a giggle.

I cringed and shook my head, laughing. "Astaghfirullah. I thought we were following the rules. That's crossing the line, sister."

"Sorry. Maybe it's because I'm thirsty too." She didn't say this in a joking way, just matter-of-factly.

We both looked straight ahead. Then Dad waved at us as he walked by our chairs, Hanna running to the water ahead of him.

Perfect timing.

"But what about if the water you're looking at is . . ." I paused, trying to think of a good way to capture my insecurities about my MS future without soliciting sympathy. "Slightly contained. Not really free like the water ahead of us."

"You mean what if the water I like is a tall, cool glass of the sweetest water?" She giggled hard now. "Sorry, this metaphor thing is driving me to break ALL THE RULES."

"No, seriously, Zayneb." I became quiet. "Are you okay with that? The MS part of me."

"Adam, I finished falling for you the day I saw you with your IV. The day you opened up to me. I'm into openness in people. *That's* what I'm drawn to. Well, one of the things."

I nodded, so crazy-happy inside but, also, tainted with worry. "And what about your family. Would they freak out?"

"You're lucky you're looking at a girl—I mean at a water—that's got super-chill parents in that department. Like, they've always told me they're okay with me meeting someone. The vast ocean this water comes from is cool, okay?"

"No, I mean would they be okay with the MS part."

"I think so? They're not cruel."

"But it's not smooth sailing."

"Life isn't?"

I sighed. I didn't know if I was getting across what I was trying to say. "I've been sort of paralyzed when I think of the future. It's, like, dark." I looked at the sand below my sneakers and then moved my right shoe through it, making grooves. "It closes in on me. It feels like I can't move. And I'm on my own."

"But why do you have to be?" She said it gently, kindly. "You don't have to be alone, Adam."

"The funny thing is, I'm not. My dad, and of course Hanna, is there for me. I've also got the coolest friends in that way," I acknowledged. "But it constantly feels like I can't tell all. Like they won't get everything, so I don't even try."

"There are forums, online and in real life, where you can meet others with MS, you know." Her voice quickened, like she couldn't wait to share her thoughts. "I've found some! I was researching MS treatments and therapy methods, and I found those forums. I'll send you links. Then we can see if there's some sort of support group right here in Doha."

"You researched MS?" I turned to her. Completely to her.

"Yeah? There's so much information! Hopeful information, Adam." She peered at me to make sure I saw how serious she was, enthusiasm taking over her face as she leaned forward in her eagerness to communicate her excitement. "You don't have to be alone."

Hope—she was trying to give me hope.

She was trying to light the way forward with hope.

Amazing. To think I'd not been alone.

That she'd been thinking ahead for me too.

"Okay, I need to look at the water." I gazed back at the waves. "Because I suddenly understand why there are rules in the first place."

"Me researching MS made you more thirsty?"

"Yeah. That, and you being you. Really thirsty."

She laughed softly. "What does this mean? 'Cause we can't drink the water, you know."

"Hello, people!"

I turned behind me to see Ms. Raymond with other teachers from DIS making their way toward us.

Ms. Raymond's face lit up at seeing our snacks. "Oh, yes! I'm so happy you got to try chapati and karak, Zayneb!"

Zayneb nodded and held up her chapati. "I approve, Doha."

We got up, and, before joining the others, I thanked the family nearby, the ones who'd lent us their chairs.

When we got home that night, we didn't text each other.

We didn't need to.

We just knew what we would both say.

MARVEL: ADAM . . . I MEAN, WATER

AUNTIE NANDY AND I WENT FOR A SWIM FIRST THING TODAY. WE swam laps together and took turns rating each other's dives, and then Auntie Nandy left for the changing room so she could go up to the apartment and put together her essential breakfast spread.

I flipped onto my back and relaxed for a bit.

My eyes were closed as I relived the moments on the beach yesterday, a goofy smile on my face—*Adam and I feel the exact same about each other, and we admitted it!*—when I got touched on the arm.

I opened my eyes and lifted my head to a déjà vu. It was the woman in the white swim cap and swimsuit from my first time in the pool, trying to get my attention again. "I'm so sorry to interrupt you again. But my husband is trying to talk to you."

Pulling myself up in order to see and clear my ears properly, I turned to where she was pointing. It was the same bobbing man who'd tattled on me before to the gym attendant, Marc. He was standing by the pool stairs, hands hanging by his sides, shorts again hitched under his stomach.

Her *husband*?

I looked at her. "Your *husband*?"

"Yeah." She nodded sheepishly then yelled at him. "Now what is it? I got her attention."

"Excuse me, but I thought Marc told you the rules of swimming here." The man's arms raised into I'm-the-boss wings as he placed both hands on his hips. He looked like an angry bird.

"We realize you may be a guest here, but there are rules at this complex, dear," the woman beside me said sympathetically, like a granny. Like an I'm-the-boss granny.

I almost lost it.

But I thought again about being on the beach yesterday.

Of sitting there in the night and the hot karak and coolness of the breeze off the water. Of Adam, when he said he liked the water *a lot.*

It made me remember something: I liked me too.

And I liked the things I liked to do, like swimming.

"I'm not breaking any rules." I spoke loudly so the man could hear. "To wear extra swim fabric is not breaking any rules."

"As we told you before, it's not proper swimwear," the man insisted, a scowl starting. He crossed his arms for emphasis, like a terrible cartoon. *Because I'm the boss, and I say so!*

His wife patted my shoulder. "My husband just likes things the way they've been. We've lived here for four years. No one's dressed like you before."

I drew myself away from her pretend niceness. "Excuse me, but I'd like to swim in peace now."

The man turned and headed toward the door.

"Oh no, he's going for Marc again." The woman tut-tutted, watching him leave. "I'm so worried what this does to his heart. Getting upset like that. He's so sensitive; I don't want him to get sick."

I stared at her. "Excuse me, but did you ever think what it does to *our* hearts? To be continuously told that how we choose to be is wrong? Like, why can't I just swim here in peace? Why do the clothes I have on my body hurt your husband's heart?"

She didn't say anything, but I could see from her eyes enlarging that the wheels were working up there in her brain.

From a distance, I went on. Not to get her to see it my way, but to help her brain out. "I'm sick of running into this so much. I'm the one heartsick, okay? Me and my sisters, my people."

She pursed her lips, so I ended with my last offer for her brain's expansion. "And you know what? I'm not going to let your prejudice, your outrage, or fake kindness, either, change one bit of me, of how I look, of who I am. Your resistance to my existence is futile, okay?"

I floated away from her.

I floated and floated, with my eyes closed, thinking of the water lapping the beach yesterday, the twinkling boat lights, and Adam.

When I decided I was done chilling, I left the empty pool.

After showering, as I sat with one white towel round my body and another round my head, drying in the changing room, I sent Adam the MS forum links I'd found.

He replied with *thanks* and *see you soon* followed by two wave emojis.

I smiled to myself.

To check whether the links I'd passed him worked right, I clicked on the first one. It led me to the MS chat subforum of a group chat site.

It was a site I hadn't heard of until I'd done the search for

Adam: Nest. I clicked around and saw that it was neatly organized into closed or open forums. I entered an open forum called CollegeDirt and scrolled the postings discussing the merits of different colleges.

I entered *U of Chicago* in the search and read the comments a bit until I stopped at a post by someone named SugarWraith.

Which reminded me of Fencer.

Fencer had used the online alias @StoneWraith14.

I searched this name in the forum and came up empty.

I methodically clicked each of the forum sites I'd sent Adam, skipping the obviously medical ones, looking for evidence of @StoneWraith14.

Nothing turned up.

But I wasn't done checking.

I pulled a black abaya on, wrapped a scarf loosely on my head, and swung my gym sackpack over both my arms before exiting the changing room, planning on getting properly and thoroughly and amazingly dressed upstairs in the apartment.

Because today was special.

On the way home yesterday from Katara, while we walked to the parking lot, Adam had told Auntie Nandy and me about the room he'd been fixing downstairs at his house. He wanted it to be done in time for Hanna's birthday as a surprise for her.

"But I haven't been able to go down there and really work on it. I was in the middle of painting it when I got the attack." He nodded at Auntie Nandy. "And, as you know, I lost a few days from that."

"I'll come over and help you paint," Auntie Nandy said. "I'm quite a pro at it."

Adam had considered for a few seconds then looked over at me. "If Zayneb comes too, then I'm in."

I watched Hanna, who'd skipped ahead with her dad and was now "tightrope" walking on the concrete bumpers edging the parking lot. "I will, but on the condition that Hanna doesn't know we're there, and she doesn't see it until we're done. So that she can be completely surprised."

"Deal. I'll just get my dad involved."

Then we'd smiled to seal it, and so today Auntie Nandy and I were going over there right after breakfast.

Right now, as I walked out of the gym, I was in la-la land, thinking of that smile between us.

Marc stood up when I reached the gym reception area. "Hi. Just to tell you, we've had another complaint about your swim-wear."

"You mean the same complaint." I didn't stop to look at him but only turned when I got to the doors, only to show him I wasn't fazed by him.

"I'd appreciate it if there weren't any disruptions here."

"And I'd appreciate it if you'd make sure I get to swim in peace like everyone else. Ciao."

I went out into the courtyard but paused right outside the glass double doors.

Then I lifted my arms to let the air blow through the billowy sleeves of the abaya.

To let Marc see that I was free of him and his interference in my freedom.

Adam had everything prepped for us: three paint trays housing paint and rollers, small brushes lying on top of closed paint cans ready for edge work, and a ladder, its legs split apart, at attention.

Even though I knew I'd be painting, I'd dressed well.

I had on jeans and a white-and-navy-blue-striped button-down shirt with a navy-blue hijab worn trim around my face.

As soon as Adam had seen me at the front door, his eyes had lit up.

As Auntie Nandy climbed the ladder to finish the ceiling edges, her wireless headphones on, and he and I began loading our rollers to finish the walls, he said, "Psst, a question in the series I Need to Know Everything About You, Volume One: Do you always wear blue hijabs? Like a shade of blue?"

"No." While picking up my paint-heavy roller from the tray, I searched his face, wondering what he meant. "I mean, that's not my thing. My favorite color is orange."

"Really? Because I've noticed a lot of blue. And I thought that was cool."

I aimed my first roll at the middle of the wall in front of me, smiling. He'd *noticed*. And liked them. My hijabs.

I pssted him, too. "I like hearing you say that, that it's cool. It's so the opposite of what I usually hear. About me wearing hijab." And then I went on to tell him about this morning at the pool.

He paused painting and drew the roller away from the wall. "That sucks, Zayneb. I'm sorry."

I paused too. "Sometimes I wonder if I'm a magnet for it. That kind of attitude. I don't know if all Muslim girls get this stuff."

"I've got to be honest—I've never asked any of the Muslim girls I've known about it. I feel bad about that." He began rolling again, but slower. "I wish I'd been there this morning, though. At the pool."

I turned to him. "What do you mean? What would you have done?"

"I would have spoken up. Maybe recorded it with my phone, so there's evidence." He reached high with the roller and smiled. "I would have been there for the water, my water, not the pool water, is what I'm trying to say."

My face tingled at the word "my," something hot spreading through my cheeks, and I wondered if I was blushing.

It felt weirdly amazing to hear him say "my water" so effortlessly like that.

I tried to continue rolling nonchalantly. Tried to douse my cheeks with practical matters. "Speaking of water, what do you think we should do? I'm returning home in three days."

He went to the cluster of paint trays and loaded his roller again. When he got back to our wall, he had a smile on his face. A secure one. "So last night I read protocol. The way to roll this out so it's right. I'm supposed to ask your parents' permission to get to know you."

"But they're in Pakistan and Springdale." I stopped rolling and thought about it. "Though my mom will be here tomorrow."

"Should I talk to her?"

I went to reload my roller and returned, thinking hard. "It sounds so official. To talk to my parents. Though I think they might know a bit already, because my sister knows."

"Well, *my* dad knows. And he likes you—I think mainly because Hanna likes you. Your aunt knows." He cleared his throat. "Hanna knows. She thinks it's weird, because we're cousins, but other than that she says she's happy. So now it's just *your* parents."

"Okay, but do it fast, all right? Like a Band-Aid. I don't want any pain from it." I imagined Dad lingering on questions and Mom wanting to be around Adam to check him out more.

"I thought they were the cool ocean." He raised his eyebrows at me from near the corner he was painting. "Completely chill parents."

"They totally are. But they might also be overly nosy."

"Concerned is another way to see it."

"I just knew you were the dutiful-son type. Mama's boy."

"Yeah. I actually am."

I removed my roller from the wall and turned away in horror. I'd forgotten again. About his mom.

Oh God, was this always going to happen?

What was wrong with my mouth?

"Zayneb? Hey?" He was pssting again, and I could tell he was close behind me.

I turned to see him rolling some patches I'd missed on the wall. I swallowed before speaking. "Sorry. To say what I did. Like the mama's-boy thing. Like alluding to you under your mom's thumb when she isn't even . . ."

"That's why I'm trying to get your attention. It's all cool. I'll always be a mama's boy." He smiled at me, completely at ease. "Because while I'm not comfortable discussing my mom's death— that, yeah, hurts me a lot . . ." His smile faltered a bit before he plowed on. "I'm completely fine talking about her life. I already told you that. She was an amazing mom, and she *continues to be*, because sometimes I bring her up in my head, the things she told me, that we talked about, when I need to figure new things out in my life now. Like my MS and stuff."

I don't know why, but I teared up on hearing that and then nodded, and he nodded, teary-eyed too, and we worked quietly side by side for a long while.

And I was so glad he'd be talking to my parents soon, because I just wanted to wrap my arms around him.

. . .

Somewhere in the soothing rhythms of painting and attaching the small pieces Adam had made over the years to add to the room, I told him all about Fencer.

At the end of it, he looked like *he* wanted to wrap his arms around me.

ADAM

THURSDAY, MARCH 21

MARVEL: CONNECTIONS

WE'D WORKED ALL DAY YESTERDAY, ZAYNEB, MS. RAYMOND, and me, breaking for lunch together, and then dinner with Dad and Hanna, who'd returned from an entire day spent at the beach. They'd been there with the one friend of Hanna's who had remained at our neighborhood compound for spring break.

With the work we'd done, the room was half-alive.

I'd woken up this morning energized to add the finishing touches—the ones I hadn't wanted to add with Zayneb there, the ones I wanted her to be surprised by.

But first I had to say good-bye to Connor, who was flying back to college in California.

We met at our favorite burger place near DIS, the one with the old-timey jukebox.

He dropped coins in the machine, and "Stand by Me" flooded the place.

"Fill me in on what's next for you," he said, sliding into the seat across from me, a triple-patty sandwich waiting for him on a tray.

"I'm finishing the room I started downstairs. Then I'm going to spend a bit of time here in Doha before I go see my grandparents, both sets, in Canada. And then, maybe . . ." I paused to take a bite of my cheeseburger and to consider how to tell him my decision. By the time I finished chewing, I'd worked it out. I'd just say it. "Go see Zayneb. In Indiana."

He took a long sip of his drink before chuckling. "Okay, this is the best. My man Adam finding his girl."

"Do me a favor?" I picked up a couple of fries and dunked them into the container of ketchup. "Keep this news out of the group chat? There was some mix-up, and Zayneb told Emma P. there was nothing between us. I don't want Emma to think she was lying."

"It's in the vault." He ate his burger, moving his head to the music in between bites. "What about with your MS? You've got a treatment plan worked out?"

"That's Friday. I'm going to the neurologist." I finished eating my fries. "How about you? You staying in your program?"

"Yeah, Nancy's going to help me figure things out. When you go to Vancouver, see if you can catch a flight to Berkeley. I want to see you, and maybe you can meet her. Nancy."

"Adding California to the jet-setting itinerary."

"I'll try to get the others to come too. Because, you know, none of our crew is coming back here, right? For the summer?"

I reached into my pocket. "Hey, I got you a Steam gift card."

I dropped the plastic card, loaded with money redeemable for use on the gaming site, in the middle of the table.

"Why?" Connor reached for it. "Whoa, that's a lot. Why'd you do that? It better not be a thank-you thing, man."

"No way. It's so we can talk," I said, undoing the seam of my empty fries sleeve, to flatten it and fold it. "You play, we talk? Every Sunday?"

He looked at me, then down at my hands origami-ing the box. "Will you play the songs I request then? On your guitar?"

"Yep." I took another bite of my burger, and he got up and added more money to the jukebox.

"Scarborough Fair" accompanied our plans to meet up in California.

Dad took Hanna out to buy her birthday decorations, and as soon as they left, I went downstairs to finish.

I hesitated only briefly before climbing the ladder, nail gun in hand.

My hands moved methodically, spacing the lights so that they crisscrossed the ceiling in a weave.

When I was done, I felt a tingling in my arms that I told myself was fatigue.

But I put the nail gun down and decided to finish the rest tomorrow morning.

Early, before Hanna woke up for her birthday.

My method for not thinking of Zayneb leaving was prepping to see her again in the summer. I'd already worked out with my grandparents on Dad's side that I'd stay with them on my own, as well as when Dad reached Vancouver with Hanna, and then go on to Ottawa to spend two weeks with my other grandparents. After which I hoped to add a trip to Indiana. And California in between somewhere.

I was on the couch looking up flight costs for these trips, jotting down notes in my marvels journal, when I got a message from Zayneb.

Can you meet me at the museum? In an hour?

Surprised because I'd written off seeing Zayneb today, knowing her mom had arrived this morning, I read the message again.

I thought she'd be spending time at home with her family. And that I'd be going to dinner with them tomorrow, after Hanna's birthday thing, so that I could meet Zayneb's mom.

But here is another day with Zayneb in it. I tapped quickly into the phone, in case she changed her mind. For sure. By the fountain?

Yes. She followed it up with a wave emoji.

Dad and Hanna were out, so I didn't have a ride.

I was about to open Uber but then remembered someone.

Zahid.

"Adam, you look wonderful." He got out of the driver's seat to look at me.

I went forward to shake his hand but then opened my arms for a hug. "Thanks, Zahid. *Uncle* Zahid, I mean," I added with a laugh.

"I'm so glad you called me. Not only for my taxi service. But also as a nephew, huh?" He broke his return hug to smile at me, and I saw that his face was a lined brown one with a full mustache and dark twinkling eyes.

It was exactly the type of kind face I'd imagined. "Yeah, thanks, Uncle."

"You feeling better?"

"Much better."

"Your family knows? They're helping you?"

"Yeah." I got in the front seat, lay my Marvels and Oddities journal on my lap, and buckled up.

He said a prayer before starting, muttering it quietly, and I joined in, my words meeting his.

Finishing, he looked at me for a second before turning the steering wheel to edge out. "You know this?"

"Yes, the dua? I'm Muslim, Zahid." I laughed. "I guess I should have said assalamu alaikum first, so you knew."

"Walaikum musalam wa rahmathullahi wabarakatha hu," he said, returning my salaam with a nobler greeting of peace.

I smiled at his benevolence.

"You are Malaysian or Indonesian?"

"No." I shook my head. "I'm Canadian. But my father's family is originally from China and my mother's from Finland."

"Ah. Okay." Zahid gave me a thumbs-up.

"Listen, Uncle Zahid. My father wanted me to invite you for dinner one day soon. He knows about how you helped me. Will you come?"

"Oh, there's no need for that, Adam. Why did you tell him?"

"It'll make him very happy. And me, too. And my sister."

"And your mother? And what about her?"

"She passed away. But she would have been happy to see you."

Zahid drove for a bit, thinking. "Okay, tell me the date for this dinner, and I'll make the time."

"Thanks."

"But then you have to come to my house too. And meet my family—my kids are young, but they will like you. They are learning to speak English."

I nodded, glad to repay his kindness in whatever way I could.

As I entered the foyer of the museum, I marveled at how different these steps of mine were compared to the ones I'd taken here on Sunday.

MS was unreliable, but I vowed to enjoy the good days. And the good in every day.

Today was a doubly special day. I was feeling fine, both physically and emotionally, plus I was getting to see Zayneb unexpectedly.

After passing the epic staircase, I looked ahead, and there she was.

At a table by the fountain, facing me, but not seeing me, surrounded by other tables bustling with people.

Her head was bent over a book on the table, the pen in her hand moving swiftly across the page.

Writing. She was writing.

Was it in her journal?

I had my own in my hand now—I'd taken it with me to show it to her finally—and felt thrilled at the prospect that she had hers, too.

"Ahem, Zayneb, would you be writing your marvels? Or oddities?" I placed my journal on the table and pulled out the chair across from her.

Her pen paused, and she looked at my journal, titling her head to read its title, a dawning, surprised expression taking over her face.

Then she looked up, stunned. "What . . . is that? Adam?"

I took a seat and smiled. "My Marvels and Oddities journal. I've been recording the good things in life since I was fourteen. And the weird things. Lately, more weird. Well, lately until I knew a certain H_2O liked me back. Now it's all marvelous."

"I'm going to scream. Like literally scream." She closed the book she'd been writing in and held up the orange cover. *MARVELS AND ODDITIES* it announced in big, capital letters. "ADAM, I'VE BEEN WRITING IN THIS FOR TWO YEARS!"

"And me, four years." I grinned at the way her eyes were wider than ever. "Well, not this exact one. I'm on my fifth note-book."

"I CANNOT BELIEVE IT." She stopped and closed her eyes. "Wait. What does this mean?"

I put my elbows on the table and leaned forward. "It means we have something in common."

She opened her eyes and nodded.

"And it's an amazing thing to have in common," I went on.

She nodded again, peering at my tiny-fonted, lowercased *marvels and oddities*, written in the top left-hand corner.

I picked it up so she could see it clearly. "I just realized this thing literally got me through the hard, alone years after my mom's death. That I was able to see the marvels around me through it all."

"Wait." She flipped through her journal. "But that's not me. So we don't have something in common. Because reams and reams of pages in this thing are about the awful things in the world. And I've got six more of these journals at home. Mostly full of crappy happenings in my life."

"You didn't record any marvels?"

"No, I did, but they were short. Except, yeah, after we started liking each other. Then it became better." She opened her journal and did a mock reading. "Marvel: Adam, blah, blah, blah, Adam. Adam, Adam, Adam, and you get the picture."

I flipped to random pages throughout my notebook. "Marvel: Zayneb. And here's another one. Marvel: Zayneb. And another one . . . so you get the picture too."

We looked at each other and burst out laughing. Then I looked beyond her, through the windows, to Doha Bay. At the sky above it.

It was perfect.

This moment was perfect. That we were so in sync and it was happening at my favorite place in the city.

"This is unreal." She took my journal and placed it beside hers and then drew her phone out to take a picture. "Why—I mean, how did you start yours?"

"Because of this museum. Because I used to come here a lot and wander through the exhibits, and one day I couldn't stop thinking of that manuscript upstairs. *The Marvels of Creation and the Oddities of Existence.*"

"Oh my God. That's why *I* couldn't move when we came here on the weekend. I couldn't believe I was in the presence of *the* manuscript. The one *I* saw online when I was sixteen."

"Upstairs. Where we had our weird fight."

"Yeah."

"Okay, I have to tell you something. But you have to promise you'll be okay with it."

"No way. How can I promise I'll be okay with something I don't know. Uh, no, I don't agree to those kinds of things." She crossed her arms, laughter in her eyes, and sat back. "I reserve the right to get upset. Proudly."

"Fine. The entire time I've known of your existence, I knew that you had a marvels and oddities journal." I leaned back and crossed my own arms. "Because it fell out of your bag. In the airport waiting area. And I saw."

"And you stalked me because of it?" She crossed her arms tighter, but her eyes twinkled with humor. "Oh, now it makes sense. That's why you wanted to talk to me on the airplane. It wasn't my magnetic eyes or smile."

"I saw that after," I assured her. "But first, it was your hijab.

Not even the color. But the fact that you had one on, and I thought, *Muslim alert.* Second, it was the color, yeah."

"You have a thing for blues, noted." She reached for her journal and her pen and pretended to write it down.

Or maybe it was for real.

I couldn't tell, because her eyes were smiling.

"Then it was your journal. That you might see the world like I do." I paused. "Then it was everything else, all at once—your smile, your eyes, your personality, like a landslide, like Zayneb."

She looked up from writing.

"Um, this is where I admit, for me, it was your looks." She cleared her throat. "I'm sorry."

"Only?"

"At first I mean. Then when you said salaam, I was like, *This guy is super cute AND Muslim?* Then it was your layers. Calm, cool, slightly sad layers. You were mysterious, and I wanted to peel you away like an onion."

"So you like sad onions."

"Yeah, they make me cry, instead of angry."

"Is this supposed to make me feel good?" I asked, laughing, but weirded out. Sad onion?

But it was Zayneb. And anything she said came from somewhere, had some sort of depth.

But *sad onion*?

"It's supposed to be real, Adam." She stopped smiling. "I like being real. Like, if I'd noticed that you journaled the same way as me, I would have just whisper-yelled, *Hey, dude, I've got a journal like that too*, right across from you at the airport in London."

I nodded. "Actually, I tried. On the plane. But you were sleeping."

"Anyway, one way of being is not better. Like, look at me: I'm the one in trouble with my mom." She sighed and closed her journal.

"I was wondering about that. Why you're here when you're supposed to be with her. What happened?" I noticed the sudden change in her. That everything about her was slumped, her mouth, her face, her shoulders. "Wait. Let me get you something. From the café."

She nodded. "Do they have karak?"

"No, but I can get you regular tea. And something to eat with that. They've got cakes and stuff."

"Thanks." She looked over at the café counter. "It looks fancy."

"It is. French-pastries fancy."

Her eyes lit up. "Oh God, that's my secret love. Okay, choose something for me. They're all amazing to me."

ODDITY: *HATERS*

We took our stuff to a newly empty table by the window.

I poured her tea and placed the plate of raspberry cream mille-feuille in front of her like a waiter, and she laughed. "Wow. Beautiful. Did you know that I watch dessert-making videos? It's my de-stressor."

"And then you try to make them yourself? The desserts?"

"No, I just like watching others making them. Less work."

"Ahem." I cleared my throat. "As a maker, I have to advise you that that's extremely wrong. To watch from the sidelines and not participate."

"I'd fail." She used the side of her fork to cut into the layers of her pastry. "Look at this delicate thing. So many steps, so many ways to get it wrong."

"You were named after a maker."

She paused with the fork halfway to her mouth. "I *was*?"

"Yeah, Zayneb bint Jahsh, the prophet's cousin. She made leather crafts, bags, and other things. Apparently, she was known for the quality of her work." I picked up the chocolate chip cookie I'd brought for old times' sake. "My father, the historian, makes sure I get this kind of info, especially if he thinks it's about something I'd be interested in. Like other makers."

"Oh, yeah, I heard that long ago about sahabiya Zayneb. In Sunday school." She nodded and took a forkful of her pastry. "Maybe one day I *will* try making some French dessert. Or maybe I'll start with my grandma's roti."

She took a knife and cut through her pastry, put half on a napkin, and passed it to me.

"For me?"

"Yeah, it's really good."

I accepted it. "So what happened? With your mom?"

"She found me looking up Fencer again." She stopped eating, put her fork down. "I didn't mean to. I meant to dedicate all my attention to her. Because I was *so* happy to see her again. Truly."

I cut half my second chocolate chip cookie and gave it to her. She took it and put it at the side of her mille-feuille plate.

"But then I remembered this comment I'd seen under this video from last week. Wait. I'll show you." She picked up her phone and clicked and scrolled and then passed it to me.

The video was titled *Muslim Girls Save World from Villain Part Two*. I lowered the volume as the intro blared, a mix of drumming and a man's deep voice saying something in Arabic. Two people in niqab, the face covering some Muslim women wear, sat at a table with a tall, obviously plastic potted cactus on a chair between them.

"Yo, assalamu alaikum. May peace *and* the Force be with you guys!" the girl on the right said. "Today, my girl Janna joins me again. And we're going to continue our interview with my ex-brother-in-law, on how he escaped getting captured for abusing my sister. Who, as you dedicated viewers know, is BACK HOME in America finally! But, inexcusably, the villain is at large, the one who kept her locked up. However, friends, never fear—he lent his alter ego, his thorny alter ego, for our interview." She poked the cactus with a black-gloved hand. "Wait, we forgot to mic him. Guys, can we get the villain miked up?"

She looked beyond the camera and gestured with another gloved hand as though she were calling a waiter.

The video went dark then came back on to reveal the cactus wired with a lapel mic clipped to one of its thorny branches, a donut stuck on another branch. I chuckled.

Zayneb waved a hand nearby in slow motion. "Adam? We can watch the epic Niqabi Ninja videos later, but, for now, scroll down to the comments."

I paused the video and found the comments. They were mostly glowing and *So happy you're doing this* and *Expose him!* and other such things until I got to one that had a lot of likes, that veered off from the sentiments previously expressed.

Why don't you admit it? Your sister was treated the way she was because of Islam. Not because of your brother-in-law. Not because of Saudi Arabia. You're peddling the same thing that got her in trouble, hypocrite. Things won't change until you give up being Muslim. On your own or by other means. I vote for other means.

I made a face. "A hateful troll."

"Look at the account."

"Stone Wraith?"

"Yeah. Click on it."

I clicked and saw a channel with one video, a time lapse of a plant. "He's got one video. But wait, a bunch of playlists. And, whoa, eighteen thousand subscribers?"

"Check when he joined."

"This month? This year?"

"Exactly. Just when Fencer deleted his other accounts."

"You think this is him?"

"I'm sure it's him. Because his subscriber count is close to what he had on his old accounts. Not as much, but close." She reached for the teapot and poured the last bit into her cup. "It's him. And he has some way to communicate to his old followers. Some forum or something. That's how they all migrated to his new accounts."

"Good sleuthing."

"But it was completely out of the blue. Like, I subscribe to those girls, the Niqabi Ninjas, and watch their videos regularly, and I happened to see this comment at the beginning of last week, but it only pinged in my mind as my mom was eating lunch here in Doha, talking about my grandma's grave, how beautifully taken care of it was. She showed us a picture of it, and it was nothing like the cemeteries we know. But just seeing it brought this grave*stone* image into my head, and then I remembered that my friends had found out Fencer's new alias was Stone Wraith, and then *ping*, the comment under the Niqabi Ninjas just flashed in my head, and I made up my mind to look into it."

I nodded to encourage her to continue.

"Then I made a mistake, because I got this idea with my mom sitting right there. I pretended I needed to go to the bathroom. But instead I went to my room and texted my friends at home and got on my laptop and was looking into Fencer's YouTube account and going down this rabbit hole of the videos on his playlists, see what he's commented on. And my mom opens the door and walks in and sits on the bed to hug me."

"Uh-oh."

"Yeah, uh-oh. I close the browser windows quickly, but then she happens to see my texts and they're like *Fencer* this, *Fencer* that. And my last one was *eat him alive for the last time*." She laughed but in a bitter way. "Can you believe it? Like my mom sees that?"

This time I shook my head to encourage her to continue.

"Then she starts asking me questions. Like what have I been doing here the whole time and why haven't I dropped it and, and . . . We got into a huge fight. And I got mad and left. And there I go again, breaking everything apart." She took a bit of the cookie and ate it. "I'm sorry. Because again, talking to you, I feel like I'm ungrateful. Because I have a mom. That I seem to always be fighting with."

I sat back and looked out the window at the turquoise water. "The thing with my mom was she preferred when I was up-front with her. I wasn't always, because I was a kid, but that's what she liked. Like she'd tell me to face my feelings."

I told her about the time we made French fries together, when she allowed me to cry.

"Wow. Adam." She sat back too. "That's unbelievably hard. Mine is like a first-world problem compared to that. My fight with my mom."

"But wait, I'm getting this new idea from that time. The Time of the French Fries." I sat up and leaned forward to get her attention, to get her to understand that what I was going to say was serious. "See, this is what I do. I go over my times with my mom and get ahas. Like I have a new one about the French fry memory:

What if she was trying to tell me that in order to be strong, you have to be weak first? Like, feel your weakness?"

She nodded, her eyes on me and sparking with interest. "Go on."

"Like we can only get to our strongest to face stuff after we've felt the lows?" I indicated her journal. "And your journal is all your lows, but now you're ready to be your strongest? Take Fencer down? Speak up about your grandmother's death? Stand strong, no holds barred? *Win?*"

I looked to see if her eyes were still sparking, but they weren't. They were tear filled.

She opened her journal and flipped through and said, "Can I read you something?"

ZAYNEB
THURSDAY, MARCH 21
ODDITY: HEART PAIN

I READ HIM THE PARTS THAT HURT. THE NOT-ANGRY PARTS.

The parts where things felt confusing, like I would never ever figure out this world. A world that didn't seem to work.

Because the moment you're feeling secure, someone hates on you.

Like being happy on the plane, headed over to Doha, and then the hateful woman shows up.

Like coming to class to learn and instead being served hate.

"It makes you distrustful. Well, it makes *me* distrustful," I said, closing my journal.

He reached his right hand forward and placed it on the teapot. "I'm going to pretend this is your hand. Because I want to touch it, but I'm not gonna, okay?" He drew his hand up a bit, then rested it again on the teapot, but lightly this time, almost hoveringly. "How's your hand so hot?"

I laughed, grateful for his corniness taking the edge off what was happening inside me.

"You know what my mom would say here? She'd say be up-front. Be Zayneb. Tell your mom everything. About the woman

on the plane, the man in the pool, everything about your teacher."
The way he looked at me, I knew he was being serious. "Like I said,
that was the thing about my mom. She liked knowing stuff."

"Maybe that's the thing with moms in general."

"Yeah. Maybe it is. So do it. Just tell her. What you're thinking, why you're doing the things you do. That's what this mama's
boy says."

I nodded and ate the rest of the cookie. "I *am* going to. After
I leave here. Because I don't think I'm ever going to stop getting in
trouble, like she wants me to. Even if I never win."

Before we left, we went and stood in front of the *Marvels of Creation and Oddities of Existence* manuscript again. Without fighting
like last time, without talking much even, except to read bits of the
caption out loud to each other in documentary-style voice-overs,
his impressions more funny than mine, because he actually did a
posh British accent, while I pretended to be an old, grave man and
ended up sounding like a talking walrus, according to Adam.

Then we asked someone walking by to take a picture of us
beside the exhibit, using both our phones in turn, and right then
and there we made the pics our lock screen *and* wallpaper images.

It was the best, because we were both holding our journals,
with the inspiration for them right between us.

And we have the happiest expressions in our eyes.

Even though we were going to be continents apart in two days,
we knew *we weren't going to be apart.*

Adam called his friend Zahid to drive us home. As we waited
outside, he told me about this friend, how he'd helped him when
he'd needed it. "It was one of the worst moments of my life,"

he said, running his fingers forward through his hair to stay it against the slight breeze. "But then Zahid was there like a guardian angel."

"Do you think you should get some sort of a medical bracelet or something? So you can get help fast?" I put my hands in the pockets of my jean jacket. It worried me. That he could just be struck with something suddenly. "Also, can I call you at any hour of the day? If I get a sudden gut feeling that I need to check on the onion in my life?"

He smiled, and with the sunlight he squinted into and the symmetry of the museum behind him, it was an image I didn't want to forget. "That's why I'm going to the neurologist on Friday. To figure that out. But yeah, you can call me whenever, H_2O."

Zahid pulled up, and when we got in the car, he weirdly seemed to know me, shooting Adam a knowing glance when he heard my name.

Adam sat in the front and chatted with him, and I sat in the back and looked at the beautiful palm trees streaming by and thought about the long arc of things.

Of how I'd begun this journal when I was sixteen, and now I'd beyond-this-world connected with someone because of it.

But then Adam had a longer arc with his journal. He'd started his at fourteen, a few years after his mom died.

But then there was an even longer arc here—with Al-Qazwini, the author of the original Marvels and Oddities, how he wrote something so long ago, trying to figure out the world he lived in.

And now here *we* were, almost a thousand years later, still doing it.

Trying to make sense of what was happening around us.

Maybe that's what life is, really.

Before I fitted my keys in and turned the handle on the apartment door, I took a deep breath and said bismillah.

Mom was sitting on the big couch beside Auntie Nandy, her scarf around her shoulders, her hair in a ponytail, her tired eyes immediately widening on seeing me.

I could practically feel the rise and fall of her body relaxing, then the stiffness of it tensing, so I made my way to her.

Auntie Nandy instinctively moved aside to open up a spot beside Mom, between them.

I laid the paper bag from the museum café in my lap before unfolding the top. Adam had secured it for me—it was in these thin, accordion-like pleats—and I smiled and calmed as I opened the bag to reveal two madeleine cakes.

Madeleines are Mom's favorite.

I held the open bag out as a peace offering.

She put her hand in and took one out and passed it to Auntie Nandy before taking one for herself. "Thank you."

I crumpled the empty bag between my hands. "Mom, I'm sorry for yelling at you. Really very sorry. But . . ."

Her body went through that relaxing-tensing thing again.

"But I'm not sorry for trying to do this thing, take my teacher down. Because I'm going to. Because if I don't, I won't be free to show myself. To say the things I think and believe and feel. Because he'll always twist it due to his views. So I'm choosing to be free of him." I remembered the breeze going through my abaya sleeves yesterday morning, how it felt to be free in front of Marc. "Like, why be different, why be Muslim, why be anything that society tells you isn't normal if you can't actually *be* it freely? Why do we have to suffer to be us?"

She didn't say anything for a bit, just looked at the cake she held in her hand. "Honey, I'm not saying you can't be yourself. I'm just saying that the way you go about it can get you in trouble. And I don't want to see that."

"Leesh, I've got to interrupt here, but *trouble* is part of changing things." Auntie Nandy put the rest of the madeleine in her mouth and finished it off. "Since when have you seen a trouble-free change for the better?"

"I don't want Zayneb targeted." Mom flashed Auntie Nandy an angry look. "And I'm sorry, but you don't have kids of your own. That's why you're talking like that. You don't get that it's making things worse for her. For her future."

Ouch. I didn't dare look at Auntie Nandy.

But I looked at Mom. And put a hand on her shoulder closest to me before resting my head on it. "Mom, please. I don't want to live like I'm not wanted around. That's not the *future* I want. And—" I couldn't stop the pain in my voice. "Right now I feel like that a lot. Like I'm not wanted when I show up sometimes."

I did what Adam had suggested and told her about the woman on the plane. And the people at the pool. And Fencer giving me a D.

About him trash-talking me to the class after I got suspended.

Then I told her the things *before* all of this; some of the events she'd known about and others she hadn't. Like the guy who tied the back of my scarf to a pole on the bus without me noticing, and when I tried to exit, my scarf pulled off and almost choked me.

But I told her in a different way than I'd told her before. With sadness, not anger.

Her arm tightened around me while she listened to each incident that had punched me.

Then I told her how much I missed Daadi.

Then I couldn't tell her any more, because it hurt like something sharp had slashed at my vocal cords too many times.

Auntie Nandy's arm reached my back too. And she put her head on my shoulder.

I realized from the slightly cold feeling on my sleeve that she was crying for me.

Mom spoke tearfully. "I'm so sorry, honey. And listening to this pain right after coming back from Pakistan is making *me* angry. I'm so so sorry." She wiped her eyes. "Dad is so broken too, Zayneb. When he learned the details of how Daadi died. Don't ask him, okay?"

I nodded against her, too sore to talk, and she went on. "Tell me what you and your friends want to do. About your teacher. I'll try to listen quietly."

Auntie Nandy sat up and reached over to the tissue box. She took a tissue for herself, then passed the box to me and Mom.

I took a while composing myself, lapsing again and again to crying when I thought I was done with tears and could start talking.

It had suddenly became hard to switch from the hurt to anger, and I realized an awful truth: Over the years, I'd built a hard, strong wall, a fortress, separating my heart from the outside world.

Now that I'd let the fortress crack, it was hard to not let my heart escape.

And feel the hurt. And be free.

This Is What You Missed, Bulletin I by Zayneb Malik, filed as FYI for Kavi Srinivasan:

I'm back, and you can't stop me. I'm back to tell you it's time to suit up.

Re-enlist Ayaan.

Prepare for battle.

StoneWraith14 has an account on a public forum from the UK called Redpillers. My reconnaissance mission yielded 87 posts from this account, 12 of which give us details connecting him to Fencer the teacher. 3 connect him to SPRINGDALE.

Send url. We are on it. Welcome back, General.

I let myself have only half an hour sending stuff to and communicating with Ayaan and Kavi. Then, for the rest of the day, Auntie Nandy and I took Mom to Katara.

We prayed together for Daadi at the mosque first and then came outside to sit and watch the birds weave in and out of the pigeon towers, with Mom holding me tight and Auntie Nandy holding *her* tight.

The Doha birds flying into the sky reminded me that I believe there is more out there, more than this small world. That Daadi will be free somewhere, her hands at peace.

ADAM
FRIDAY, MARCH 22
MARVEL: DAD

I WOKE UP WITH TINGLING IN MY ARMS AGAIN, MORE THAN yesterday. And the first thing I did was reach for my phone to call Dad.

He helped me sit up, to check my movements slowly, before lending his shoulder for me to try to stand.

My legs were okay. My steps were okay.

Joy rushed inside, and I let it out by hugging Dad. "Thanks. Thank you, Dad."

"Do you want to rest again, or are you ready to start the day?" He rubbed my back before letting go, and I was relieved his voice was happy, not stressed.

"I wanted to finish the room for Hanna. But I'm not so sure with my arms." I kneaded them to get at the feelings of pins and needles coursing throughout. "I just had a bit more to do."

Dad leaned back against my dresser. "How okay is it if I do it? If you direct me?"

"Completely okay."

"Then let's do it. Before Hanna wakes up."

• • •

Dad rigged the light system, finished attaching the remaining cut-outs, and secured the fake moss to parts of the stone chips I'd glued on the floor. Then he hung the mobile of tiny geese flying in a V formation in the far corner of the room.

When he went to wake up Hanna, I closed the door and turned the lights on.

The entire room, except for the floor, was made up of blues, ranging from the lightest white blue near the floor to the darkest, inkiest blues swathing the ceiling. The whole place was also lit by various kinds of lights—from streams of small, flickering lights to strong spotlights—and they highlighted different parts of the room, different things to be examined.

I lay on the beanbag chair Dad had carried down from the living room before he went to get Hanna.

I let myself completely chill, head back, hands behind my head, breathing even.

The world in the room surrounded me with its signs of life, the ones I'd noticed and amassed over time.

There was even a potato in a display box on a pedestal in the corner. A plastic potato, yes, but I'd painted over it with a matte-brown acrylic and rubbed dirt into it.

That had been one night three years ago when I couldn't sleep and went to get water and saw the potato sticking out of Hanna's toy box.

A lowly potato was a marvel if you thought about it.

The door burst open, and Hanna walked in, hands covering her eyes, with Dad following behind.

"ADAM!" she screamed when she opened them.

I laughed and stood up. "Look all you want, then sit back on this throne to really enjoy it. Happy birthday."

"Oh my gosh, oh my gosh, oh my gosh. This is amazing!" She moved around like a Ping-Pong ball, drawn from one object to another. "A path!"

She stepped on the stones gingerly, bending down to touch the moss here and there, and stopped and straightened up at the potato stand at the end of the path. "A POTATO?"

Her laughter was so worth it.

I went to stand beside her, and she turned and threw her arms around me. "This is the best, Adam. Thank you a million times! Can this be my room?"

"I don't know about that. It's kind of like the world. It kinda belongs to everyone." I turned her to face the potato. "Although, this potato *is* yours. I stole it from your toy box when you were a simple, young girl."

"Whaaat?" She peered at it. "Well, I donate it to this museum of the world, then!"

"Thanks. Speaking of potatoes, I'm getting something to eat. You enjoy the room."

"I'm going to lie on the throne and enjoy all the lights!" She made her way to the beanbag chair and lay down, a sigh rising from her as she took in the ceiling. "Does it say something in Arabic?"

"Yeah. It's a verse from the Qur'an. About the sky. I copied it from one of the pictures in Dad's office."

Do they not look at the sky above them, how we have built it and adorned it, and there are no rifts in it?

I brought down French fries, Mom's French fries, for Hanna and Dad, and we puffed up the beanbag chair as much as we could in order to use it as a backrest for the three of us, and then we sat on the floor and leaned on it and ate while I told them about when and how I'd made each item in the room.

"This has been a three-year project?" Dad sounded surprised.

"Well, I didn't know they were going to end up in the room. I just kept making things." I pointed at the Canada-geese mobile. "Like *that* I started making last summer before I left for London."

"And I have one of them. That's why there's only four geese," Hanna announced proudly. "I got the leader."

"Canada geese choose one partner for life. And they show extraordinary commitment to their mate," Dad said, staring at the mobile. "Sometimes they mourn their partner forever."

"They also are super protective," I added.

"Of their entire community," Dad finished, maintaining his gaze on the dangling geese.

"These fries are good but kind of soggy, too." Hanna reached for another ketchup pack.

"They're exactly the way Mom used to make them," Dad said, his voice tinged with pride. He glanced at me quickly before glancing away just as quickly.

But I didn't let it distract me.

From telling Hanna the French fries story. Telling Dad, too.

Both of them.

Both stories: the time I thought I'd made Mom go into premature labor by asking for fries and the time we made them together for the first time.

I shared them because I felt strong enough to bring us all together—me, Hanna, Dad, *and* Mom.

Hanna brought down my guitar, and while we waited for her friend to arrive to eat cake, I played whatever she asked me to.

It was fun, but the best was when Dad requested "Seasons in the Sun."

I smiled at him when I finished, and he smiled back.

Dad was in on me meeting up with Zayneb, her mom, and Ms. Raymond, so he gave me a ride to the Malaysian restaurant where they were waiting.

Hanna came along for the ride but refused to get out of the car because the restaurant was at Souq Waqif.

She'd been on an active boycott of the market since the conditions of the pet section had begun bothering her more than her desire to take in the wonder of the colorful stalls.

I waved good-bye to them before following the cobblestoned main road through the souk to the restaurant with its polished black tables spilling onto the street.

Zayneb waved at me from a table just inside, on the restaurant's porch, and I smiled back at her and nodded at Ms. Raymond and the woman sitting beside her, who sort of looked like a smaller version of Ms. Raymond, but with a head scarf on. She wasn't smiling much, and I felt the beginnings of fear gnawing at me—did she already not like me? Or had she heard about my MS?

But then I remembered that she'd just come back from dealing with Zayneb's grandmother's death. She had a reason for that solemn face.

When I got to the table, she stood up, and I was immediately reminded of Dad.

It's just something he does when a guest or someone he's been waiting for arrives. Stand up and hold his hand to his heart before and after shaking their hand.

Zayneb looked over at her mom saying salaam to me and slowly stood up too.

I put my hand to my heart instinctively after greeting them.

And her mom smiled the gentlest smile, and everything in me that had begun to tighten as I'd walked to the table—nerves, fears, worries—just dispersed, and I sat down as my calm self.

Zayneb didn't talk much, but as the evening wore on and her face beamed more and more, I knew things were going to be okay.

When dessert was being served—we'd each chosen types of ice kacang, mounds of shaved ice drizzled with various flavors and toppings—her mom asked the dreaded question. "What are your plans for the future, Adam?"

"I'm planning on visiting family and working on a few projects before reassessing what to focus on for my education." I moved the ice drenched with bean paste in my bowl, not looking up. "I may study industrial design or even carpentry."

"Like our father," Zayneb's mom said. "Back home."

"He's good, too, like Daddy. Did you finish the room you've been working on, Adam? For Hanna's birthday?" Ms. Raymond asked.

I nodded. "Yeah, you're welcome to come by to see it, if you're up to it."

"Let's?" Zayneb put a hand on her mom's arm. "It's so amazing!"

"Do you mind if I call a friend to join us?" Ms. Raymond hadn't finished her dessert, but she stood up, her phone in her hand, awaiting my answer.

I said sure, but I was unsure of why she was so intense all of a sudden. "If Dad would be okay with it."

"He's a friend of your father's, too, actually," she said before walking away from the table to use the phone.

Zayneb's mom, Ms. Malik, smiled at me. "I can't wait to see your work."

I took a picture of Zayneb when she saw the room lit up. "OH WOW. There is only one word for this. *Enchanting*," she said, coming up to me to look at the picture on my phone as Ms. Raymond went around with Zayneb's mom, looking at the details. "And you *do* have a thing for blues, Adam Chen. I know it a hundred percent now."

"Is that why you're wearing my favorite blue hijab again today?" I took my phone back from her and looked at the picture I'd taken. Sure enough, it was a mix of blues in the background competing with her scarf—but not her face, not her smile. I favorited the picture. "Because you know it's my thing?"

She shrugged her shoulders. "Maybe. Or maybe it was the only clean scarf I had."

The door to the room, ajar previously, opened wider, and a man walked in with Dad. He was dressed in traditionally Qatari clothes, a long white thobe and a shemagh.

I went forward to greet him, with my hand out, but he didn't notice me.

He was looking at the room, his eyes widening.

It was the first time I saw someone looking at something I'd made the way I looked at things I was interested in: like he wanted to take in every single detail.

Adam, his dad, and Hanna came to the airport to see me and Mom off.

I hadn't wanted Adam to come, because then Mom would see how much we meant to each other.

And she wasn't ready to see that.

Last night, when we were returning from dinner and his house, Mom had told Auntie Nandy that she thought Adam was a "very mature and responsible young man with a peaceful, kind aura" but that he was still trying to figure out things and that we were young, and so what was there to come but going our own, separate ways.

I hadn't said anything, because I didn't want to show my hand.

To reveal the truth: that I wanted to get to know one person more than I'd ever wanted to get to know any other person in the entire world.

That I carried something in me, a little piece wedged inside my heart, that knew for certain he felt the same way about me.

That we were connected beyond what Mom was saying in the front seat beside Auntie Nandy.

I knew for certain that the long arc of things included me and him, Adam and Zayneb.

The long arc went from A to Z, across continents and oceans, across time, and I didn't need to protest or speak up or get angry at Mom for discounting Adam, for discounting us.

I believed there was more out there, more than this small world, so I stayed quiet and confident in the back of the car and just whispered a prayer out the window into the night.

But he came to the airport, and he had something in his hand that he held out to me as we stood to the side of Mom and Auntie Nandy saying their good-byes.

He unfurled his fingers, and there was a small carved goose with . . . was that enameled orange eyes?

It was beautiful.

He turned his palm over carefully, and the bird dropped into my hand, just as my tear did too. "I'd begun making it for you, but then Hanna saw it and loved it, and I gave it to her. But she wanted you to have it. Because it was meant for you in the first place. It's a Canada goose."

"Oh my God, it's unbelievable. And the orange eyes."

"I did that part last night after you left."

"You remembered. That I liked enameling. And the orange." I closed my fingers over his gift as I closed my eyes. "I won't forget anything I know about you, either, Adam."

"Geese are protective of their communities. Just found that out." He paused. "Like you."

"And I won't stop being protective."

He responded with "assalamu alaikum." When I opened my

eyes to say salaam back, he'd stepped back as Auntie Nandy came to say good-bye to me.

I got more teary-eyed as I thought of not seeing her again, but she whispered something into my scarfed ear that made me smile. "I'm coming to visit this summer. And Adam is too—his Dad told me, with Hanna, who apparently loves you as well."

When she stepped away, I looked at Hanna standing a bit apart with Adam's dad. She saw my glance and smiled and waved. I opened my arms.

She ran into them. When we broke away, I said, "Wait. I have something for you."

Right there, I lay my big suitcase down and opened it up. Luckily, it wasn't a mess inside, and I was able to find what I wanted to give her.

I held out the Blues, the Angry Bird that became three. She took it, her eyes wide with happiness. "It's from the game we played in the car!"

"Yeah, and look," I said, taking it back to show her how it launched into three birds. "Three times as powerful. Kind of like you, your dad, and Adam."

"And you, Zayneb." She hugged me again.

"And me, always. You can be the big bird and Adam, your dad, and I are your power boosters." I smoothed her hair and tucked in the stray clumps. "Keep in touch, Hanna Chen. I expect Ariel pictures every so often."

She nodded and squeezed the Blues to her before hopping back to her dad.

Mom spoke to Adam, who'd straightened from closing and righting my suitcase. "Congratulations. Natasha just told me. What amazing news."

I looked at Adam, then Mom, puzzled.

"Oh, you didn't tell her?" Auntie Nandy asked him. "The friend of mine who came over last night to see the room Adam made is actually the director of art exhibits at Katara. He wants Adam to make an installation there. It's going to be a permanent exhibit, so it's quite a big contract. Congrats again, Adam, on your season in the sun." She winked at him.

"Thanks, Ms. Raymond." He smiled at her and then turned to me, his eyes dancing. "Katara is doing a feature on ancient manuscripts from the Muslim world. And the director wants my installation to focus on the same manuscript I based the room on."

"*The Marvels of Creation and the Oddities of Existence*?" I said, unable to contain the joy bubbling in me.

"That's the one," Adam said, joining me in laughter.

It was Auntie Nandy's and Mom's turn to look puzzled, but between me and Adam, all of it made sense.

The world made complete sense for once.

Dad wasn't home yet, and Sadia and Mansoor were returning to Springdale next weekend when Dad did, so Mom and I hung out together, talking and watching things and talking some more.

It was so amazing, just to be home with her. To turn to her as we laughed at something crazy on a show or lean my tired self into her open arms at the end of a movie. It felt like the fortress had cracked in two, and my heart was peeking out.

I also spent a lot of the weekend sleeping.

I wanted to be completely awake for school on Monday.

I WALKED INTO FENCER'S CLASS ON MY OWN, AS I'D COME STRAIGHT over from Communication Technology, not from stopping by Kavi's locker.

She and Ayaan would still be busy. They both had had a prior spare period and had used it wisely. At the principal's office.

Fencer was writing something on the board and didn't see Noemi stand up when she saw me enter the class, walk over to the seat I'd just taken, and give me a high five.

"All hail the queen," she whispered before sitting back down.

Everyone else drifted in, and I studiously avoided their gazes, choosing not to see their curiosity or, worse, their animosity.

Fencer turned around. *How does oppression begin? What are the roots?* was written on the board behind him.

I turned my eyes down, drawing a goose on my notebook paper.

"Welcome to the beginning of session two." He cleared his throat. "You people in the back, it shouldn't take this long to settle down."

I'd read that Canada geese couple for life. *Is that why Adam gave me the present, now in my jean jacket pocket?*

"This term we're looking at the most repressive regimes in modern history. And, when I mean modern history, I mean happening *at this moment*."

Last night, Adam and I had texted each other. Our long train of news had ended with a wave emoji from him and an onion pic from me.

"Can anyone give the class examples of repressive governments?" Fencer walked by my desk and then came back again, slowing down as he got near. Then he stopped right beside me. "Places where to speak up freely will get you in trouble. Where to be a woman is to be condemned. Where religious laws, like sharia law, result in stonings and honor killings."

I drew an eye on my goose, a beautiful, long-lashed one, and raised my hand.

"Welcome back, Zee-naab. Yes? Are you going to give us the name of a repressive regime?"

"Why did you have to refer to sharia law specifically?"

"It's an example. I like to use real-world examples."

"Can you give European real-world examples of repressive laws?"

"I don't remember anyone appointing you as the principal, Zee-naab."

"I see your use of the word 'sharia' as an addition to the long list of ways you try to negatively portray people of my faith." I stood up. "And I'm not taking it. I exercise my right to speak up freely. And my right to leave a place where I am subjected to discrimination and hatred."

My voice shook at that last part, but I carried it out with me, with my books and my backpack. And my goose in my pocket.

In the hall I looked to my left, then right, and saw the windows of the library.

I'll go to the Situation Room.

Ms. Margolis was on our team, according to Kavi.

Where is Kavi anyway?

"Where you go, I follow." It was Noemi's voice. Behind me.

I turned to see her, with her books and backpack.

"My speech wasn't as eloquent as yours. I said something like, *Suck it, Fencer. I'm done with your Islamophobia.*" She laughed, and I caught her laugh, because it was the most contagious laugh I'd ever heard.

The door opened behind her, and two others came out. One was Darren, from the school newspaper, and the other was a girl named Violet.

"We'd been whispering in the back, and Fencer lost it on us, so we walked out too," Violet said. "We're sick of his dumb-ass comments."

A few more people spilled out. Noemi high-fived them. "These are my girls from lacrosse."

"He was about to call the office when the phone rang. He's talking now," one of the lacrosse girls said. She glanced around. "Maybe the office can see all of us in the hall from the cameras. So they're checking what's going on."

I leaned against the wall across from Fencer's classroom and looked at everyone.

The door opened, and Mike stood in the doorway with his iPad. "Are you guys doing a protest?"

"We're simulating the effects of a repressive regime in the classroom," Noemi said. "It's part of the lesson."

Through the doorway, I could see Fencer on the phone.

The reddening of his face told me something amazing: Kavi and Ayaan must have advanced on the battlefield.

. . .

Just as Ms. Margolis came over to us assembled in the hall, Fencer stormed out of the classroom.

He was headed to the office.

"Okay, let's gather everyone up, and we'll go to the library," Ms. Margolis said, giving me a gentle glance.

I waited until everyone went ahead, and then I fell back with Noemi. "Thank you."

"Please! Without you, this would not be. This exodus to freedom. So thank *you*." She put her arm around me, and I let her.

Kavi and Ayaan joined us in the library, and all four of us—Kavi, Ayaan, Noemi, and me—went to the Situation Room, where they told us that Fencer was under investigation by the school for his online activities.

That the school board was involved.

That he most likely would be fired.

Noemi gave a hoot so loud that Ms. Margolis knocked on the Situation Room door.

I let her in.

Because, now, this was what it was all about.

I was ready to let people in.

I'd still keep some people out.

But I saw—in this room, out through the window into the library, even in my pocket, with the small goose—that there were so many more that wanted in than out.

And that was one of the most marvelous things in the world.

EPILOGUE

THE WORLD IS A MYSTERIOUS PLACE. ON THE ONE HAND, ITS SIZE can be measured and recorded and verified. Its marvels and oddities captured in complex, empirical detail.

On the other hand, its size is relative to our mind's perception of it. Its marvels and oddities only extending to how far our vision goes.

For some of us, this means the world is small, including only those we see as belonging to it. People related to us, people who look like us, dress like us, think like us.

For others, it's medium-size and includes those we connect to through some similarity, some trait that pings familiarity within, which then allows us to overlook the differences between us and them.

And then there are those who see the world as huge, as the actual size it measurably is.

Huge enough to include vast differences, people with nothing in common with one another except a beating heart and a feeling soul, these two—heart, soul—being the strongest connection between us all.

・ ・ ・

Adam and Zayneb were on a course to becoming the third type of people.

And they were doing it together. Four years of faraway togetherness, with brief, exhilarating glimpses in between getting a political science degree at Northwestern (Zayneb) and working on six art installation projects around the Middle East (Adam) and through visits to MS support groups (Adam and Zayneb).

Then they met for real—heart, soul, and body—the summer of their katb el kitab, the summer they exchanged their vows, after a short engagement.

They met up in Istanbul, only emerging from their hotel room for bites to eat and breaths of fresh air and breathtaking views.

After four days, they traveled seven hours to visit the grave of the girl killed by her father and grandfather.

Their world had become so large that it was necessary.

To end our story, they will tell you why themselves.

ADAM

MARVEL AND ODDITY: KISSING ZAYNEB

Who knew kissing Zayneb would be such a problem while being necessary to my living healthily on this planet? As necessary as how I've learned to keep my MS attacks at bay?

Kissing her took skill.

You had to know when to move in. And that was hard.

Like right now: We were paused by our hotel room door as Zayneb stood in front of the long mirror outside the bathroom, stuffing her hair into a scarf—the hair I'd woken up with my face buried in.

I wanted to kiss her one more time before we left the room, so I waited with my back against the door.

But I wasn't waiting for her to finish hijabing.

She'd also been talking nonstop since we woke up, sharing her eagerness to start our excursion today.

"The only way to make this scarf work is by wearing it with plain clothes and tucking it in neat and trim, like so." She turned to me, her face framed in the print of vivid blues I'd bought for her at the Grand Bazaar in Istanbul. "Thanks again for the BLUIEST scarf in the world, Squish."

"Are you done talking?" I took my patient hands out of my pockets and reached forward and brought her close to me, until the only space between us was for our words. Well, my words. "Are your lips done? So I can kiss them peacefully?"

She nodded and tilted her head up, closed her eyes.

As our lips met, a curl of hair fell from her scarf. Her hands rose to the back of my head, pulling me in hard.

Zayneb, interrupting Adam's journal here: Fade to black.

Adam, taking my journal back: We delayed our excursion, the one I wanted to come to this part of Turkey for, because Zayneb tore off her hijab in a fit of passion and, yeah, fade to black.

Zayneb: THE SCARF WAS SUPER SILKY AND FALLING OFF. YOU DO NOT KNOW HOW TO CHOOSE THE RIGHT FABRIC FOR A GIRL'S HEAD YET.

Who knew that four years ago I'd see a girl at the airport, and she'd end up being the part of me that had been missing for so long.

There was a reason *love* was a round-sounding word.

It completed you and then some, like treading a circular path, the way it was immemorial. Whole.

But also . . . infinite.

It went on and on as long as you went on and on, to meet it, keep it, treasure it.

And I would.

ZAYNEB

Before I placed flowers by the grave of the girl buried alive, the girl who'd started this whole journey that led me to my heart, I said two simple prayers.

First for her, for her soul to be freer than it had ever been on earth, and then for me. *Please, God, don't let the hatred through which others see the world distort my own sense of justice.*

I smoothed the grave before laying the flowers down.

It felt like I'd laid down my last guard against vulnerability.

I was okay seeing things through my own eyes. Not defensively, the way people who hate saw me. I was done with that.

I needed to be done with that now that I was starting law school in the fall.

I would be studying the only thing I wanted to know the most about: human rights.

For everyone.

Because that was the only way the world made sense. When the arc of care went far and wide.

So wide it journeyed and battled to exclude none.

Beside me, Adam straightened up after saying his own duas, and I glanced at his eyes, glittery with tears.

There was no one around, just us two in this desolate location, so I sank into him, and he stretched his arms to engulf me, his kisses covering my own tears.

Oh, I forgot to record my marvel today. It's the greatest one of all.

You probably guessed it.

MARVEL: LOVE

On MS, Conversion, and Islamophobia

Adam's multiple sclerosis experiences were written with the help of a family member who was diagnosed with relapsing-remitting MS early on in his life. With support, especially from his wife of more than twenty years, and good health care, he lives a life of resilience with a positive outlook rooted in his strong Muslim faith.

However, it must be noted that MS experiences vary and the circumstances described in *Love from A to Z* do not typify nor communicate the full extent of people's experiences living with the illness.

The depictions of Adam; his father, David; and Zayneb's mother, Alisha, as being converts to Islam were also guided by family members of West Indian and white backgrounds, including my husband, who converted to the faith at the age of nine (under the guidance of his convert mother). A member of my Muslim community, the Canadian journalist Steven Zhou, read the manuscript to ensure accuracy regarding the representation of converts of Chinese backgrounds (as Adam and David are).

The Islamophobia described in this book is based on true incidents. Zayneb's scenes on the flight, at the swimming pool, and online were written calling upon memories of painful personal experiences—ones that will resonate with many.

As an educator for more than twenty years, I wish I could exempt Zayneb's classroom experiences from this litany of hateful incidents, but in bearing witness to truth, I really cannot. Three years ago, a high school teacher at a school board just outside Toronto was fired after a group of students discovered the Islamophobic content he'd been posting online. The bravery and courage of these students to go to the school board, to speak truth to power, inspired parts of my book. I wish I'd been as dauntless as a teen when I'd sat in classrooms, wincing from the Islamophobia I heard again and again.

While writing *Love from A to Z*, I often wondered if all this would seem too incredulous to some readers—but then I knew for certain that so many other readers would nod their heads in recognition. I write for all of you—those who know what it feels like and those who don't, *but want to*.

Onward, readers, into a better world born from empathy, lit by the sparks of truth, courage, and love.

ACKNOWLEDGMENTS

When I was young, it was a cool thing to call into radio stations and request the DJ to play a song dedicated to someone special in our lives. *Love from A to Z* includes music, so to acknowledge those who've helped bring this book to life, I hereby ask the DJ to dedicate these ten songs in the book to these ten groups of amazing people.

Love from A to Z Top Ten Countdown

10. "I Will Survive"
Dedicated to the Canada Council for the Arts and Ontario Arts Council for giving me grants so I could take a leave from work and still pay my bills and survive while finishing this book.

9. "Wild World"
Dedicated to the awesome people I've met in the YA writing world, especially the following authors who gave me the gift of their hand to hold, mentorship, and check-ins: Kate Hart, Emery Lord, Akemi Dawn Bowman, Rachel Hartman, Kiersten White, Jael Richardson, Cherie Dimaline, Sandhya Menon, Karen M. McManus, E. K. Johnston, and S. F. Henson.

8. "Leaves from the Vine (Little Soldier Boy)"
Dedicated to my Muslim squad of writers, we who come from the same vine, whose woven web of support I cherish so very much. Time to admit that during the hard periods of writing this book, I'd sometimes re-read the wonderful things you said about *Saints and Misfits* in order to believe that I *could* actually write. There are so many of you, but I want to especially mention these friends who

made my debut year so special with their expressions of love: thank you, Hanna Alkaf, Rukhsana Khan, Shannon Chakraborty, Ardo Omer, Nafiza Azad, Jamilah Thompkins-Bigelow, Fartumo Kusow, Asmaa Hussein, Hajera Khaja, London Shah, Nadine Courtney Jolie, Fatin Marini, Melati Lum, Umm Juwayriyah, Sabina Khan, G. Willow Wilson, Sabaa Tahir, Hind Makki, Maleeha Siddiqui, Na'ima B. Robert, Nevien Shaabneh, Hafsah Faizal, Saadia Faruqi, Karuna Riazi, and Alexis York Lumbard.

7. "Aap Jaisa Koi"

Dedicated to two new friends who walked into my life recently and who became so very dear to me: Aisha Saeed and Safiyyah Kathimi. Aisha, your kind texts and our phone chats always provided the bolts of clarity I needed to hear, and Safiyyah, our train of funny e-mails, messages, and late-night calls kept me going while I wrote *Love from A to Z*. You're both cherished.

6. "Seasons in the Sun"

Dedicated to old friends who've been with me through the winters and summers of life over the years, even when I've gone silent for long periods as I hid in the writing cave. Thank you for consistently cheering me on through this lifelong journey of mine with true friendship, Shaiza, Zakiya, Rania, Amie, Farzana, and Nhu. Thank you, Naseem, for re-entering my life—growing up as kids, you and I shared our mutual love of books, and now we get to share our mutual love of writing.

5. "I Like It"

Dedicated to those who brought this book to *actual* life, or supported my author career from the very beginning of my experience working with Simon & Schuster. Mekisha Telfer, Brian Luster, Jenica Nasworthy, Alexa Pastor, Lucy Ruth Cummins, Lisa Moraleda, Justin Chanda, the entire S&S library team, and, up here in Canada, Rita Silva, Michelle Skelsey, and Felicia Quon: I like it that you are all amazing!

4. "Have You Ever Seen the Rain"

Dedicated to my literary agent, John Cusick, and my editor, Zareen Jaffery, because both of you get my words so very much—and so instantly. You understand that I write the rain *and* the sunny days into my stories. I am beyond grateful that I get to work with you both. John, you are the same incredibly supportive agent I signed with three years ago, and, Zareen, if someone had told me to dream up my perfect editor when I was starting out as a writer, you would have been it—and my dream came true, alhamdulillah.

3. "Let It Go"

Dedicated to my writing soul-sisters, Uzma Jalaluddin and Ausma Zehanat Khan. I love that I can let go of all my writer vulnerabilities and just be free with you both. I love that we talk about everything and anything, writing or not. Thanks, Uzma, for our daily chats, for reading just about everything I write, for being brilliant and compassionate you. Thanks, Ausma, for being the star of a recurring thought of mine, WWAD: *What would Ausma do?*, and then answering this question for me with big-sister love and wisdom, all the way from the mountains of Colorado.

2. "Can You Feel the Love Tonight"

Dedicated to my army of a family, who shows up for me always, ready to take up the entire front row if need be, with phones out to capture the moment, with encouraging smiles and claps at the ready. I feel your love—all of your love so very much. Thank you, Faisal, Shakil, Anwaar, Johanne, Sakeina, Sahar, Amanda, Sana, Muhammad, Dawood, Bushra, Alain, Khalil, Khalid, Zenyah, Chiku, Saira, Aasiyah, and Maleeha.

1. "Stand by Me"

Dedicated to my parents, Ahmed and Zuhra (the kindest people on earth); my children, Hamza, Bilqis, and Jochua (a trio who inspires me); my sister, Hajara (a dynamo in all ways); and my husband, Jez (my rock). You all embody virtues I aspire to, and I want to stand by and with you always. Thanks for shaping this book and my life.